SLAUGHTERHOUSE
MOAN

DANIEL J. VOLPE

Front cover art by Nick Justus and Len Danovich

Formatted by Matt Wildasin

Edited by Mary Danner.

Printed in the United States of America.

For signed copies, visit DJVHORROR.COM

SLAUGHTERHOUSE MOAN

DEDICATION

For Aron Beauregard

PART 1:
ALL THE MASKS WE WEAR

2003

CHAPTER 1

1

It would've been difficult for Davey Grainer to know how big of a piece of shit he was if he didn't have his father constantly reminding him. But waking up at the crack of noon, hungover, with a disgusting barfly beside him, was a pretty good reminder.

The afternoon light lanced into his bloodshot eyes, a tangle of cheap sheets wound through his legs. The coolness of the faux silk chilled his nude body.

He looked around, unsure where he was, which was nothing new. It wasn't his place, which was a plus. He'd made the mistake of bringing home a few crazies in his day, and it didn't end well. Usually the sex was decent; getting them to leave was the problem. If Davey weren't flat broke, relying on his looks and loose morals to get him drunk, he'd be sober. Which, according to his probation officer, he was supposed to be, but Davey didn't care, and since he was tall, tattooed, and a complete scumbag to women, the ladies flocked to him.

His apartment wasn't the best place, anyway. The living room—if it could even be called that— had a small TV with rabbit ears. The VCR attached to it was his pride and joy, along with the stack of tapes he'd taken when he left home a decade prior. His parents were happy to see him go, letting him take whatever he wanted. They even gave him a few bucks to find a place, which he quickly spent on booze.

Davey's bedroom had an old mattress that had seen better days. It stunk of piss and various other bodily fluids. Some were from him, and others from the ladies he brought home. It wasn't quite the bachelor pad he hoped it would be, so he ended up elsewhere.

The woman next to him snored.

He couldn't see her face and didn't know if that was a blessing or a curse.

She, too, was nude, but no part of the sheets covered her. A cheap tattoo of a sun and moon adorned her left shoulder, faded with years of age. It more closely resembled spiky blobs of runny ink. Her bare ass was flat and pocked with divots of cellulite.

Davey rubbed his hands over his face. His beard felt crusty, and he sniffed his upper lip.

Please tell me I didn't eat this skank's box.

The odor wafting off his face said otherwise, but to be sure, he stuck out his tongue and ran it around his lips. It was sour, with just a hint of oniony tang to it. Not the worst he'd woken up to. Davey wriggled back, sitting up.

The headboard groaned when he did. He couldn't remember the night before, but if that thing made noise from him adjusting, he could only imagine the sound it made when railing the barfly.

An open beer and a pack of cigarettes were on the nightstand. He grabbed the beer, happy to feel some heft to it. It was piss warm, but he didn't care. He needed something to get the taste of dirty pussy and hangover breath out of his mouth. Davey chugged it down, happy it was beer and not something else. He'd made the mistake of chugging from a random beer bottle once, only to find out it was old dip spit. The sour, thick tobacco drool made Davey projectile vomit. Despite that, he didn't learn his lesson.

Putting the empty can on the nightstand, Davey grabbed the cigarettes. He noticed his clothes in a heap on the ground, which was a plus. Waking up naked was fine as long as he could get dressed and leave, which he planned on doing as soon as he lit his smoke.

Taking a deep drag of the cigarette, he relished in the chemicals flooding his brain. Slowly, he drew the sheet off him and put his feet on the slightly-damp carpet. He didn't see an ashtray, so he flicked the tip of his cigarette onto the floor.

Davey sat and could smell his nuts. He touched his cock and balls, feeling the grime of sex on him. Not only that, but he could smell it, too. Showering wasn't always a priority, especially if he'd been drinking, and from the combined smells wafting up from his crotch, he didn't think it was a priority for a few days at least. But that didn't stop women from going down on him. He knew the ones—the dirty ones—who would do whatever he wanted.

At thirty, with the body of a pro-athlete, the tattoos of a biker, and the face of a model, Davey had his pick of the ladies. He usually went for the low-hanging fruit. The older, divorced, and not very attractive women who had the money to keep him drunk all night, they were his targets. Of course, he could still take down a co-ed if he wanted, but those younger ones could be prudes. They wouldn't let him do the nasty shit he liked, and a lot of them made him wear a rubber.

Davey braced himself to stand and felt long nails on his back.

"Where ya going?" a raspy voice asked.

2

Fuck!

Davey took a drag on the cigarette and flicked more ash onto the ground, careful not to get any on his clothes. His mind raced to remember what this woman looked like before he turned around. He had a feeling, but he'd shocked himself before. There was no chance he would remember her name if he'd even known it in the first place.

His head swam with the nicotine and hangover as he pushed his black hair back so he could cover the shock on his face if she was hideous.

She wasn't, at least compared to some others he'd woken up next to. Mid-forties, too-thin plucked eyebrows, a weathered face from too much smoking and drinking, dyed hair showing bits of gray and dark roots. She didn't bother covering herself, showing her pooch, which had held a child or two. Her tits hung low, resting on the flab of her gut, but she had no shame. She'd earned every mark on her body, which turned Davey on.

He was disgusted with himself for the arousal, especially sober, but he'd always been a sexual creature. Most people would've called him a sexual deviant, but he just thought them to be jealous. A small glimmer of shame washed over him, but he chased it away.

"I was just gonna go take a piss." Davey put the cigarette in his mouth.

She took it from his lips, putting it to her own. Leaning on one arm, she laid back down. Everything drooped to the bed, and she gave him *fuck me* eyes through the haze of smoke. "Hurry back."

Davey stood. He wobbled for a moment and caught himself before staggering toward the bathroom. What he really needed was another beer, or maybe a shot of whiskey, but he didn't see any in the few feet he traveled to get to the pisser.

The tile floor was cold on his bare feet. He pushed the door closed, but it didn't even make it halfway. Avoiding the mirror, Davey stood in front of the toilet. He didn't put the seat up, nor did he control his dick as a split-stream of piss sprayed out. Warm urine hit the floor, the garbage can, and the seat before he could rein it into the bowl. It burned coming out, but he didn't think it was the burn of an STD, just dehydration. He hoped. The last few drops of his acrid piss landed on the floor mat. He didn't flush.

Turning to leave, he caught his reflection in the mirror.

"Look at you," his father said from the cracked glass.

Davey blinked, trying to focus and force the view of his father from the mirror. It didn't work.

His dad stared at him, looking him up and down. "Pathetic."

Davey pressed the heels of his hands into his eyes. "Fuck you." Starbursts exploded in his vision, but it was better than the accusing view of his father.

"Hey, did you fall in?" the barfly asked from the bedroom.

Davey pulled his hands away and saw his reflection in the mirror; his father was gone. "Fuck you, Dad," he whispered.

3

She was lying on her stomach, facing the bathroom. Her hair was a rat's nest and stuck up at every angle. The makeup on her face was smeared, and Davey could see her mascara had been running. He had a feeling he knew why.

Davey's cock twitched, a familiar sensation as it filled with blood. Seeing her perched on the edge of the bed gave him an idea, one he'd had many times in the past.

"Mornin'," he said, and shot her a grin as he stroked his cock.

The barfly licked her lips. "It certainly looks like a good morning to me."

"Flip onto your back," Davey said, still rubbing himself. "And hang your head off the edge of the bed."

"I was hoping we could get right to fucking. Start the day right." She perched on her elbows.

Davey grinned. It was a grin that had taken many women out of their panties. "Oh, don't worry, we will, but I want to fuck that mouth first. There's nothing hotter than watching my cock fill a throat."

He was fully erect with a glimmer of pre-cum oozing from his tip.

Still apprehensive, but not wanting to miss the opportunity, the barfly flipped over. Her hair had either too much hairspray or spunk that it barely even dangled. A pair of deflated tits snaked down to her armpits.

He used his pre-cum to loosen the discharge that dried on his shaft overnight. The smell of his musty crotch wafted up, and he didn't know how long she'd be able to handle it. If his balls smelled that bad, he could only imagine what his ass stunk like.

"Open wide," he said, tapping his helmet on her forehead. Davey thrust his dick into her waiting mouth. His balls hit her nose as he fucked her face.

Guttural noises and wet slurping escaped from around his meat as he pounded her throat. She gagged and writhed, pushing herself away from the facial violation.

Davey was on the verge of cumming when he felt the sharp stab of teeth on his tender flesh. He wanted to bust and run, but he didn't want his dick bitten off. Reluctantly, he slid out of her mouth, allowing her to crawl away.

The woman's mascara ran even worse, mixing with the darkness around her eyes from lack of sleep. Her mouth was coated in drool and cock slime. She wiped it away with her hand, but didn't spit. She was pissed, but Davey didn't care.

The way she looked at him was something he'd seen before. Yeah, she was annoyed that he hate-fucked her mouth, but it wasn't a deal-breaker. Davey stood there nude, tattooed, and hard-bodied, with a smirk that made women drip. He'd been an asshole his entire life and never suffered from lack of pussy.

"I think the mouth has had enough," she said. "How about you give this pussy a pounding like you did to my fucking throat?" There was no sarcasm in her voice.

For a moment, Davey considered getting dressed and leaving. *Who the fuck do you think you are, you old bitch? You haven't had a lay from a guy like me in twenty years.*

Before he could retort, the barfly rolled over and propped herself on all fours. She pushed her ass back, spreading her cheeks as she did. Davey had a perfect look at her pussy and hairy asshole. He was pleasantly surprised. Her pussy—at least from behind—wasn't half bad.

"Are you gonna fuck me, or just stare at it?"

Davey didn't have a rubber, but he didn't care if she didn't care. From the coating on his cock only minutes before, he didn't think he'd worn one the previous night. With one hand on her flabby ass and the other on his saliva-slicked member, Davey slid into her.

She was wetter than he expected, which was a plus. He knew he wasn't holding out long. Davey rarely fucked when sober, and forgot how good it felt when the alcohol wasn't numbing his senses.

The barfly moaned and pushed back against him, which would not help him hold out much longer.

He didn't care. Bust and run, that was his plan, and the feeling growing deep in his body was letting him know it was happening.

She steadied herself on one arm and reached back with the other, rubbing her clit. "That's it. I'm almost there! Don't stop."

Yeah, that's what you think. Davey was cumming, and there was no chance of stopping it. With a grunt, he pulled his cock out of her. He spread her ass, aiming his load for her hairy asshole. Thick ropes of cum spurted from him, landing on her back and in the wiry hairs around her anus. In his lust, and because he thought it would be funny, he squeezed her ass cheeks together, making his load seep out.

"Fuck!" She stopped touching herself and collapsed on the bed. "You couldn't have lasted another minute?"

A minute? Bitch, you're lucky I let you stop me from fucking your mouth.

Davey was sweaty, even though the ordeal had only been mere moments. His abs glistened, and he pushed his black hair out of his face. "Sorry, babe." His cock was wilting, and a drop of cum landed on her bed.

She crawled over to the nightstand and pulled something from it.

Davey smirked when he saw the purple vibrator.

"Eh, you're not the first one to disappoint," she said, her anger disappearing. She stood and tried to kiss Davey on the mouth, but he turned his head, letting her thin lips hit his cheek. "Make me some coffee, would ya? I'm gonna shower and take care of this." She held the vibrator in front of his face.

Davey could smell it hadn't been cleaned in quite some time. "Sure thing, babe," he said as she walked to the bathroom.

Cum ran down her back and her ass was tacky, but she didn't seem to care.

Standing nude, he waited a moment. When he heard the water running and the tell-tale buzzing sound of the vibrator, he made his move. Davey grabbed a handful of her sheets and wiped his cock on them. He didn't know if she normally had a thick discharge or if he'd nutted in her the night before, but his shaft was a slimy mess. Maybe he'd shower later.

After he was somewhat clean, Davey threw his pants on. His underwear—if he'd worn any—were missing, so he free balled it. Fully dressed, he left the bedroom.

The rest of the apartment was just as dumpy—cheap furniture in the living room, with a fresh pack of cigarettes on the coffee table.

"Don't mind if I do." Davey grabbed the smokes and a lighter. He ripped open the pack and popped one into his mouth.

Smoke billowed up as he lit it, but he saw something else: her purse. Quickly, and without a moment of hesitation, he pulled open the faux-leather bag. Her wallet was small but had almost eighty bucks in it. "Been a pleasure, my dear." He stuffed the money into his pocket and walked out of the apartment.

He didn't bother closing the door.

4

The afternoon sun burned Davey's eyes. His hungover brain was mad he didn't steal a pair of sunglasses along with the cash and cigarettes. Shading his face with his hand, he looked around.

He hadn't lived in River Grove for too long, but long enough to realize where he was. Davey's apartment—which wasn't any nicer than the one he'd just snuck out of—was at least a mile or two away. He considered splurging on a cab, but he couldn't afford a cell phone to call one, and doubted the barfly would let him back in to use her phone. So, he started walking.

It was warm, bordering on hot. Virginia was one of those states that could experience all four seasons in a single day, but when it was summer, you knew about it. July was in full swing, and the days were only getting hotter.

As Davey walked, sweat ran down his back and chest, wetting his black shirt. In hindsight, black wasn't the best option, but he didn't give that a thought when he'd dressed the night before.

An oasis stood down the street—a corner store. Davey realized how thirsty he was, and water was the last thing on his mind. An ice-cold beer, or maybe two, would hit the spot and take the edge off his hangover. Usually, he bought his suds with change he found, but he remembered the wad of cash in his pocket.

The bell above the door jingled when he entered. A cool blast of A/C hit him, and Davey sighed, almost sounding like the barfly after she realized he came first.

Perusing the beer cooler, he tried to decide the cheapest way to get drunk. He knew he shouldn't buy any of it and just get a bottle of water, but that wasn't going to happen. A little niggling thought burrowed through his mind and into his forebrain: his probation officer.

Davey was a year into a three-year probation stint. After a night of drinking and whoring, Davey didn't know when to call it quits. Well, he found out quickly when he ended up with a face full of pepper spray, handcuffed in the back of a police car.

The glass shone on the cooler, casting back his reflection, but it wasn't his; it was his father's. Before the voice of his dad could speak up and tell him what a piece of shit he was, Davey yanked the cooler open. An arctic chill hit him as he grabbed three of the strongest IPAs. The beer wasn't his favorite—he preferred an ice-cold Miller Lite—but he was on a mission to get hammered fast.

"Is that all?" the clerk asked as he scanned the tall beers.

Davey's stomach rumbled, and he tossed a bag of pork rinds on the counter for good measure. "Yeah, and these too."

The clerk rang him up, and Davey handed over a crumpled ten-dollar bill.

With a couple of loose bills and a pocket full of change, Davey walked back into the sun.

An old picnic table was on the side of the store. It wobbled and was covered with graffiti and splinters, but it was in the shade.

Davey's head felt like he'd gone a few rounds with Mike Tyson. He hoped the beer would take the edge off. The first sip told him he was right. Leaning his back against the table, looking out at the street, he lit a smoke and opened the pack of salty, artery-clogging pork skins.

Slowly, a cop car drove by.

He couldn't tell if it was Officer Kirby behind the wheel, but in his mind, every cop was that sonofabitch. He and Kirby had history, even though Davey hadn't been in River Grove long.

When Davey first set foot in the rural town, he was an outcast to the men, but a luxury for the women.

Many folks in the town could trace their roots back a few generations, and everyone knew each other. Families had old alliances, and strangely, people were almost destined to marry.

That's what Kirby thought. After chasing Loretta Sanders since high school, Kirby finally had his shot. Well, he thought he did. That was until Davey turned on the charm one Friday night at the local watering hole.

Kirby had picked up an overtime shift, planning on using the extra money to take his date somewhere fancy and out of town.

Loretta ended up on Davey's cock in the backseat of her car in the parking lot of the bar.

When Kirby did his parking lot checks—making sure no one was getting ready to drink and drive—he saw the love of his life riding a stranger. Her tits were buried in the face of the new man, and with a look of ecstasy on her face, Kirby sped away, not bothering to call her again.

Davey wanted to wave at the police car, but thought better of it. He wasn't supposed to be drinking as part of his probation, and drinking in public was illegal anyway, so he sat back and enjoyed the shade and his beer.

Not even a minute later, another police car—this one belonging to a deputy sheriff and not RGPD—drove by.

Even in River Grove, which was hundreds of miles from New York, the increased police presence was felt.

It had been almost two years since terrorists had flown planes into the World Trade Center, the Pentagon, and crashed one somewhere in Pennsylvania, but the country was still on edge.

Davey didn't concern himself with politics, but even he felt the after-effects of the attacks. Mainly because he was afraid of a draft. He'd just turned thirty, but stranger things had happened in the history of the world. Tension was ramping up in the Middle East, with the crosshairs shifting from Afghanistan to Iraq. The only thing Davey knew and cared about was that the government, on all levels, had increased their police presence. Even in little towns like River Grove, more cops were on patrol.

Finishing the first of three beers, Davey lit a cigarette. He stood and cracked another can open. The first beer was already working, and a slight twinge of euphoria hit his bloodstream. He knew it would be short-lived, but he didn't care.

5

With each sip he took, his mind drifted back to his probation officer. The last six months had been smooth sailing, so to speak. His PO was a dumpy, married, middle-aged woman with a shitty haircut and a cheap ring.

How she looked at Davey resembled a dog looking at a steak.

When he had his first appointment with her, he knew there would be no issues with reporting or her checking in. He could practically smell the pheromones coming from her pussy, and he made it a point to lift his shirt to 'wipe something from his eye.'

When she saw his ripped stomach, lined with cheap tattoos, she all but came in her granny panties. But, last month, she was transferred.

He didn't know why, but it could've been that she blew him in her office. Davey certainly didn't tell anyone (even though it was one of the worst blowjobs he'd ever received), but it could've gotten out. Either way, easy street was ending.

His new PO was anything but a pushover. An older bull dyke with a buzz-cut, she was a hard-box bitch.

Davey tried turning on the charm in their first meeting, and she almost violated him just for that. Luckily, his piss had been clean, and he was sober for a few days, a small miracle in his life, but he knew he was playing with fire. The piss tests would only detect booze if he drank within 12 hours, or so he'd been told. He didn't think she'd test him at his next visit, but there was one thing she demanded of him: to look for work.

Never much of an academic, Davey skated through high school on his sports ability and looks. College was not something he ever considered, nor did he have a fucking chance of passing. Manual labor had been the only thing he could do. It wasn't the best job in the world, but one of the few where drinking at work wasn't frowned upon.

He worked odd jobs over the years, and they had sufficed until that point. With his new bitch of a PO, he knew that wasn't an option. He needed something concrete, with a boss that wasn't as much of a scumbag as he was.

A gentle breeze cut through the warm day, and the fluttering of fate came with it. Davey heard paper blowing and turned to look at the front of the store.

Flyers littered a corkboard attached to the wall.

He never really paid it much mind before as his brain was usually focused on grabbing beer, but with a possible probation violation looming, he took notice. Davey looked over his shoulder, ensuring no cops were around, and took a swig of his beer.

He perused the papers, but most of them were outdated or bullshit he'd never do. And then, he saw it.

Wanted:

Farm help at the Winslow Farm. Manual labor, animal tending, and general maintenance. Lunch provided, cash payment. Lodging optional (at reduced pay). Contact Beulah for info.

Davey had never worked on a farm, but he'd been with some women who could've lived on one. He took another deep swig of beer, tore a scrap of paper with Beulah's number, and stuffed it into his pocket before beginning his walk home.

CHAPTER 2

1

JD wished his father had the A/C fixed in the car before he and his friends started their road trip. Unfortunately, his dad told him there was no way he was going to spring for a repair on the old Honda. So, JD and the three others in the sweatbox car had the windows rolled down and the radio up.

The Honda ate up the pavement ahead as JD did his best to focus on the road and not the others in the car. With the wind blowing, and all of them trying to talk over the radio, it was difficult. Plus, Arianna was wearing the low-cut tank top he liked. Even though he'd seen her naked what felt like a million times, his teenage brain couldn't stop thinking about her tits. He couldn't stop thinking about her at all, not just sexually.

His older brother told him not to fall in love with the first piece of pussy he put his cock in, but JD lost that battle.

"Here, put this in," Danielle yelled from the backseat.

JD looked at her in the rearview, even though she was talking to his girlfriend and not him.

"What is it?" Ari asked, looking back at her friend from the front passenger seat.

"It's the mix we play when we fuck," Rich said. "I burned a bunch of songs off Limewire. I probably fucked up the computer, but it was worth it; these songs get the blood flowing." Rich's hair didn't move an inch, even with the windows down. His black mane had so much gel that a hurricane wouldn't touch it.

Danielle handed the CD titled *Fuck Songs* to Ari.

Ari looked at the handwritten title and laughed, showing it to JD before ejecting the CD that was currently playing.

"Summertime" by Beyonce cut out as the disc slid from the player.

"Nice. Maybe we should make a copy for ourselves," JD said. His eyes drifted down Ari's shirt as she leaned over slightly to switch out the music.

Ari looked at him and raised an eyebrow.

The new CD slid into the player, and her hand touched his thigh. "Honey, I don't think we need any more encouragement." She grazed his crotch and nipped his earlobe with her teeth.

Blood rushed to JD's dick, and the beginnings of a half-chub started.

Moving away from him, the warmth of Ari's hand left with her.

JD looked as she scooted against the door.

The breeze pulled at her chestnut hair.

She pushed it back, raking it with her fingers to keep it from her face. Blue-green eyes shimmered in the sunlight, eyes that would turn greener when she'd cum. A few freckles dotted her round nose, accenting her creamy skin. Her mouth opened, allowing her to roll her bottom lip. She caressed it with her top teeth, leaving gentle indentations on the flesh.

JD loved her. It wasn't just the sex, which was

amazing, but he truly loved her, which made the road trip even more bittersweet. There was an elephant in the car with them: college and the long-distance relationship that came with it.

A horn blared, and JD ripped his attention away from his seductive girlfriend and went back to the road.

"Fuck!" he yelled as he jerked the wheel. The car had drifted into the other lane, and JD snapped his attention back to the road.

Ari laughed, but Danielle shrieked.

"Jesus Christ, JD," Danielle said. She put a hand to her chest in fright and looked at Rich.

Rich took the hint. He grabbed the driver's seat and leaned in. "Hey, lover boy, there will be plenty of time for fucking on this trip, but not if you kill us. Comprende?"

JD cleared his throat. The fear of death had softened his cock, and the coolness of pre-cum chilled his leg. He looked at his buddy in the rearview. "My bad."

2

Ari unfolded the MapQuest directions and shuffled through them. She looked at the passing signs and matched them up to the route before her. Modern technology made things so much easier, and she didn't know how people got around before the internet. With maps like a damn pioneer? No thanks, she'd stick with MapQuest. "It looks like we're on this road for another sixty miles or so." She pointed at the line of directions on the paper. "You're looking for exit 215." She scanned the directions again. "That'll put us closer to the coast of Virginia and in the good ole town of River Grove."

JD nodded. "Got it."

Ari knew he'd studied the directions the night before, but she wanted to make sure he was still on track. Everyone knew the front seat passenger's job was to help navigate.

"Hey, when you see a rest stop, pull in. I have to take a piss," Rich said.

"Yeah, I wouldn't mind a pee break either," Danielle added. "We've been on the road for like six hours and only stopped once. What's the rush?"

JD adjusted his grip on the wheel. "No rush, just trying to get us on the sunny Florida beaches before we turn ninety. Trying to make some memories, that's all."

"I told you we should've just gone to Seaside," Danielle said. She pulled a piece of gum from her purse and popped it into her mouth.

Rich looked at her and laughed. "You watch too much shitty TV. Seaside is a dump. Besides, half the class of '03 will be there. This road trip is perfect. If only I could take a piss sometime this year."

"Yeah, yeah. Pinch off that little cock of yours. I'll find a spot in a minute," JD said, looking back at his friend in the mirror.

Ari watched him smirk, but the playfulness that was there only moments ago was gone. He was thinking about them and what the future had in store. She was, too. It had been a big topic of discussion for the past few months, and since high school ended, it had become reality.

She received her acceptance letter first. Boise State was her first pick for college, and because of her grades and extracurricular activities, Ari thought she had a decent shot. But, as always, a kernel of doubt worked its way into her subconscious. Maybe she wasn't good enough for such a big school. And if she did get in, could she cut it?

When she showed JD the letter he hugged her, the pounding of both their hearts in sync.

And then, they cried.

JD was smart, but didn't have the grades to get into a school like Boise State. Even if he passed the admissions board, there was no way his parents could afford to send him. Student loans were an option, but his parents weren't too keen on taking out a mortgage worth of debt for an education halfway across the country. JD had his pick of the many SUNY schools in New York, but that would put him 2000 miles away from her.

They talked and cried about their life and what college would mean for their relationship. Video chatting was becoming popular, so they discussed that as an option. Planning 'online date nights' to see each other was also talked about. And, of course, trying to ensure they could spend the maximum amount of time with each other during the holidays. The optimism grew, and both were committed to making it work at that moment, but deep down, they knew it was far-fetched. They'd seen it with older friends and other classmates who tried it.

It would start the same way: they'd stick to the plan and talk as much as possible, even video chatting when they could. And then, one of them would have to reschedule. Then, there would be more missed calls or brief, informal chats. Seeds of doubt would grow and flourish. A bond of trust that formed in high school would start to crack and seep the blackness of jealousy. Accusations would be made in jest, but with truth behind them. They would turn from jokes to serious in a matter of weeks, if not sooner. Proclamations of love would be made, and tears shed, but still, the niggling doubt would continue to grow. And then, the dreadful call would be made—the one full of tears and shouts of regret.

I cheated on you. I'm so fucking sorry!

That would be it. The division would be permanent, and the relationship would be killed. The odds were against them; they knew it. But they would try.

"There." Rich leaned between JD and Ari, pointing at the sign for the gas station as if they didn't see it. "For the love of God, pull over so I can piss."

Ari swatted at his hand. "Stay back, beast."

Rich shrieked in mock pain and jumped back to his seat. "Hey, I was just ensuring our chauffeur saw it before my bladder explodes in the backseat."

The blinker in the Honda clicked.

"Lucky for you, we're making good time. And I have to piss too."

3

The bell above the door chimed as the four of them walked in.

Rich and Danielle made a mad dash for the bathrooms tucked in the back of the store. As badly as he had to go, Rich took a moment to admire the thick ass of his girlfriend. He grabbed her by the arm, stopping her short.

She turned with a hint of annoyance, but didn't stop him.

Rich let his free hand slide down her back to her ass. He pulled her close to him and kissed her.

Their tongues met, seeking one another in passion. The road trip had been going well, but neither could wait to get to a hotel room and have some real fun.

Blood rushed to Rich's cock, swelling it ever so slightly. With his growing erection and the burning desire to pee, Rich broke the kiss. He licked his lips, tasting his girlfriend.

"To be continued," Danielle said. She gave him a peck on the mouth, letting their saliva mingle one last time before turning and disappearing into the ladies' room.

Rich turned and almost bumped into a man exiting the bathroom. He dashed in, settling in front of a urinal. A wave of relief washed over him. When he finished, Rich stood in front of the mirror. His hair, his beautiful hair, was still looking good. He thought the wind might have messed it up a little, but the hefty amount of product he'd coated it with held firm. It was his ticket in life, or so he hoped.

Unlike JD and Ari, he and Danielle weren't venturing far away. Hair was his passion, and even though his father didn't think much of it, Rich knew it had a future. Only one town over was a decent barber college which he was enrolled in. In no time at all, Rich would be a licensed barber running his shop. He knew the clientele list would take some time to grow, but he had faith in his skills. Plus, he understood hair. Traditional college wasn't for him. He never had the grades for it, always concerning himself with other things—girls. That's where Danielle came into his life.

They'd only been together for a year, but their lust made it seem longer. Rich and Danielle worked at the Polar Bear, a local ice cream shop, the summer before. After a bit of casual flirting, and a couple of innocent touches here and there, Rich made a move.

Their first kiss was in the backroom amongst stacks of ice cream cones and sprinkles, but it was one he'd never forget. The taste of her lips, and the subtle hint of perfume mixed with sweat, were the most powerful aphrodisiacs in the world. From that moment on, he knew he had to have her. It only took a few months before they started talking about the future and what it held for both of them.

Rich didn't know if it was the sex that made him love her, landing him in the honeymoon phase, but he was hooked.

When Danielle decided to stay close to home and attend community college, Rich nearly jumped for joy. Of course, he kept his reaction to a minimum in front of her, but inside, he was ecstatic.

Looking again at his hair, he made sure the black locks were perfect before stepping out.

"If I hadn't seen your dick like a million times, I'd swear you were a woman," Danielle said, waiting for him outside of the bathroom.

Rich smiled at her and put his arm around her waist. He pulled her close, pressing the side of her hip against his as they walked. "I can't wait for you to see it again."

She kissed him and guided him toward the snack aisle. "If you want me to touch and not look, buy me these." Danielle grabbed a bag of Corn Nuts and handed them to her boyfriend.

Rich smiled and took them from her. "Anything for you, my love."

She pulled away from his grasp. "Good. I'm gonna add more to that order. But don't worry, I'll be sure to *pay* you back." Danielle winked and blew him a kiss before browsing the rest of the store.

Rich wasn't one to miss an opportunity to check her out, and he watched her walk away. He hoped they would make it to the hotel soon or he was going to nut in his pants.

4

With bladders empty and the gas tank full, JD guided the Honda back onto the road. Songs were sung, and snacks were passed around. The old import ate up the roadway.

"I still don't know how you guys like that rap shit," JD said. "I mean, I can tolerate some R&B, especially if it gets her," he nodded toward Ari, "in the mood. But the hardcore rap? Nah, that's not for me."

Rich leaned forward. "You have to expand your mind, buddy. Stop with the sad emo shit and get into some real beats. When I open my shop, I'm only playing the best music. Latin dance, some classic hip hop, you know, shit that makes people want to be there. Not your sad cut-my-wrist bullshit," he laughed.

JD smiled at his friend in the mirror. Whenever they rode together, it was always a battle for the radio. Finally, they reached a truce. Whoever was driving picked the music selection. It was only fair. In reality, they talked more than they listened to the radio anyway. The music was just fun material to banter about.

Over the last few months, Rich and JD had become closer. Friends since middle school, they hung out quite a bit. But with the finality of high school, they found themselves together more often. It was as if they were trying to make up for lost time as college loomed.

"Yeah, yeah. Just keep listening to guns, bitches, money, and drugs," JD said.

Rich nodded. "Doesn't sound like a bad life to me." He smirked at his friend. "You know I love my bitches." Looking out of the side of his eye, he glanced at Danielle.

She hadn't been paying much attention to them. She and Ari were having a sidebar conversation. But her boyfriend talking about other women pulled her right out of that. "Excuse me?" Danielle asked with a hint of sass. "Bitches? First of all, I'm not your *bitch*. Second, there'd better not be multiple bitches."

Her eyes and the little smirk were enough to let JD know she was joking, but it was a risky move by his friend. Then again, that was Rich. Always the risk taker, especially with his mouth. It had landed him in trouble before when a joke didn't hit right, or he spurted out the first thing that came to mind. He would have a rough trip if he pissed off his girlfriend before it even started.

Rich slid closer to her and wrapped his arm around her shoulders. "Oh, baby, you know what I mean." He went in for a kiss, but she turned away.

"You get the cheek, and that's it," Danielle said, offering the side of her face.

Rich smiled and kissed her. "I wish my face was buried between your other cheeks."

She turned with a grin on her face and kissed him quickly. "I'll think about it, but only if you're a good boy."

JD laughed. He felt the warmth of Ari's hand on his thigh and looked at her. If he could've lived in that moment—his friends happy, his girlfriend staring at him like he was the only person in the world—he would have.

He heard the pop before he felt the car jerk violently into the other lane.

A chorus of gasps and screams echoed through the car as he fought to keep them all alive.

5

"Fuck!" JD yelled, looking at the blown-out tire.

He'd kept them from crashing, guiding the limping Honda onto the shoulder.

They were all okay, but the car wasn't. Shredded rubber stunk in the bright sun of the Virginia highway. The tire wasn't just flat, it was fucked.

JD paced, kicking at debris on the shoulder. "Fuck!" he yelled again, as if the profanity would help the situation.

Ari walked over to him and rubbed his back. "It's okay, babe. We'll just put the donut on and keep going."

JD knew she was just trying to help, but at that moment, he felt his ire growing. The trip was supposed to be perfect, and before they were even halfway through, they were screwed. He took a deep breath, knowing she was only trying to help calm him.

"Do you want me to call for help?" Danielle asked. She pulled a cell phone from her purse. It was blocky and large, an older model compared to the sleek flip phones on the market. "My dad gave me his old phone, but said it was only for emergencies. There's only a handful of minutes on it, but more than enough to call 911 or something."

JD's blood pressure descended to somewhat normal, and he began thinking rationally. "No, we don't need 911 or anything. We just have to change it and keep moving." He popped the trunk and removed the donut and jack.

Cars flew by them on the highway, creating small gusts of wind.

JD cringed when the semis drove by, and with them, a storm of road grime. He was crouched down, doing his best to keep his knees from the hot asphalt, when he heard tires crunching on the rocks.

The four teens turned and looked at the pickup truck that pulled up behind them.

After activating his hazard lights, the driver of the dusty Ford climbed out. "Need a hand?" he asked.

The man wasn't much older than them, looking

to be in his mid-twenties. He was whip-thin and wore a sleeveless shirt with a faded NASCAR logo. He was already putting on a pair of work gloves as he walked over to them. "New York?" he asked, looking at the license plate.

JD stood and wiped his hands on his shirt. "Yeah. Heading down to Florida for summer break. And well…" he pointed at the shredded tire.

The man looked at all of them, letting his gaze linger on the chests of Ari and Danielle before squatting down to inspect the damage. "She's fucked, alright." He turned and looked up at JD, using his gloved hand to block out the sun. "And not in a good way." He pointed to the small scissor jack that had come with the Honda. "I have a bigger jack in the truck. These little shits rust out over time, and the last thing you want is the car dropping on the rotor." He walked away from the group, digging around in the bed of the truck.

"That's not just a flat, dude," Rich said.

JD looked at him with a *'yeah, I can see that,'* look. "Let's see what he has to say. We sure as hell can't drive to Florida on a donut."

The good Samaritan returned, dragging a large jack behind him and a tire iron in his hand. A lit cigarette dangled from his lips, and he allowed himself a long glance at the girls' asses this time.

"Whelp, there's a decent shop not far into town," he said as he slid the jack under the car. "Pretty reasonable prices, but I'm not sure what they have in stock." He cranked on the lug nuts, loosening them before lifting the car. "Le'me get this changed and I'll give you directions."

Within moments, he had the destroyed tire off the car and the pathetic-looking donut in its place.

The car groaned when he lowered it to the ground.

"There. That'll get you back on the road." He pulled the dirty gloves from his hands and stuffed them into the back pocket of his pants. "Got a pen?"

Ari grabbed the MapQuest directions and a pen from the glove box, handing them to the man.

"Thank ya, darlin'," he said, taking the pen and paper. "It's not hard to find," he said, the cigarette bobbing as he spoke. "You tell 'em Gremlin sent you."

Gremlin? That's a fucking stupid name, JD thought, but said, "Thank you, Gremlin." He took the paper even though Gremlin was trying to give it back to Ari. He was grateful for the help, but the strange man's leering made them all uncomfortable.

Gremlin, taking the hint, pulled the cigarette from his mouth. He threw it on the hot asphalt and ground it out with the toe of his boot. "Don't mention it."

The loud pickup truck kicked up a storm of road grime and dirt as he sped away.

"Well, he was kind of an asshole," Danielle said.

"Yeah, real creep," Ari replied.

Rich put his arm around Danielle's waist and pulled her close, kissing her neck. "Eh, he's just a horny dude with two hot, sweaty chicks on the side of the road. Plus, it was free, so sneaking a peek at your titties was a good price to pay."

Danielle sucked her teeth and pushed him away. "You're an asshole."

Rich put his hands up in mock surrender. "I'm just saying—"

"Well, don't," Danielle snapped.

"Hey, can we get moving?" JD asked. He handed the directions to Ari, who was trying to decipher Gremlin's chicken scratch.

"After you," Rich said, letting his girlfriend go ahead. He made an exaggerated move to look at her ass as she walked by, which she knew.

Danielle looked over her shoulder at him, but the scorn from moments earlier was gone. "Perv."

"Oh, baby, just you wait."

The Honda sputtered back to life and merged back onto the highway.

6

"Yup, this tire is mighty fucked," Chet said. He was tall, with a belly that pushed against his oil-stained work shirt. His name tag used to be white, but was the off-shade color of grime. A red rag was in his hands, which he used, in vain, to wipe at years of filth. "But I can order you up a new one."

JD leaned on the counter with Ari at his side.

Rich and Danielle opted to stand outside, hoping to catch a breeze.

The shop was hot, with only a small fan lazily spinning away overhead.

Beads of sweat ran down JD's back, and he noticed a dark patch forming on Ari's shirt, too. Even though the situation was serious, and he was trying to figure out how to get them out of their current predicament, he could not help but think of Ari's sweat running down her nude back. He knew it would follow the contour of her spine, trickling down to the crack of her ass. JD would've given anything to run his tongue along the length of her body, tasting everything she had to offer.

"—morrow, but probably closer to two days," Chet said, pulling JD from his sexual fantasy.

JD looked back at the sweaty mechanic. "Two days?"

"Yeah, we don't keep many tires in stock here. And most of the ones we do have wouldn't fit an import." He continued wiping his hands as if they would miraculously get clean.

JD and Ari looked at each other.

"What choice do we have?" Ari asked.

She was right. They couldn't get far on a donut, whether it was back home or to their vacation spot. The tire was a must, but it cut into their small budget.

"If it takes two days, we need to find somewhere to stay."

Ari nodded. "Fuck, you're right." She looked at Chet, who'd finally given up on cleaning his hands. "Are there any cheap motels in the area? We're not looking for anything crazy or expensive, just a spot to sleep until the tire is ready."

Chet sucked at something in his teeth and looked at the teens. "We're not known for our tourism, so there's not much in town. The only hotel we had closed up after a fire in '96, and nothing else has sprung up. You'd have to get back onto the interstate and go about," he scrunched his face in thought, "thirty miles or so. But that's a newer chain, so it ain't gonna be cheap, that's for sure."

JD wanted this trip to go well and have fun with his friends and girlfriend—one last hurrah before the inevitable stress of college and the breakup that was sure to come. With each word that tumbled out of Chet's mouth, JD saw that dream slipping away.

"Oh wait, there might be a spot that's local," Chet said. He took the rag from his pocket and wiped his balding pate, leaving a streak of grease. "There's an old farm just outside of town. I know the lady who owns it. Bit of a kook, but decent enough. There's a hunting cabin on the property that her daddy used to rent out when he was around. I'm not sure if she still lets people stay there or not, but I know everyone in these parts could use a few extra bucks. Let me give her a call and see what I can do." He disappeared into a back room.

Ari hugged JD who was biting his nails and seemed lost in his thoughts. She kissed him and rubbed his back. "It'll be okay, babe. This is just another bump in the road, but we have a bright future ahead of us." And almost as an afterthought, she said, "Together."

JD looked at her. *Really* looked at her. He wanted to believe what she was saying, but knew the chances of success. Try as he might, pushing the thoughts of their future from his mind was difficult. He smiled at her and kissed her forehead. "Let's not think about the future. Let's just focus on us here and now."

Ari smiled and jumped as the door where Chet had disappeared to banged open.

"Good news," Chet said, wiping his hands again. "I got you folks a room at the Winslow Farm. And for about a quarter of what that chain hotel would've charged you. I was right, Beulah needs the cash, so she was happy to have some guests." He grabbed a pad of paper and scribbled some directions on it.

"A farm. That doesn't sound bad," Ari said. "I've always been hypnotized by the rows of corn or wheat, so it'll be cool to see it all up close."

Chet grunted and looked up from the pad of paper. "They ain't growing corn on the Winslow Farm."

"Oh, no?"

"Nah, it's a livestock farm. Pigs, mostly, but I know they dabble in other beasts as well." He tore the directions from the pad. "And the best part is, they slaughter them there, too. Yup, a one-stop shop." Chet held the directions out in front of him.

JD took the paper but could see the change in Ari's expression at the thought of staying at a slaughterhouse.

"Have fun," Chet said as he put down the pen and picked up his rag.

CHAPTER 3

1

Beulah Belle Winslow wedged the phone between her shoulder and ear as she fumbled with a lighter. The old Bic spat sparks, but no flame caught. "Come on, you piece of shit." She shook it as if that would give new life to the lighter. With an unlit cigarette dangling from her lips, Beulah tried again.

Success!

The flame kissed the tip of the cheap cigarette, and she adjusted the phone. "No, I wasn't talking to you, Chet. I couldn't get this damn lighter to work." She pulled the long, curly cord of the phone and sat at the table.

An ashtray in the shape of a pig, with the words *King of Pork* enameled across the rump of a cartoon animal, sat waiting on the battered table.

Beulah flicked the ash into the tray. "Four of 'em?"

Chet's voice was mumbled, but she didn't know if it was an interference with the lines or if the fat fuck was stuffing his face. "Yup. Two boys and two girls. They ran into some trouble on the interstate with a tire blowout. They ain't going nowhere for a day or two, so I figured I'd ask and see if you still rented out that old cabin your daddy used to use."

Taking a drag, Beulah looked down at the *King*

of Pork ashtray. If her daddy was the king, then she was the princess. She looked around at the weathered kitchen, her pork palace.

The tile floor was dingy, the grout the color of mud. Her sink was the original, or damn near close to it. The fridge was a hand-me-down she bartered for at the salvage yard. Even the cabinets—real wood and not press board—were swollen with years of moisture. Most of them stood ajar or fully open.

Beulah didn't care; there wasn't much in them. "And they can pay, right?"

Chet wheezed through the phone line. "Yeah. Not much, I'd reckon, but you could get something from 'em, that's for sure."

Something's better than nothing.

It was nearing lunchtime, and she knew the farmhands would be coming in soon. She hoped they liked dry tuna on stale bread because that's what she had.

"Look, thanks for thinking of me," Beulah said. She twirled her finger in the phone cord just like she'd done when she was younger and on the phone with boys. Boys she actually liked, not a greasy mechanic. Or even better, when she was on the phone with talent scouts, a time in her life that seemed ages ago. "Send 'em over. I'll have Hattie run out and straighten the old place up. Chase out any critters that might have taken up residence."

"I'll tell 'em." Chet paused, breathing heavily. "Oh, and about payment for the tractor—"

Beulah hung up.

The bells in the phone's plastic body chimed when she slammed the receiver down.

That was her life: people standing there with a handout, or sometimes their cock, waiting for Beulah to take care of them. Chet was just another one on the long list.

Heavy boots thumped on the porch, followed by deep voices.

"Fuck," Beulah muttered. It was lunchtime, and she didn't have the sandwiches ready. "Hattie!" she yelled.

Nothing; no response.

"Hattie!"

A thump sounded above her, and footsteps moved quickly through the house.

Opening the refrigerator that was just barely cold, Beulah pulled out a bowl of mushy tuna. It wasn't a lot, but if she made the sandwiches and didn't let the hands make their own, there might be enough to go around.

2

Hattie jumped when she heard her mother scream her name. She put the old dress on the table, careful not to lose the needle. The last thing she wanted was to step on that later. A part of her wanted to ignore her mother's call and finish up the repair, but she knew better.

There was always something to work on, and she knew that finishing one dress meant moving on to another garment. Whether it was the pastor's Sunday slacks that needed to be let out a bit or a bundle of used socks that were to be sold at the thrift store, River Grove always had work for her.

The second time her mother yelled, Hattie was already getting off her bed. She hit the ground hard, and for a second, almost didn't grab her mask. But one look in the mirror changed her mind.

It wasn't just the severe cleft palate that bothered her; it was the scars too. Her face was nearly split in two, with each half sharing rows of crooked and stained teeth. Bits of black rot tucked themselves into the crevices of the enamel. But the scars lining her face and her body were the real sources of shame.

Hattie fought the urge to hate herself, but it was a losing battle. Her hair was long and needed a trim. She wanted to grab the brush and run it through the brown locks, but knew her mother was waiting. It would take her a moment or two to ensure her mask was tied well.

She picked up the old Halloween prop and positioned it over the lower part of her face, covering her mutilated mouth.

The ancient plastic creaked and groaned each time she put it on. One day, it would shatter, and so would her façade. Bits of tape held it together, and the elastic band had long since been replaced with braided thread. It was something so stupid, yet important to her, and fitting for her and the farm.

The pig mask was a faded shade of pink. Its vibrance had long since drifted away like so many of her hopes. The nose was the shape of a marshmallow with two dark nostrils. Small holes allowed a little amount of air to pass into Hattie's misshapen face. A cartoonish mouth sported three teeth, two on the top and one on the bottom, along with a few breathing slits.

It smelled of her—of her shame and the curse she was destined to live with—a curse brought on by the woman who'd already yelled her name twice.

With the mask tied tight, Hattie pulled her door open and ran downstairs.

3

All three of them smelled like shit, but that was the norm for a farmhand on the Winslow Farm.

The farm consisted of only a few buildings: the house, the row, the cabin, and the slaughterhouse.

All the men had just come from the row, a long building that housed pens of pigs. From sows, to boars, and even piglets, all manner of curly-tailed beasts lived on the farm.

The row was where the pigs spent most of their lives, crammed into metal pens, covered in their shit and that of their pen-mates. That was, until it was time for the slaughter.

For anyone who says animals aren't smart, they've never been around pigs. They know, oh they know when it's time to die. The panic sets in as they're herded away from the grotesque comfort of their pens and the slop they're fed. Seemingly dumb eyes fill with panic, and shrill squeals rip through the air.

A chute was constructed, leading the swine from the row to the slaughterhouse. The brick building stunk of death. Years of spilled blood and offal soaked into the masonry, sealing in the torment.

They bite and fight, trying their best to escape the inevitable. In larger commercial slaughterhouses, the pigs were well cared for, avoiding undue stress. On the Winslow Farm, compassion didn't exist.

The pigs were shuffled into a holding chute one at a time.

An antique set of stunners—what look like giant tongs, except with wires hanging from them—were plugged in and ready.

Each pig is stunned when the electrodes hit their skull, knocking them out. Their back legs are tied, then they're hung upside down from a rotating pulley system.

A farmhand waits at the apex of the loop with a long knife in hand.

Each pig's throat is opened, bleeding them out.

Slaughter.

Rinse.

Repeat.

"Lunch is ready, boys," Beulah yelled from the kitchen.

"How much you wanna bet it's shitty tuna again?" Wayne asked Brett.

"Shit, I ain't betting you nothin'. With the amount she pays us, one lost bet will put me in the hole even deeper than I am," Brett said.

Wayne looked at Ralph, the oldest and most experienced of the trio. "What about you, old timer? You wanna take me up on that?"

Ralph chuckled. "Boy, I've been working this farm since before you were in your daddy's nutsack." He picked an errant piece of chewing tobacco— leftover from his earlier dip—from his lip and tossed it on the floor. "I damn well know it's tuna."

The men entered the kitchen, and the smell of

canned fish and onions hit them. It wasn't the best lunch, but it was free and smelled better than pig shit, although that was a smell they never seemed to get away from.

The stench of animals followed them like a leech. It stuck to their clothes, their hair, and even their skin. No matter how many showers they took, the smell lingered.

"Wash up and I'll have these sandwiches done in just a minute," Beulah said. She mixed a bowl of tuna with a wooden spoon before setting it down on the counter.

An opened bag of bread sat in front of a few paper plates.

All four looked toward the second door leading into the kitchen as footsteps approached.

Hattie walked in wearing a sundress and her mask.

Silence fell over the room, and the sound of her wet breathing could be heard through the plastic.

Wayne shook the excess water from his hands and dried them on his soiled shirt. He didn't waste a moment, nor try to hide his gaze, when his eyes landed on Hattie.

The dress the deformed girl wore was at least two sizes too small, pulling snug against her teenage breasts. Puffy nipples were visible through the fabric, and she wasn't wearing a bra.

Looking her up and down, Wayne took a seat at the table. "Afternoon, Miss Hattie," he said, still taking in the girl's shape.

Hattie looked away and mumbled something.

Wayne didn't know if it was a curse or a

greeting, but he didn't care.

Ralph looked at the lust in Wayne's eyes. He dried his hands on a towel set by the sink and sat across from the lewd man.

"Somethin' on your mind?" Wayne asked, his attention snapping from the girl to the older man staring at him.

Shaking his head, Ralph said, "Nah, just thinking about what else needs to be done after lunch. What about you? Something you want to talk about?"

Wayne sucked his teeth and grabbed the pitcher of watered-down lemonade on the table. He poured a glass for himself and set it down. "Nope. Not a thing in the world. Just happy to be here and away from the pigs." He sipped. "Although, I don't mind making a mess sometimes." Wayne shot a wink at Hattie, who looked away.

Beulah turned from the sandwiches she was making and looked at her daughter. "Grab a broom and some rags and clean up the old cabin. Chase out any critters that might be living there."

"Ohay," Hattie muttered through the mask. She opened the small closet and grabbed a broom that had seen better days. With that, along with a handful of rags, she walked out.

Wayne didn't miss a beat, leaning past Ralph to get a look at her ass. "They sure do raise some fine stock on this farm."

Brett sat next to Wayne, seemingly oblivious to his friend's gaze. He was the youngest of the trio, just over twenty-five. He'd only worked the farm for the last year or so, unlike Wayne and Ralph who spent a few years in the service of the Winslow Farm. His eyes weren't on the teenager, but squarely resting on her mother.

Beulah's dress was tight, but not because it wasn't the right size. No, its snugness was by design. She had Hattie tailor it specifically, leaving it just a little loose in the belly, while making sure it was tight on her chest and ass. Even as she approached forty, Beulah still had a body most women half her age would've killed for. Although, in her eyes, she was a pig, she knew what she had and how to flaunt it. Her looks had gotten her into, and out of, trouble her entire life.

"Getting hot in here," Beulah said. She leaned over the counter and opened the window allowing a warm breeze to blow through the kitchen.

It came from the south and with it, the smell of the row.

She took a rubber band from her wrist and threw her blonde hair into a messy bun atop her head.

Brett stared at her glistening neck. "You expecting hunters?" he asked.

They all knew hunting season didn't start for a few months. Even so, she hadn't rented that cabin out in some time.

Beulah put a sandwich on each plate and turned to the hungry men. "No, not quite." She set one down in front of each of them. "Some kids had some car trouble, and Chet thought they could stay in the cabin." She pulled out a chair and sat with them. "Not for free, of course. They'll be paying for their stay. Lord knows I can use the money." Beulah lit a cigarette and pulled the piggish ashtray closer to her.

Wayne, with his mouth full of fish and bread,

spoke. "Yeah, about money." Crumbs flew from his lips, some getting snagged in his wispy mustache. "When are we getting paid?"

All three men looked at her, each with the same look in their eyes.

Beulah took a long drag on her smoke, as if trying to buy time. She flicked the ash into the pig and licked her lips.

4

Beulah knew the question was coming. It was only a matter of time before they started bitching about their money. But each of them knew the farm life; they knew how it worked and how a bad season or poor market could slow down or even kill a farm.

The year prior, some bad pork made its way into the US market from overseas. A lot of people got sick from it, with a few of them dying. The pork market took a big hit, knocking out many small farms. Of course, the factory farms made it through, but family farms, like the Winslow Farm, felt the impact. It wasn't until recently that the Americans decided to trust the pigs again and the market rebounded.

With the summer in full swing, many families sat down to barbeques, pig roasts for graduations, and celebrations. The pig was, again, on the rise, and Beulah knew this was her only shot at making the farm survive.

She took a risk, another gamble in a life full of them, and postponed her slaughter. Many other farms began their butchering around Memorial Day, capitalizing on the popularity of the holiday. Beulah knew most of her stock was ready for slaughter, but another few months would add more hogs to that number. And with the price of pork slowly rising, as many of the farms had sent their animals to slaughter, these circumstances would, hopefully, create the perfect storm for her, giving her fresh stock at a premium price.

Beulah just needed the men to stick it out, one way or another.

She took another drag, albeit a smaller one. "Soon, I promise. You know the slaughter is coming in the next week or so. I already have buyers lined up and ready to pay a premium price."

Brett washed his bite of sandwich down with some lemonade. "Yeah, but that doesn't help me now. I have bills to pay."

We all fucking do!

Ralph pushed his plate away, leaving behind a few scraps of crust. "I told you we should've gone to slaughter at the end of the spring." He took out a can of chewing tobacco and put a fat wad of the brown mush into his mouth. "I've been on this farm since before you were born. Trust me, I know the market and the pigs."

Beulah crushed her cigarette into the ashtray, scattering ash around the table. "Yes, you've told me many times, Ralph."

"I'm just saying, your daddy wouldn't have waited so long."

Glaring at him, her nostrils flared, Beulah breathed deeply. "Well, if you see the old fucker, please let me know."

Shortly after Beulah returned home to help her

father run the family farm, the old man decided to up and leave—no note, no nothing. He just took a handful of clothes and hit the road. No one had heard from him since. At least, that's what she told everyone. Only Beulah knew the truth about what *actually* happened to her father.

"He would've had the good sense to not gamble with the farm's future. He would have gone to market with everyone else and secured enough payment for another year." Ralph stood and brushed the crumbs from his shirt. "We need to get paid, Beulah. *I* need to get paid. I have mouths to feed."

Yeah, that fat cunt of a wife eats more than a football team, Beulah wanted to scream, but held her tongue.

She did her best, knowing she needed Ralph. Each man was valuable, and she needed them all. Just losing one would cripple the farm. They needed another hand to help with the slaughter. Beulah posted a flyer at the gas station a while ago, but no one knocked her door down looking for work. It was another gamble, but one more worker would make the slaughter go quicker, thus getting her pork to the market in time. And, hopefully, hitting that window she needed for maximum profit.

Ralph's short speech inspired the other two men as well.

"I don't work for free, darlin'," Wayne said. He leaned in the chair with his arm draped over the back. "I can leave today and find work on another farm. A farm that actually pays its staff."

Brett didn't speak but nodded along.

"Look, I told the three of you, I'll make it worth

it. You'll each get an extra ten percent after the slaughter. Just wait it out until then."

"Hmm, I'm not so sure I can do that," Wayne said.

"Am I supposed to ask the gas station to fill my truck based on promises?" Brett finally added.

Ralph glared at Beulah. "You'll have the money from those kids staying in the cabin. Use that and pay us." The other two men nodded in agreement.

"You know that won't be a lot. How much can I charge 'em to stay in that dump? I'm not even sure if the power still works or if the pipes haven't burst."

"It's better than nothin'."

Beulah licked her lips, not as if she were nervous, but seductively. "Look, you boys know I have *other* ways of paying you." She looked at each of them in turn.

The two younger ones, Wayne and Brett, stared with hunger while Ralph had sadness in his gaze.

"I'm gonna be blunt here, because I think it's important. I'll fuck you or suck you—all of you—right now. Just stick it out until the slaughter."

Ralph shook his head. "What would your father think of you, Beulah? Huh? How would he feel knowing you throw your body around so easily? Or Hattie? What would she think?"

She stared at him, letting his words hit but not sting. Her smile was wavering, but she held it tight. *You don't have to like it, you just have to do it,* the voice in her mind said.

It was a voice she hadn't heard in years, not since crawling back home to the family farm.

Think of your smile as a mask. Each emotion is

*a new mask. Each groan of fake pleasure is a mask,
something to disguise the pain we're in. Just think of
all the masks we wear.*

"Well, if you find Daddy, tell him I said thank
you. He made me this way, Ralph. And if you think
otherwise, you're not as smart as I thought," Beulah
said. She felt the mask—the façade of lustful calm—
slipping. But, using the skills she obtained while
acting, she pulled it back together.

Ralph wouldn't leave the farm; she knew that. If
anything, he was loyal. He might talk a big game, but
he knew the slaughter would make them a lot of
money. If he left then, he would miss out on a
payday. Even if another farm hired him, he wouldn't
make shit. Most other farms already went to market;
he'd just get paid farmhand wages, not a bonus for
the slaughter. No, he had no choice but to wait it out.

Ralph looked at the other two men staring at
their boss. "I'm going back to work. We still have a
lot to do in the row."

Wayne didn't look back at him, just raised a
hand, waving him off. "Yeah, we'll be back soon, old
timer."

Beulah met Ralph's eyes one last time. There
was judgement in them, but something else lurked:
temptation. She remembered his gaze at her when
she was only a girl, the way his eyes would linger on
her teenage breasts the same way Wayne's lingered
on Hattie's.

He couldn't hide the bulge in his pants when
he'd get a glimpse of the vanilla mounds of her
young tits, or if her dress would ride a little high.

At first, she was disgusted by it, but then, she

realized what control she had.

And then, her daddy realized it.

Ralph stomped out, slamming the door behind him.

5

Wayne's cock was swelling tight in his denim pants. He stared at Beulah, knowing it was going to happen eventually. He'd worked on the farm long enough to have fucked her and gotten his dick sucked more than he could remember. Most of the time, it was in lieu of payment, but he knew Beulah had a horny streak in her occasionally.

With no steady man in her life, she had desires that needed fulfilling.

Not that Wayne cared much about her needs, but if she got off during one of their fuck sessions, so be it.

Brett, on the other hand, was still new to the farm—new enough that this was probably his first run at the owner.

Wayne couldn't be sure, but guessed the younger man would've told him if he'd fucked the boss at some point. And Wayne didn't hold back. The day Brett said something about how good Beulah looked, Wayne told him to wait; it would happen eventually. At some point, she'd get horny or desperate and throw pussy at them, and that time had come.

As Beulah leaned against the counter, a few strands of hair fell from her messy bun, framing her face. The breeze blowing through the window was warm, but cool enough to make her nipples erect.

Maybe she's horny too, Wayne thought. He didn't mind fucking and busting quickly, but if she was horny, he knew it would be that much better.

Beulah raised her arms high, stretching, and the hem of her dress rose, exposing the creamy skin of her thighs. She ran her hands down over her chest, accenting her tits and pulling her dress taut.

"Yeah, yeah, that's good and all, but what about the money?" Wayne asked. He cared about getting paid, but he had something else on his mind.

Beulah smiled. "Wayne, you've been here long enough to know what I can do for you is better than a few days' pay."

Wayne scrunched his face and shrugged. "Eh, it's good and all, but let's face it, you're not getting any younger." It was an unnecessary barb thrown at her and Wayne could see it landed.

Beulah was a hell of an actress, but that one cracked her just a little.

"And I really could use the money…"

"I just told you; you'll have your money, and then some, in just a little while. I'm just trying to cover the bills until then," Beulah said. There was just a hint of frustration in her voice.

Good, get upset. It'll make this easier on us all. Well, maybe not everyone.

"Well, there is a way we can make this right. If not…" Wayne shrugged with a shit-eating grin on his face. "I'll find work elsewhere. I'm sure another farm would pick me up." He rubbed at his wispy facial hair. "I am quite the catch."

The realization of what he would ask showed on

Beulah's face.

Wayne loved to see her transformation. He was sure it was the same for her when she was a girl and her daddy was put in the same predicament.

"I want the freak. I wanna fuck her, not you. That's my offer. Take it or leave it," Wayne said.

He could see Brett staring at him from the corner of his eye, but he didn't give a fuck about the other man. He'd learn farm life sooner or later. And right then, he was getting his first lesson: supply and demand was the lifeblood of agriculture.

"You sick fu—" Beulah started, but Wayne cut her off.

"I'm not negotiating with you, nor am I arguing. That girl has blossomed over the years. Maybe not so much in the face, but she has a body like her mama. Just not old and used up, but firm, young and untouched." Wayne's erection was growing, and he made sure Beulah saw it framed in his pants.

Beulah's nostrils flared and her eyes moistened, but she waited a while to speak.

Wayne could see the tempest in her—the urge to grab a knife from the butcher's block and stick it into his crotch.

Her lips quivered, but she steeled herself. Without saying a word, Beulah nodded. It was slight, but it was there.

With his face split into a grin, Wayne walked over to Beulah. He put his lips near her ear.

Feeling the tingling of his beard on her skin, she didn't flinch.

"I'll be gentle, but you know how big it is." He sucked air through his teeth with a hiss. "Oh boy, it is gonna be snug." Wayne reached up and grabbed her left tit, plucking her nipple before walking out of the kitchen and toward the backdoor.

6

Hattie didn't mind cleaning. The old cabin wasn't in too bad of shape, and she could thank herself for that. Oftentimes, she would use the old building for her solace. If she saw something that needed cleaning or repair, she would do it.

The old cabin was just as she left it, with a fresh layer of dust on some surfaces. She sat on the old couch, watching the dust motes flutter up as she did. They danced in the sunlight.

Hattie, lost in her reverie, made up a story for each of the flickering bits. Her eyes drifted to the cold fireplace, imagining it full of roaring flames. There could be a storm raging outside, but the thin glass and fire were enough to keep her warm.

She got off the couch and went into the kitchen/dining area, which was reasonably clean. The bedrooms—there were only two—had two twin beds that were stripped and wrapped in plastic. Hattie pulled the protective cover from them and was digging sheets out from the boxes in the closet when she heard boots walking up the steps.

Her ears tuning into the odd sound, she froze. Her breath became ragged behind the mask. She considered taking it off to clean, but never did.

The front door swung open on unoiled hinges.

"You in here, Hattie?" Wayne asked.

Hattie's heart raced. She wasn't stupid,

regardless of how she looked. She'd seen the farmhand staring at her and felt almost nude wearing the sundress.

Without realizing it, Hattie had worked up a little sweat that dampened her brow. She wiped her forehead with her arm before poking her head out of the bedroom.

Wayne stepped into the cabin and closed the door behind him, locking it. "Ah, there you are."

"U'm keening," Hattie mumbled. Her speech was usually pretty good if she focused on it, but when she was nervous, her cleft made her stumble over words.

Of all the farmhands her mother had hired over the years, she disliked Wayne the most. He was crude and mean to the animals. She knew they were being raised for slaughter, but there was no reason to be mean to them.

The things he said about her mother was another nasty habit of his. Hattie had heard, and even seen, things her mother did.

Beulah wasn't a shy woman, and often—usually drunk—told Hattie stories about her childhood. The things her daddy—Hattie's grandad—used to make her do for the family.

Hattie always thought about the song "Fancy," by Reba McEntire, and compared her mother to the title character.

Moving back into the bedroom, she hoped it would give Wayne the hint it was time to go.

She was wrong.

Her back was to the open door, but she didn't need to look to know he was standing there. As if his gaze was something solid, Hattie could feel it on her behind.

"Oh my, how you've grown over these last few years," Wayne said.

Hattie turned and faced him. Her breath stunk in the mask. It smelled of fear and old plastic. She was trying her best not to show her fear, but she was scared.

The bulge in Wayne's jeans made her heart race, and not with excitement like her mother told her it would. Thumping behind the breasts Wayne was glaring at, the powerful muscle pulsed.

"Yeth, Wayne. We all gwow up. Maybe yoo should twy it."

Wayne laughed and stepped closer. "You got a smart mouth on ya, girl. A smart, fucked-up-looking mouth. Not like your mama's. She's got a sweet mouth."

Moving backward as he stepped closer, the backs of Hattie's legs hit the bed and she let out a little shriek.

"But my oh my, you've definitely grown in ways that put your mama to shame," Wayne said as he reached out and grabbed one of Hattie's breasts.

Hattie swatted at his hand.

He let it fall away, but she felt the power in his arm.

She knew if he wanted her, he'd take her. "Geth yer futhing hands off me!"

Wayne put his hands up in mock surrender. "Relax, Hattie girl. I'm just sampling the goods is all."

Hattie pushed against his chest and created a

little distance, but not enough to escape the small room. If she tried to run, he'd be on her instantly. "Leave me alone or I'll tell my motha," she said. Her breath was coming faster and harder, bringing tears to her eyes.

Wayne made a sound like he was trying to console a child, which he was. But his consolation wasn't for a skinned knee or broken toy; it was for something far worse. "Hattie, she sent me here. She said it's time for you to pull your weight on the farm. And there's no way in fuck you're gonna be out in the row with us hauling pig shit." His hand rose again, this time landing on her hip.

A shudder ran through her flesh, but Hattie didn't push it away.

"There comes a time when everyone has to chip in. It's the farm life. You think I want to break my ass from sunup to sundown? Hell fucking no. But it's what I have to do." His hand rose higher, just touching the bottom swell of her breast.

A squeak came from the pig mask covering Hattie's mouth. She thought she was going to puke. The warmth of his flesh through her thin dress made her shudder. His calloused thumb rubbed the swollen nub of her nipple, and her body betrayed her by allowing it to grow erect. There was no pleasure or lust, only fear.

"Now, I'm not gonna force ya to do anything, but just know if ya don't, I'm quitting. And if I quit, the farm dies. Ya understand that, don'tcha?"

Hattie felt like she had a frog in her throat, something wet and alive, begging to get out.

Wayne was right; the farm was on the verge of

collapse. They needed more help than they could get.

She knew her mother was trying, but bills weren't paid in happy thoughts. Slowly, she nodded, but didn't speak; she didn't know if her voice would betray her.

Wayne licked his lips. "Smart girl. And loyal, too. I like that in a woman." He brought his other hand up and cupped both of her breasts. "And let me tell you, you're a woman, Hattie." He slid his hands down her waist, stopping at the hem of the dress.

She wanted to scream, kick him, hit him, bite him with her mangled, deformed mouth. But she didn't.

It was a warm day, but when Hattie's dress lifted, her skin bristled with goosebumps. Downy hair rose with the bumps of flesh. The scars on her body, the ones given to her by her mother, felt even colder.

Reluctantly, Hattie lifted her arms, allowing the dress to go over her head.

The collar of her dress tugged at the mask, threatening to pull it free.

Once the dress was off, she adjusted the old costume piece and brushed away the tears. She stood there, in only her panties, with her nude breasts exposed. Quickly, she moved to cover her scarred chest, but Wayne's hand was faster.

"No, let me see them." He pushed her hands away.

Hattie's nipples puckered with the cold fear of knowing what was about to happen next.

Wayne stared with hunger.

She didn't think any man would look at her that

way. And at that moment, she wished no man would ever look at her again.

Unbuckling his pants, Wayne pulled his cock free.

Hattie gasped. She'd never seen a penis before, at least not in real life or so close.

The thing jutting from Wayne's body looked like it belonged on a donkey or maybe a horse.

She shook with anticipation, knowing the pain she'd soon be in.

"Lay down," Wayne said, moving forward.

Hattie lowered herself onto the bed, shaking. Her panties were still on, and part of her hoped this was all just a cruel joke. Surely, they couldn't have sex if she was still wearing them.

Wayne kicked his boots off, his jeans and underwear close behind them. He bent down and hooked his calloused fingers on Hattie's cotton panties.

A clear drop oozed from the tip of his cock, sliding down his shaft.

Hattie went rigid as her panties were removed. The bed felt like sandpaper under her nude flesh. Her eyes were locked on the bulbous tip of Wayne's penis, but his eyes were on her pussy—the eyes of a predator looking at his prey.

"Oh my, how you've blossomed," he said, stroking his dick as he crawled onto the bed.

7

Beulah wished Brett would hurry up and cum. The linoleum of the kitchen floor was hurting her knees.

Brett fucked her mouth. His dirty fingers were wrapped in the messy bun atop Beulah's head.

She tried to keep up with his rhythm, ignoring the smell of unwiped ass, sweaty balls, and pig shit. It wasn't the cleanest cock she'd ever sucked, but it was far from the dirtiest.

"Oh shit," Brett moaned. His pace increased.

Beulah was glad it was his cock in her mouth and not Wayne's. Brett was on the smaller side of average, which she could easily deep throat, while Wayne's meat belonged on a barnyard animal. If she took a face fucking from Wayne like Brett was giving her, her jaw and throat would be sore for days.

Her mind wandered back to Wayne and Hattie, and she pushed the guilt away. She knew what had to be done to keep the farm afloat. If anyone knew what it took to keep that place open, it was Beulah Belle.

"Fuck!" Brett grunted, shoving his cock so far into her mouth his balls rested on her chin.

Beulah gagged as a thick rope of cum shot down her throat.

Brett's grip was tight, keeping his shaft in her mouth until the pulsations stopped.

Swallowing it down, Beulah did her best not to vomit.

Finally, Brett released her head, allowing his boss to take a breath. His eyes were closed as he leaned against the counter. The open window let in a breeze that smelled of nature and animals. "Mmm, that was the best fucking blowjob I've ever had."

Beulah stood up. Her eyes were watering, and she wiped a tear with her pointer finger. "Yeah, I know." She rubbed her hands on her dress. "Now put that thing away and get back to work."

"You're the boss," Brett said, flopping his softening dick back into his pants.

A scream cut through the hanging silence. It was shrill and guttural, one of pain. One that sounded like a macabre blend of girl and pig.

Hattie!

Beulah and Brett looked through the open window toward the old hunting cabin.

"Sounds like Wayne will be joining me soon," Brett said with a smirk. He buckled his belt and sipped his glass before leaving the house.

Staring toward the cabin, Beulah knew the pain Hattie was feeling all too well. It was a pain she felt over and over, something brought on her by the man who was supposed to be her protector. But in her father's eyes, everyone had to pull their weight on the farm. And now, it was Hattie's turn to help the family.

Beulah cleaned the few dishes that were left over from lunch. She closed the window so she didn't have to listen to the screams.

1982

CHAPTER 4

1

Shepherd "Shep" Winslow looked at the cards in his hand.

Three sixes looked back at him.

His eyes wandered to the pile of money in the center of the table. *Three sixes—the mark of the beast,* he thought.

If he'd been playing cards with his father, the man who named him after the most righteous players in the bible, his dad would've dropped to his knees and prayed for salvation. But Shep's father, who'd been dead and buried for nearly ten years, didn't play cards. Nor did he drink or whore around, two of Shep's favorite things.

The senior Winslow died pushing pigs through the pen, landing face down in the muck. His doctor said he was dead before he hit the ground, but Shep liked to think the old bastard suffocated on pig shit.

Shep grabbed his last few bills and tossed them in the center. He put his cards face down and picked up the cigarette burning in the ashtray next to him. "Raise." Shep took a drag, letting the smoke flow from his mouth. He looked at the other three men around the table.

Ralph and Bruce folded, tossing their cards in the center, each with a huff.

"I gotta piss, but let me know who wins," Bruce

said, pushing his chair away from the table.

"Yeah, I might as well drain the lizard, too," Ralph said.

Both men left the room without another word.

Micky, the fourth player at the table, eyed his cards. "I know they call you the King of Pork, but that's an awful lot of money, Shep."

Smiling, Shep took another drag. He hoped his hand wasn't shaking too much. It was a lot of money. In fact, it was all of his money, the last bit of his cash he had until the next slaughter, which wasn't for a few weeks. But he felt in his bones he would win. His luck had to turn around at some point.

"Too rich for your blood, Mick?" He put the cigarette in the pig-shaped ashtray and grabbed his beer.

The longneck bottle was empty.

"Goddamn it! Where the fuck is Beulah with my beer?"

On cue, the door creaked open without a knock.

Beulah, Shep's eighteen-year-old daughter, walked in cradling a few beers and a bag of pretzels. Her faded t-shirt was stretched tight across her chest, and the condensation from the bottles wet the fabric.

Mick looked at the girl, his rheumy eyes locked on her chest.

Beulah set a beer down in front of her father, along with the pretzels.

"Damn girl, what the fuck took so long? My buzz almost wore off waiting on you."

"Sorry, Dad," she grumbled, then walked over to Micky and set his beer down. She jumped when he pinched her ass.

Beulah looked at her father to say something, but he was chugging his beer. Not that he would've said anything anyhow. "That it?"

Shep put his half-empty bottle down and burped. "Nah, we're good."

"Speak for yourself," Micky said. He patted his knee. "Why don't you come sit on my lap? You can be my good luck charm."

Forcing a smile, Beulah said, "I've too much work to do to be playing games. Besides, I have to study."

Her father was stifling another belch, giving her enough time to leave the room before he could stop her.

Micky made no qualms about watching her tight ass framed in a pair of cutoff jeans as she walked away. "You have a mighty fine daughter. Mighty fine. She's always been a cute girl, but my oh my, has she turned into a woman. I mean, she's had the tits for years, but she's filled out nicely."

Shep lit another cigarette, looking at his friend. "Gets it from her mama. That woman had the best set of tits I've ever seen."

"She get fucked yet? I'm sure the boys in town are sniffing after that pussy like a bunch of hounds."

Shep eyed him, but the lewd talk was nothing new, especially from Micky. And the man was right. His daughter seemed to grow up overnight, blossoming from a gangly teenager into a busty woman before his eyes. He'd even *accidentally* walked in on her a couple of times, letting his eyes linger on her tight body for a few seconds longer than any father should have.

"Nah, I don't think so. The girl has her nose in a book all the time. Studying to be a vet, or something like that, as if I have the money to pay for college." Shep laughed. "With the body on her, I just keep pushing her into the pageants. Get some attention for the farm and maybe raise a little money."

"The Princess of Pork, right? She's definitely a prime piece of meat," Micky said. He took a drink from his beer. "Hell, I know I'd pay quite a bit for a roll with her. Especially for a taste of virgin pussy."

"Hey! She might be a looker, but that's still my daughter you're talking about."

Micky put his hands up. "I'm just saying, she could make you some real money. Not pageant bullshit."

"Are we playing cards, or what?"

The door opened and Ralph and Bruce came walking back in. "What did we miss?" Bruce asked.

"Nothing much, just making some side bets is all," Micky said. He picked up his cards and grabbed a stack of money. "I call." He put his cards down face up, showing a flush.

Shep looked at his three sixes. "Fuck." He didn't show his cards. "It's yours. I'm going to bed, but you boys have fun and lock up when you leave."

He wanted to scream at the loss, to flip the fucking table. Shep gripped his beer bottle, thinking about smashing it into Micky's face, cutting him with the shards of brown glass.

"Think about the side bet, Shep. A lot of money could come your way."

"Fuck you." Shep slammed the door on his way out.

The door opened behind him, and he turned.

Micky stood there with a fist full of money. "I know the farm is hurting, so let me help."

Shep held the bottle at his side, but didn't swing.

His friend was right. The farm had been doing well for a long time, long enough that he became comfortable—too comfortable. He sighed.

Micky grinned. "I won't pop 'er cherry, but I need a little something. Nothing crazy, just a little relief. I'm lonely, Shep. You're not the only widower of the bunch." He pushed the money into Shep's chest. "Just a few minutes, that's all I need."

Shep didn't touch the money, only looked into the other man's eyes. Finally, he took the crumpled, warm bills. "What do you have in mind?"

2

Beulah sat in front of her mirror brushing her hair. She hated it when her father had poker games. She couldn't stand the leers and crude jokes, especially from Micky. After years of comments and groping, Beulah should've been used to it, but she wasn't; far from it.

The older she got, the more it bothered her. In a way, she wished she was ugly. She wished she didn't have a body like a model that attracted men's attention, but she did. Part of her liked the power, but the conscience she tried to bury fought against it. The attention was something she loathed, yet loved.

When she entered her first pageant, she was mortified. Dubbed the Princess of Pork, Beulah won and won, gaining more attention for her looks. But she didn't want the attention for her looks; she wanted it for her mind.

One day, she'd leave River Grove and go to college. There, she'd study and become a veterinarian, a member of society that helped animals, not led them to slaughter. But until that day came, she used her looks as a crutch.

A light tapping on her door made her jump. Usually, her father didn't knock; he'd just barge in. There were more than a few times he'd walked in on her naked. Rather than apologize and leave, he'd stop and stare until she hastily covered herself. His knocking was almost more alarming than him just walking in.

Beulah changed from her shirt and wore a loose-fitting tank top and sweatpants. "Come in," she said, crossing her arms over her chest.

Shep walked in. He had the glare of intoxication on his face and sadness in his eyes.

Beulah's heart raced. Something bad was going to happen.

"Hey, darlin'," he slurred. "Look, I need you to help me. To help *us*."

Micky moved in next to Shep, his drunken eyes locked on Beulah. His weren't just filled with intoxication, but with lust. "Why, hello, beautiful," he said, pushing past Shep.

"Dad, what's going on?" Her heart was the staccato of a machine gun.

"He's not gonna hurt you. Hell, he's not even gonna touch you." Shep looked away from her. "He's only gonna touch himself. You, ah, just need to show them to him. That's it."

Beulah stood, uncrossing her arms. Her breasts swung under the loose material, which she realized wasn't the best idea. "What the fuck? No, I'm not showing this old fucking pervert my tits! Get the fuck out of my room! Now!"

She didn't think her father could move as fast as he did, but when the slap struck her face, she was left in shock. A burning rose up her face, part from pain and the rest from betrayal.

"How dare you talk to me that way, you ungrateful cunt?" Shep stood over his daughter as tears fell onto the red handprint on her cheek. "This is a family farm, and you're part of the family. If you're not willing to help, get the fuck out. You think this is bad? Try living on the street. You'll be doing much worse than showing your udders, that I can guarantee you."

Micky just smiled, one hand massaging his cock through his pants.

"I'm leaving, but I can tell you this, Beulah, if this doesn't happen, you'd better be gone by sunrise." Shep was shaking as he turned. He locked eyes with Micky before slamming the bedroom door behind him.

"Look, darlin', I'm not gonna hurt you. I'm just a horny old man who ain't seen a set of tits like yours in forty years. Just let me shoot a load of spunk on 'em, and we'll be done. Daddy can pay his bills, and the farm will be good until the slaughter. All you have to do is take 'em out and I'll do the rest. Hell, I'll probably shoot off within a few seconds, anyhow. A couple wipes of a tissue, and it'll be like nothing ever happened."

Beulah cried. Not softly either, but wept. She was trapped. She had no options, and she didn't know if her father was serious. He couldn't throw her out, could he? Would he? As if on autopilot, Beulah grabbed the bottom of her tank top.

"Atta girl," Micky said, still rubbing at his shaft. A wet spot darkened the denim. "Show Uncle Mick those beauts."

Beulah lifted her shirt. The tears flowed faster, running down her face as she exposed herself.

Micky began unbuttoning his pants. "Good girl. Now, kneel like you're in church. I'll take care of the rest."

Lowering herself to the ground, Beulah obeyed. Her room was usually warm, but it felt like she was in a refrigerator.

Micky's cock was in his hand, pointed at her like a weapon. In a way, it was. It was the tool that would steal her innocence. Slowly, he stroked himself. "Push 'em together for me."

With shaking hands, Beulah pressed her breasts together.

"Atta girl," Micky grunted, his strokes growing faster and longer. "Squeeze 'em for Uncle Mick."

Beulah cried.

His right hand was a blur, jerking himself feverishly. Grunts erupted from his throat like that of a pig. And he was a pig. A fucking human pig. Micky's left hand shot out, groping her right breast like it was an udder.

Beulah shrieked, and Micky's pig-like grunts became primal.

His old face scrunched up like he'd eaten

something sour.

She couldn't help but look at the hole of his dick as a shot of cum burst forth, hitting her in the eye.

Beulah screamed as the semen burned like soap.

She screamed, and he grunted.

2003

CHAPTER 5

1

JD eased the Honda down the dirt driveway. Each bump made him shudder, and he prayed the donut would hold up to the rough terrain. A large pothole made the car scream and clunk.

Dusk was settling over the farm, and JD couldn't see all of the potholes.

After getting lost for nearly two hours, stopping to grab something to eat, and a piss break, they finally arrived at the farm without a moment to spare. He'd gotten lost in the daytime, and wandering around after dark wasn't something he wanted to try.

"Jesus," Rich said from the backseat.

"Fuck off," JD said, doing his best to navigate around the divots in the dirt.

Their destination was ahead. An old farmhouse loomed in the distance, and close to it lay a squat, white building. A few trucks could be seen in the gloom of the approaching night.

"That must be the slaughterhouse," Rich said, leaning forward. "They're probably in there right now cutting throats and shit."

"You're fucking gross," Danielle said, pulling her boyfriend back to his seat.

JD looked at Ari from the corner of his eye.

She was focused on the slaughterhouse, not taking her eyes off it. "It's kinda depressing," she said. "Those animals go their whole lives just to be killed and turned into meat. Makes me never want to eat a burger ever again."

JD nodded. He agreed the slaughterhouse was depressing, but nothing would keep him from chowing down on a burger or steak. "I guess we should head to the house," he said, taking the conversation away from animal death. "Hopefully my car will make it out to the cabin, because I certainly don't see shit out here."

Beyond the house and slaughterhouse was a dark tree line. The fading light couldn't pierce the shadowed woods.

Pulling the car to a stop in front of the house, JD killed the engine.

Danielle and Rich wasted no time jumping out, but JD and Ari lingered.

He looked at her, really looked at her, and took her hand.

She smiled at him, the dimples in her cheeks growing deeper.

He loved her, and she loved him, but they both knew their futures were uncertain. JD tried his best to live in the moment, make memories with his girlfriend, and enjoy the trip, but it was difficult. He felt like he was on death row without an execution date. The time was coming when it would end, but would he see it before the blade fell, or would he be blindsided by betrayal?

It was a conversation they'd had many times and not one he wanted to bring up again. Rather, the two teen lovers stared at each other for just a moment before leaning in to kiss.

"Hey, let's go!" Rich yelled.

"Yeah, come on. There'll be plenty of time for kissing and fucking later," Danielle joined in.

Ari looked at JD. "It'll be okay," she said.

"What will?"

She kissed him on the nose. "Everything." She opened her door. "Come on, before they have a tantrum."

He followed her out. JD knew he'd follow her anywhere.

2

Beulah stood at the window watching the teens exit their car. It was a Jap car, which she had no use for. They weren't practical, and if something wasn't practical, it had no business being in her life.

"You finished up the cabin, right?" Beulah turned and asked her daughter.

Hattie stood; it hurt to sit. Her mask was tied snuggly to the lower half of her face and her eyes were finally dry, albeit red. "Yeth. I finithed afta...afta Wayne—"

Putting her hand up, Beulah silenced the girl. "Yes, I know. I get it." She turned to her daughter. "You're a woman now, whether you like it or not. What's done is done, Hattie, ya hear."

Hattie looked down, ashamed. "Yeth, motha."

"Now listen, you learned a very valuable lesson today. We are ladies. Men are stronger than us, bigger, faster, but we have something they want. Something that has ended empires and created new ones." She stepped up to Hattie and grabbed her sore crotch. "This. This slit between your legs and the tits on your chest. Even with a face like yours, men will still fuck you. But don't let them get it for free, ya hear? No, always get something from them. They get to bust their nut, and you get something. We're smarter than them, my girl. That pussy is power. Never forget it. Now, let's welcome our guests."

Beulah walked toward the front door, checking herself in the hall mirror. She looked great, with just enough cleavage, and her hair was messy, but in a sexy way. She could've used some makeup, but that wasn't in the cards.

These teen boys would shoot their load for a strong breeze.

She'd show her daughter how a woman snared a man.

"Welcome to the Winslow Farm," Beulah said as she walked out the front door.

A teenage boy, who looked like he used more product in his hair than most women she knew, was walking toward the door.

Just behind him was a girl who had a resting bitch face like Beulah had never seen. *Oh, this little one can already tell that I would fuck her little boy-toy. He'd get one suck job from me and that would be the end of them. I'd change that kid's life with this mouth and pussy.*

Beulah may not have the body she once had as a girl, but experience was worth more than a firm chest and tight snatch. At least, that's what she told herself.

"You must be the travelers that Chet called me about earlier." She looked up at the darkening sky. "I was expecting you much sooner."

Another teen boy and girl emerged from the car.

"Either way, the cabin is ready for you. I'm sure you'll find it to your liking, I hope." Beulah batted her eyes and made it a point to lean just slightly, emphasizing her chest.

"Yeah, that was us," said the boy with the slick hair.

His girlfriend moved close to him, not taking her eyes from Beulah.

Instinctively, he put his arm around her waist, letting his hand fall to her ass. "We had a little trouble along the way, but we're here now."

The other pair of teens joined them. The boy who exited the driver's seat walked in front of his friend and bitch-faced girlfriend.

"Oh, hi. I'm JD. Yes, we're the ones who need the cabin for a few days. We hit a little car trouble." He pointed at the donut on the front of the car. "Thank you for taking us on such short notice."

Beulah could feel the boy's innocence. He might have been a virgin, but she doubted it.

His female companion was staring daggers at her, but the girl had an air of confidence. Unlike bitch-face who just looked like a cunt.

Even if this kid had tasted pussy before, Beulah could do stuff to him that would change his life.

"Not a problem at all. It's not quite hunting season, so the cabin was available. My daughter prepped it nice for you." Beulah cringed when she heard the door open behind her.

Hattie could be shy around adults, and especially kids. But for some reason, her deformed daughter decided to make an appearance.

Turning, Beulah looked at Hattie as she stood behind her, pig mask and all.

There was an audible gasp from the teens when her daughter stepped out. Even though the girl wore her mask, they could tell something was wrong with her face.

Beulah looked back at the four teens and plastered on a fake smile, a talent she'd all but perfected over the years. "So, where are y'all from?"

JD opened his mouth to respond, but his girlfriend stepped forward.

"I'm sorry, and I'm not trying to be rude, but we're really tired. Can you just show us to the cabin?"

Beulah let out a little sigh. "Oh yes, dear. I should've thought better of it. It's quite simple to get to." She pointed to a rough-looking road that was truly more of a trail. "Just drive down through the trees and you'll see it. If it wasn't so dark, you'd see it just fine. Can't miss it." Her smile was painful.

"Thanks," JD said as his girlfriend led him back to the car.

The other pair of teens were right behind them.

The small import started up with the whine of a four-cylinder engine.

Dim headlights cut through the night as they slowly made their way to the cabin.

Turning on her heels, Beulah faced Hattie. "Why did you come out? You scared them away. I was going to invite them in and show you just how easily dumb boys could be manipulated."

Hattie looked at the ground. Her rough breathing was raspy through the mask. "Thorry mama."

"Get inside and wash up." Beulah watched the car park at the cabin, the headlights just visible through the trees. "And stay away from them, ya hear? Those kids are nothing but trouble."

Hattie's head was still down as she walked back into the house.

The sound of American trucks made Beulah turn and look back at the slaughterhouse. The day was done, and the farm hands were leaving for the night.

Even though it had been hours, Beulah could still taste the remnants of Brett's load in her throat. But that was far from the worst thing that happened that day. She crossed a line with her daughter, and it was a line that could never be redrawn.

Beulah still remembered the day that Micky shot a load in her eye at her father's authority. It was the first of many blasts of cum that would grace her face over her lifetime, and she didn't think those days were over. Not while she had a farm to run and no money to do it.

Her father was a fucking joke. The King of Pork? Even more of a joke. He was king of nothing, and she was his prize pig. The Princess of Pork, always there to fuck or suck a creditor to make good on his debt, her innocence stolen by the man who was supposed to protect her.

Was she any better? She did the same with Hattie, but worse.

Her poor daughter's first sexual experience was with a big-dick farmhand in a dusty cabin—virginity robbed in the blink of an eye—and for what? A few weeks of wages until the slaughter.

And now that Wayne knew Hattie's sex was an

option, would he take it when he wanted? Would this be a daily bargain with the man, or would Beulah fall back into her role as the Winslow whore?

3

The cabin was musty, but to JD, it looked pretty good. A small, open living room with a kitchen and woodstove dominated most of the space. Two small bedrooms occupied the rest of the structure, with an even smaller bathroom.

They had electricity and water, plus a cheap roof over their heads; JD considered that a win.

"Well, that was kinda fucking creepy, if you ask me," Danielle said as she set her duffle bag on the couch.

"Yeah, what was up with the girl in the mask? So fucking weird," Rich replied. "Did you see the way she was looking at us? *Blech*, gives me the creeps."

"I'm sure you didn't notice the fact she had giant tits, right?" Danielle looked at him with a half-serious glare.

Rich shrugged. "Eh, I guess they were decent, but looking at the chest of a freak doesn't do it for me, ya know?"

"Boys are pervs," Ari said. "You'll look at any tits, even if they're attached to a mannequin."

JD shrugged. "I've seen some stacked mannequins before." He flinched as Ari playfully swatted him.

"Well, I guess you don't need to play with mine anymore. Maybe we can find a slutty mannequin for you to grope."

JD smirked and wrapped her in a hug. "Oh, don't do that to me, baby. You know how much I love your titties. In fact, why don't we go check out our room real quick? Maybe you can give me a show."

Ari moved in like she was going to kiss him and tapped him on the nose. "Nope. I'm going to see how the hot water is and take a shower."

JD opened his mouth to speak.

"A shower *alone* and behind a locked door." She turned and walked away, then paused and looked over her shoulder. "But if you're a good boy, maybe I'll let you see them later." Before he could say a word, Ari disappeared into the bathroom.

4

Ari turned on the shower and gave it a second to warm up, hoping the old cabin had hot water. Cold showers were not pleasant, but she needed one. She wanted her pussy eaten, and JD was pretty damn talented. Not that she had anyone to compare him to, but since she came almost every time he ate her out, she considered that good. After this first leg of the road trip, she could use a good oral session.

Among many things, that would be missing from her life when they separated for college in only a few weeks. Try as she might to calm her boyfriend's nerves, Ari was just as anxious about the distance.

JD tried so hard to make their trip perfect, and she loved him for it. She knew it was an obstacle they could overcome. She hoped.

Steam rose from the shower, filling the room with mist.

Ari cracked the small window to let some of it escape before stripping down. It felt good to be out of her bra, and she rubbed at her free breasts. There was no sexual pleasure in the act, just relief—like scratching an itch you couldn't quite reach.

She stood nude and looked down at her crotch. The small patch of hair she kept was getting a little long, but that wouldn't stop JD from going down on her. Just the thought of his rough tongue on her throbbing clit made her slick with lust. She stepped into the shower, the hot water only made her hotter.

As she quickly washed, the desire to touch herself was mounting. Fucking in a new place was always fun, but even masturbating was thrilling. Ari rolled the swollen nub of her clit between her fingers, teasing more blood into it. She edged herself, touching and pressing on the pink button of pleasure.

The window creaked on the old tracks as if someone was opening it.

Ari stopped and quickly rinsed the soap from her body. She was flushed from the water and the clitoral stimulation. Knowing her boyfriend was outside the window made it even hotter. She was tempted to call him into the bathroom and have him go down on her right then and there.

She opened the curtain, and rather than grabbing her towel and drying off in the shower, she stepped out nude. If JD made it a point to go outside and open the steamy window, the least she could do was give him a little show. She kept her back to the window and could hear his lusty breathing.

JD loved her ass, and when he was ready to cum, he'd always fuck her from behind. She'd usually already gotten off from his mouth by that time, so her pussy would be drenched. If JD was feeling frisky, he'd spread her ass and put a wet thumb in there, rubbing his cock from the inside as he fucked.

Ari bent over to dry her legs and gave him a perfect shot of her pussy from the back. She'd had enough of teasing him. "You like what you see?" she said, turning around.

A mutated pig stared back at her. No, not a pig, but a person in a pig mask.

Ari screamed, covering herself with the towel as she realized the deformed girl was the one spying on her.

The girl disappeared as a loud knock hit the door.

"Ari, are you okay?" JD asked as he tried the locked knob.

Realizing she wasn't in danger, Ari wrapped the towel around herself and opened the door.

"That…that fucking freak was watching me shower."

"What? Who? The girl in the mask?" JD asked.

"Yes. Fucking bitch was standing outside of the window watching me. Not only is she fucking ugly, but she's a dyke bitch, too."

Rich opened the front door and looked out into the darkness. "I don't see anyone."

"Trust me, she was there."

"Well, she's gone now," JD said, hugging his wet girlfriend.

"Good. I hope they get this tire soon and we can

get the fuck out of this place."

Even though none of them said anything, she knew they were thinking the same thing.

5

The back door shut. It was quiet, and Hattie did her best to make as little noise as possible, but Beulah had been sneaking out of the house since before her daughter was even a glimmer in her eye.

The stairs creaked as Hattie, again, did her best to sneak up to her room.

Beulah knew where the girl had gone: to spy on the kids in the cabin. Yes, she could've stopped it, but why bother? The girl was curious, especially about kids her age. Besides, the worst thing Hattie might see was some fucking or weed smoking, both of which might be good for the girl. If she could at least see somewhat pleasurable sex, it might give her hope for the future. Beulah knew her daughter's first sexual experience wasn't the best, and she hoped it hadn't ruined it for the girl.

Beulah listened as the door latched shut, signaling her daughter was in her room. She needed to talk with her daughter, explain everything to her, and warn her about bad people.

Bad people were everywhere, and for a long time, they'd been a big part of her life. It felt like the life of a different person when Beulah thought back on those days. They didn't seem real, but she knew they were.

She stopped outside of Hattie's room. Beulah was getting ready to talk to her daughter about bad people. People who would take advantage of her. People who would use her for their gains. She raised her hand to knock and stopped.

Beulah couldn't do it. She knew herself all too well. She was one of the bad people. And she remembered how she became that way.

1987

CHAPTER 6

1

Even though Beulah had lived in New York City for nearly a year, she couldn't quite get used to the noise. After living almost her entire life in River Grove, the move to the Big Apple was jarring. The country's silence was something special that she'd taken for granted. She didn't think she'd ever sleep again if it weren't for earplugs.

She hadn't slept well the night before; not because of the traffic, but due to her nerves. Without an agent, getting an audition was next to impossible. But sometimes luck was better than anything else, and when a photographer saw her crossing a busy street, her luck changed.

The man, Bruno, worked for an exotic car company and was in the city for a photoshoot. The executive decided he needed more girls for the spread at the last minute. Bruno, with his eye for beauty, set out looking. He talked with all the agencies, but none of their girls fit the bill or were already booked.

That was when fate struck.

Beulah, who quickly decided she would go by B, trusted her gut and met Bruno in a warehouse near the World Trade Center.

She'd heard horror stories from other girls about

men in the industry. The old saying, *'It's not who you know, it's who you blow,'* made her cringe. She was twenty-two, and not a prude by any means, but the thought of sucking a strange cock just for the opportunity to get a few pictures was absurd.

The other girls in the business laughed at her.

Luckily for her, Bruno was as gay as the day was long.

The photoshoot went well, and Beulah made her first bit of money as a model. She thought that would be it for her, that the world would know who she was, but she soon discovered the harsh reality of the business.

That paycheck went fast, leaving her broke once again.

Beulah picked up a few more modeling gigs, but they didn't pay nearly as much. And they weren't what she considered *legit*. Lingerie, leather, nude, she took what she could get. She even had offers of getting into adult films, but it wasn't something she could bring herself to do. Beulah had a difficult time just posing nude, praying that no one, especially her father, would ever discover the pictures.

But that was just about a year ago—a year since she broke away from the Winslow Farm and bought a one-way ticket north to New York.

She sat in a waiting room with a script in her hand. It wasn't a big role, but it was a shot at something other than modeling.

A new sitcom was filming nearby, and the producers were hunting for some unknowns to fill in spots and keep the budget down. The gig didn't pay much, but like modeling, Beulah needed a foot in the door with the acting scene.

Tapping her foot, she read the lines repeatedly, hoping she had the New York accent. There wasn't much of a southern drawl in her speech, but enough that it was noticeable.

The door opened.

Beulah felt like she was going to puke. Her nerves were almost as jangled as the day her father walked into her room with Micky in tow. She stood and straightened her dress, put on a fake smile, and went in for her audition.

2

"How'd it go?" Candace asked. She sipped from her drink and played with the straw. Her dark hair was teased and tortured and held with enough hairspray to put its own hole in the ozone layer.

Beulah played with a drop of condensation on the side of her glass. It was her third drink in the last half hour. She needed to slow down. Not from fear of getting drunk, but because she was on a budget. She could count on a few guys buying her drinks most nights, which was nice. She'd even flirt and occasionally fuck some of them, but usually just accepted the drinks, gave them a minute of her time, and dismissed them.

If she was really feeling good, she'd even turn down the hot ones. The guys she'd normally take somewhere and fuck, she'd shoot them down just to let them know she could. Everyone had an ego, especially a male model in the big city, but nothing hurt more than rejection. And she knew all about that.

"Well, you know how these things go. *'Don't call us, we'll call you,'* kinda stuff. I thought I did well, but you never know what they're looking for."

Candace nodded and drank. "Oh, I know it, honey. This is just a big fucking game." She waved her hand around the bar as if Beulah didn't know what she was talking about. "The entire city is fake, and the industry is the fakest of them all. Fake tits, fake teeth, fake friends—except me, of course—fake fucking everything." She was starting to slur as she finished the rest of her drink and looked around, hoping to catch the eye of some bum to pay for her next round, but the bar wasn't as packed as she'd hoped.

With alcohol racing through her bloodstream, Beulah was feeling good. She wished someone would hit on her. She wasn't in the rejection kind of mood, but more of a, *'I'll fuck anything,'* mood.

It was rare for her, but lately, she'd been hornier than usual. She even noticed when she showered earlier that her nipples were extra sensitive. The hot water felt like warm fingers rubbing her down. She thought about pleasuring herself before going out, but she knew if she came, there was a good chance she was putting on pajamas and staying in for the night. Which, at that moment, didn't sound like a bad move. Her funds were running low, and the guys in that place weren't paying her much mind.

"Are all these guys queer?" Candace asked as she slid money to the bartender.

Beulah laughed. "They must be, because we look fucking hot tonight."

And they did.

Her shirt was low cut, exposing her ample tits, and she purposely didn't wear panties to outline the shape of her pussy. Not to mention, Beulah liked the sensation of the zipper against her. She crossed and uncrossed her legs more times than she could count that evening.

Ordering another drink, she rubbed her forearm against her chest. She winced as she touched the tender flesh of her breast.

"What? Is your bra too tight? I'm sure with tits the size of yours, you'd need some serious support." Candace chased her straw with her lips before catching up to it.

"No, it's not that. My nipples were a little sensitive earlier, but it felt good. Now my boobs hurt like I just ran a marathon without a bra."

"Hmm, you're not pregnant, are you?" Candace asked with a grin.

Beulah paused, her drink just about to touch her lips. *When was my last period?* She couldn't remember, but she didn't think it was that long ago. *Was it?* Most of the guys she fucked wore condoms, but some nights she'd been so drunk, she wasn't sure if they did. She knew she told them to, but what if they didn't listen?

Shaking off the shock of the possibility of pregnancy, Beulah put on a smile. "No, not possible." To emphasize the point, she took a sip of her drink.

"I Wanna Dance with Somebody," by Whitney Houston, blared over the speakers.

Candace all but jumped out of her chair. "I love

this song!" She grabbed Beulah's hand. "Come on, let's get on the dance floor. Maybe if we shake our asses, someone will buy our next few drinks."

Beulah let her friend lead her to the dance floor. Their gyrations attracted the attention of a few men, but no matter what, Beulah couldn't get the thought out of her head.

Could I be pregnant?

3

A guy poured a line of cocaine just below Beulah's belly button, and she giggled gleefully.

With a rolled-up dollar bill in his nose, the guy snorted the line of coke from her skin. He pressed his finger to his opposite nostril and snorted harder, forcing the narcotic deep into his sinuses.

There was a bit of residue left on her creamy skin, and Beulah looked at him with lust in her eyes and hunger in her cunt. "Lick it up, baby."

The man, who was probably a model but not one she knew, smiled at her. He pushed his hair back and licked her.

Beulah's eyes rolled back as she arched her pelvis. She put her hands on his head, like so many guys had done to her, and pushed his face lower. It had been a while since she had her pussy eaten, and eaten well, but she was drunk and high; a stiff breeze would make her cum.

Pretty Boy got the hint and slid around so he was between her legs.

She allowed him to wrap his arms around her thighs.

A bead of nectar ran from her, sliding down the crack of her ass.

His warm, welcoming tongue found it just as it reached her asshole.

Beulah arched her back, driving his tongue into her open sex. She needed him to run it up her cleft, find the aching nub of her clit, but hearing him moan as he tasted her essence was almost as good. Not quite, but almost.

Wiggling lower, she pushed his nose against the engorged swell at the top of her pussy. Just that pressure alone began the climb of an orgasm she knew would be mind-blowing.

His nose, still powdered with cocaine, slid with her wetness as his hot tongue lapped at her aching clit.

Beulah melted in the warmth of alcohol and cocaine as the orgasm started. Like a flood of honey, her entire body was dipped in pleasure as it built and built. She grabbed his long hair and ground her pussy into his face, willing his tongue harder against her as she came.

In that second, nothing else mattered. Not the auditions, not her former life as the Princess of Pork, and not even the fact she may be pregnant. No, in that instant, all she cared about was the stranger's face between her thighs. She let the world drift by as she dripped with pleasure.

4

Vomit swirled down the toilet as Beulah looked at her swelling belly in the mirror. She looked like shit.

The saying that women glow when they're pregnant was bullshit, at least for her. And the morning sickness? She thought that was supposed to end after the first trimester.

It had been nearly six months since her oral escapades with the model in his apartment. That had been the last good thing to happen to her. Since then, she'd been on multiple auditions, but hadn't had a call back.

The modeling was drying up, at least the tame stuff. It seemed like the only work she was getting was in skin mags, which she couldn't stand, but that was the only thing that kept the lights on.

A baby would complicate things. Having an abortion was her plan A, but with just enough money to barely scrape by, she couldn't afford one. Since she didn't know who the father was, there was no way to get him to help pay for it.

She figured enough alcohol and cocaine would kill the life inside of her, but the baby continued to grow. It wouldn't be long before the modeling gigs stopped. Few men wanted to see a pregnant woman, even if she had fat tits. Soon, she wouldn't be able to hide the bump, and before long, it would look like she swallowed a watermelon.

The phone rang in the other room.

Beulah walked nude through her small apartment and snatched it off the ringer.

No one usually called her except for Candace, but they'd grown distant over the last few months.

"Hello."

"Is this Beulah Winslow?" the woman on the phone asked.

"Ah, yes, this is her."

"Hi, Ms. Winslow, this is Marina Gaskins. You came in for an audition a few months ago."

Beulah perked up. She remembered the audition well. It was for a spot on the sitcom, but she was certain they'd filled the spot.

"Oh, yes, I remember it well." Her heart was thumping.

The baby—the fucking baby—kicked and moved.

"Well, I'm calling because one of the leads in the series suffered...let's call it a setback, and has separated from the show. Your audition stood out to us, and we'd love to have you back to re-audition for a much larger role."

Beulah's heart sank with dread. She knew she'd be perfect for the show, but the role was a co-ed working at a yoga studio, not a fucking pregnant whale.

"Hello? Are you still there?"

Beulah hadn't realized how long she'd been standing in disbelief. "Yeah, yeah, I'm here. Wh- when is the audition?"

There was a ruffle of paper through the phone line.

"Um, we have an opening a week from Thursday. Will that work for you?"

Her mind raced as the baby rolled over again.

Why? Why couldn't you have fucking died? Didn't I drink enough or do enough coke to kill you?

It was clear she hadn't. Inside her, life was growing. Again, another dream of hers was to be killed by a Winslow.

Her father ensured she didn't get to follow her first dream of becoming a veterinarian, and now her bastard child was robbing her chances at acting—stealing her youth and mutilating the body that won beauty pageants and brought her modeling contracts.

She wouldn't let it happen. *Couldn't* let it happen. She had a week to figure it out. Beulah wouldn't lose another dream, even if it cost her everything.

5

The wire hanger felt flimsy in her hand. Flimsy, yet heavy at the same time.

Beulah had soaked it in rubbing alcohol after straightening it out, and hadn't touched it in hours. She just let it sit in the clear liquid that would, hopefully, purify it.

Now that it was in her hand, the gravity of the situation was unlike any she'd ever felt.

Nude on the toilet, covered in goosebumps, she stared at the hanger like a talisman of doom. But she knew the object could bring hope. It would set her back on the path she started—a lifeline to get her back where she belonged, walking her way to stardom. She just had to do it.

She filled the tub half full of warm water. No one told her to do that, but she thought it might help. She did not know why, but it seemed right; call it maternal instinct.

Sweating and racked with chills, Beulah got in the tub. The water enveloped her like amniotic fluid, and she wondered what her baby was feeling at that moment.

Did it know it was about to die? To be ripped from the womb with an old hanger and left to rot, if it wasn't dead already?

No, it floated, oblivious to anything besides the soft voice of its mother.

Beulah spread her legs, resting her heels on the tub's rim. The last time she was in that position, she'd been receiving some of the best oral sex ever. Now, she was about to receive a kiss of cheap metal invading her womb.

Looking over the mound of her belly and down at the thick pubic hair around her vagina, her breathing was ragged and tears stung her eyes. This was just another sacrifice she had to make for her chance at stardom. Her entire life had been about sacrifice, but not for her.

She gave up so much for her father and the farm, and where had it gotten her? About to self-abort her child in a cheap apartment in New York. She should've been a veterinarian, working with animals she loved, surrounded by a strong family. Instead, she was forced into killing the animals and becoming a bargaining chip for a father who didn't love her.

Gently, she put the hook of the hanger against her vagina and pushed it in.

"Ah," she grunted as it scraped her. Her tears flowed faster and harder. Her chest heaved with every pained breath. Farther, she pushed.

The rough edge of the hook gouged the soft walls of her womanhood.

"Fuck!"

The water pinkened as she plunged deeper.

Beulah didn't know how far she had to go. Deeper she went.

Warmth ran from between her legs as if she'd pissed in the tub, but it wasn't urine; it was blood.

Still, she needed to go farther.

The hook hit the soft wall of her cervix, the last barrier before her womb.

Grunting, she pushed, shivering with pain.

The hanger slithered through.

The baby kicked.

It wasn't the soft kick of mommy eating spicy food or listening to calming music. It was a kick of primal fear, of survival that all living things possessed.

The baby resisted the hanger, pushing further into the womb.

Beulah felt as if the fetus was in her chest as she fished with the instrument of abortion. "Gahhh!"

Blood poured from her, turning the water from pink to red.

Still, the baby fought the expulsion.

Finding purchase on flesh that was not hers, Beulah sunk the hanger into it.

The baby flailed, blooms of panic surging through its forming brain.

Beulah pulled and screamed.

The hanger ripped free from the meat of the fetus and lodged into the soft flesh of her womb.

"Fucking hell!" Beulah's throat was raw.

Chunks of gore floated in the water. Clots that resembled bits of jelly bobbed within the red slurry in the tub.

She worked the hanger from her muscle, and

once again, fished for the body of her unborn child.

The pain was unbearable. Nausea rolled over her in waves as her injured child pressed against her internal organs in a vain attempt to escape the invading hanger.

"One more time." Beulah dug around inside of herself, but her vision was clouding. Darkness was starting to envelop her, closing off her periphery.

A sound—a banging—was coming from somewhere.

There was a voice.

"Beulah!" the voice yelled.

She was slipping into delirium. Her fingers had lost their dexterity, and the hanger slipped from her grasp. Half of it was still buried in her vagina.

"God, is that you?" she mumbled as the banging increased.

No, it wouldn't be God who came for her, but Satan.

Beulah slipped into unconsciousness and slid under the red water. It wasn't quite the rose-colored lens she was looking for.

6

There were voices as Beulah came to.

"… a lot of blood. Get the transfusion set up now!"

"Honestly, fuck her for what she did. We need to save the baby."

"We will, but the mother needs to live too. It's our fucking job."

Beulah's eyes fluttered.

Bright lights and masked faces loomed above her.

More pain tore through her, and it felt like the lower half of her body was on fire.

"Th-the baby," she croaked.

One of the masked faces looked at her and placed a wet cloth on her forehead.

"Shh, we're going to save the baby," a soft, feminine voice said.

"N-no, don't save it. Please don't," Beulah whined.

The other masked faces looked at each other with disgust in their eyes.

A cramp like nothing she'd ever felt before ripped at her guts.

Something was happening.

"The baby. It's coming," one of them said.

"Beulah, I need you to push. Just pretend like you're trying to poop."

Beulah didn't want to push, but she needed the torment to end. She bore down and pushed.

Fluid ran from her, and with it came more pain. And then, something came out of her—something large.

One of the masked doctors backed away with fear in his eyes.

She did it. Beulah had killed her child, and the doctor was reacting to that. It had to be.

And then, the baby cried. It didn't sound right.

She had heard newborns scream before, and something about that cry was *off*.

"Congratulations. It's a girl," the doctor said before laying the monstrosity on her belly.

Beulah screamed when she saw the deformed child.

The baby's face was split with the worst cleft she'd ever seen. Gouges and cuts riddled the pink body of the newborn baby—wounds from the assault with the hanger.

Before Beulah could throw the deformed child onto the floor, the doctor pulled the infant from its mother's stomach.

"Now, she has to go into immediate surgery. I hope you're proud."

She wasn't. She was angry. Angry at a life lost and a life gained. Angry at herself, but mostly at the world. Beulah didn't think her life could get any worse.

She was wrong.

2003

CHAPTER 7

1

Davey's blood alcohol content was on its way up as he threw back another shot of cheap whiskey.

He wiped his mouth with the back of his hand, feeling the rough stubble against his skin. The scent of soap lingered, which was a plus.

After fleeing the barfly's apartment and grabbing the number for the farm, Davey went back to his decrepit abode. He slugged down the beers he'd bought with the stolen money, smoked some of the stolen cigarettes, and took a shower.

Feeling refreshed after washing the slime from his cock, he treated himself to a nap on his sagging couch.

The nap did wonders for him, and with the prospect of a new job on the horizon, he celebrated with a trip to the local watering hole.

Davey put a $20 bill on the empty glass and caught the eye of the bartender. "One more, if you don't mind," he said.

The bartender took the cash and upended a bottle of shitty booze, pouring a sloshing shot into the glass.

Davey grabbed the cup and tossed back the drink. "Eh, pour me a beer, too."

Knowing Davey wasn't leaving a tip, the bartender rolled his eyes. He poured the beer and gave Davey back his change, which he promptly pocketed.

Two guys who smelled vaguely like a barn bellied up to the bar next to him.

"You almost made her puke?" one of the men asked the other.

"Yeah, if she had been wearing mascara, that shit would've been running down her face. Full raccoon mode."

"Dude, that's wild. I had a pretty good day on the farm myself." Then, to the bartender, "Two drafts and two shots."

The bartender set the drinks down and took the offered money.

"I could tell. We heard you and the freak all the way at the house."

The guy threw back his shot, grimaced, and laughed. "Oh yeah, the freak was a screamer. And a bleeder."

"I guess that's a fringe benefit of working on the farm, right?"

"Gotta get something to smell like pig shit all day."

Davey sipped at his beer and stood up behind the two men. "You boys working at the Winslow Farm?" he asked, jutting into their conversation.

They both turned and looked him up and down. "Yeah, why?"

Reaching into his pocket, Davey pulled out the tab of paper. "I was thinking about getting a job there."

"That fucking bitch can't hardly pay us besides getting our cocks wet, and she's out there looking to hire?"

Davey was confused, but waited for their fit of laughter to die down.

"I'm Wayne, and this is Brett."

"Davey."

The three of them shook hands.

"So, the owner doesn't have the money to pay you? Why would you work if you're not getting paid?"

Brett took a sip of his beer. "Eh, she pays us, but sometimes it's light or sporadic. The big money is coming from the slaughter, which is probably why she's looking for some new workers."

"That, and she's afraid we're gonna quit," Wayne said. He drank half his beer in a gulp. "Bitch always jerks us around for cash, but she makes good on it most of the time. And when she can't, she makes up for it in other ways."

Davey smirked. He'd been paid in *other* ways before. Cash was king, but pussy was a close second. "Oh yeah, how so?"

Both men raised their eyebrows.

"Dude, do we have to explain it to you? The bitch will drain your nuts in every which way possible. She's a bit older, but a good lay," Wayne said. "She has a freak of a daughter, and when I say freak, I don't mean in the sheets. Like a legit sideshow creature."

"Yeah? What happened to her?"

"Well, for starters, she has a fucked up cleft palate. Like kid-in-a-third-world-country bad. I haven't seen her face in a while, but when I did, I nearly shit my pants. Her mouth is split, right up the middle, all the way up her nose. That nasty shit is full of crooked ass teeth, but she does the world a favor and wears a mask." Brett finished his beer and signaled for another.

"A mask? That's kinda fucked up," Davey said.

"Yeah, well, she needs it," Wayne said. "She's got a smoking body for a freak, but that face is fucked up. There are a few nasty scars on her body too, but it doesn't take away from the fact she's stacked." He put his hands up to his chest, mimicking breasts.

"But the mom isn't bad, though, And she's a *freak* freak. Like sexual deviant," Brett said.

"Sounds like my kind of gal," Davey said.

"My advice," Wayne spoke, "come work the slaughter, fuck Beulah, the owner, get paid, and leave. Honestly, I think that's the route I'm headed down. I need to get the fuck out of River Grove."

Davey nodded. That didn't sound like a half-bad idea. He needed to pull up his shallow roots and take off; let the wind carry him wherever it may.

"Sounds like a plan. I've had my fair share of freaks, so I don't mind one more."

On cue, the door opened and in walked a woman.

"Oh fuck," Davey said as he recognized the barfly from earlier in the day. He still had a wad of her stolen money in his pocket.

2

The barfly looked a little better than when he'd last seen her, with a fresh shellac of makeup and clean hair. But it was, no doubt, her.

She had a smile on her face as she scanned the

bar.

Davey tried to avert his gaze, but her eyes found his.

Her demeanor changed from happy to bitch really fast.

"Fuck," he said again.

The echo of her heels was loud as she stomped toward him. "Hey, asshole," she said as she walked up to him. "Nice departure this morning. First, you fuck my mouth with your nasty cock. Then, you give me two pumps and a load in my ass crack without a thought of getting me off. And then, you have the nerve to steal from me? Huh, a real piece of shit you are."

Brett and Wayne fought a losing battle to withhold their laughter as the barfly ripped into Davey.

"Hey, I might've been a shitty lay, but I'm no thief," Davey lied. "Come on, I work for a living, my dear. I have no need to steal from you." He turned to Brett and Wayne, who finally controlled their laughter. "Look, these two boys are my co-workers."

Brett swallowed a chuckle. "Yup, that's right. We all work on a farm. The three of us are as thick as thieves."

"And that's why I had a little odor. Because of the farm."

The lies just rolled from Davey's mouth. He knew it sounded like bullshit. There was no reason working on a farm would make his cock smell like death unless he was fucking the animals. He'd done a lot of nasty shit, but beastiality wasn't one of them.

Women believed the lies of hot men a hell of a

lot easier than someone ugly; Davey knew that was a fact. He could see the anger melting from her face.

"Well, if you didn't take my money, I must've spent it."

Davey nodded along, convincing her of his false innocence. "Yeah, babe, we were having a good time last night. And this morning." He shot her a cheesy wink, and he knew it was making her wet. Davey put his arm around her and nuzzled her ear. "My cock is much cleaner now if you want to suck it again."

She turned and playfully swatted his chest. "Oh, you're bad."

He looked at Brett and Wayne and thought, *What the hell*? "How about a little action for my boys too? I told them how hot your pussy was and the things you can do with your mouth."

A look of real offense shot across her face. "I'm not a fucking whore," she spat.

Davey grabbed her arm as she tried to pull away. "I'm just playing. That pussy is all mine." He flagged down the bartender. "Four beers, please, and keep 'em coming." He tossed another stolen $20 bill on the counter and draped his arm around her shoulders. "We're gonna have a good night."

3

The wet, squelching sounds of sex echoed off the outside of the building.

Davey was, once again, getting his dick sucked by the barfly, while Wayne rearranged her insides with his hog of a cock.

Brett stood off to the side watching, waiting his

turn as he played with his semi-erect dick.

Davey looked at Wayne and they smiled and laughed as they fucked her from both ends.

The rush of an orgasm was building in Davey's sack. He pulled out of her mouth and came in her hair.

"Hey, motherfucker," she yelled, her head bobbing as Wayne pumped harder. "Did you just fucking cum in my hair?"

Davey shook his cock, flinging the last glob of cum onto the tip of her nose.

Wayne grunted and pulled out, shooting a load onto the back of her shirt.

"What the fuck?" she yelled, stumbling forward. Her pants were around her ankles, and she tripped, falling face first onto the dirty ground.

Laughing, the drunk men tucked their dicks away and darted back into the bar.

Davey knew he was going to enjoy working on the farm.

CHAPTER 8

1

Hattie stood nude in front of the mirror. Her body, one that made men like Wayne want to hurt her, was riddled with scars.

The mask sat on her dresser, waiting for her to don it again.

She touched her heavy breasts, lifting them, squeezing them. It felt different when she did it as opposed to Wayne.

His touch was hard and rough. He didn't rub her like the boys in the cabin would. She knew they would be gentle. They probably touched the other girls like that, very soft so it felt good.

Hattie looked at the thatch of black hair between her legs; it was matted with dried blood. She touched herself and winced. She knew touching certain spots could feel good, like, really good.

What Wayne had done did not feel good. Not at all. He was too rough, and didn't treat her nicely. It was like she was an animal, and he was breeding her.

Hattie didn't know if she ever wanted a man to touch her again, at least for a long time.

There hadn't been many men in her life, and the ones who came usually left soon after. But there was one who said he'd never hurt her, never leave her, a man her mommy said was a bad man. But after what

Mommy made her do with Wayne, she didn't think anyone could be worse.

It had been years since Hattie and her mother talked about Shep Winslow, the *real* owner of the farm.

She hadn't thought about her grandfather in a while, but the image of him burst into her brain and refused to leave.

Her mother said her grandfather was gone, but Hattie wasn't stupid. She heard the sounds, the squealing, coming from the basement.

The heavy locks made it impossible for her to go down there, but Hattie knew where the keys were. She knew more than her mother gave her credit for. And, she knew the truth about what happened to her grandfather all those years ago.

The lies her mother spewed were nothing but nonsense. But the pain and betrayal she felt were real. Her mother hated her, and she knew. No, she never said it outright, but Hattie was smart. She could feel the hatred like a physical thing.

Hattie didn't remember her grandfather much, but what she did were happy thoughts—good times between them, even if her mother didn't approve. It wasn't fair that she couldn't see him anymore. The more she thought about it, the more enraged she became.

Well, Hattie Winslow was about to change that.

2

The house was dark and quiet.

Hattie wore only a long shirt and nothing else,

not even her mask. She let her monstrous face breathe without the restriction of the plastic covering.

The moon was bright in the sky, shining silver light through the windows. She imagined the kids at the cabin bathing in the moon's light, naked and fucking, enjoying their lust. Something Hattie longed for. In the future, possibly, but in that moment, she wanted something else.

To see *him*.

Hattie climbed up onto the counter and grabbed an old bag of coffee. It was full of damp beans, but she wasn't looking for a pick-me-up. She dug through the coffee until her hand touched a ring of thick keys, then she pulled them free.

The house was silent, but she expected the sound of angry footsteps any second, yet nothing came. No yelling or charging, just the sounds of the house and pigs outside.

Hattie walked silently to the basement door. She touched the cool locks and found the right keys. Slowly, she opened the door.

It whined in protest, and again, Hattie thought she'd be caught.

Something moved in the dark below.

With shaking fingers, she reached into the inky gloom, landing on the light switch. She flipped it up, illuminating the bottom of the steps.

More movement came from the basement, but nothing could be seen.

Hattie knew he was down there, but didn't know how to get him out.

The sound of a squealing pig echoed up the wall and into Hattie's ears.

A large shadow—the shadow of something misshapen and cruel—stepped closer.

Her grandfather stepped into the light.

Hattie smiled.

PART 2:
THE SLAUGHTER

CHAPTER 9

1

The sun was rising behind the old farmhouse as Davey rolled up to the Winslow Farm.

His truck creaked and bounced over the potholes in the dirt road leading to the house.

Davey drank a warm beer, chasing it with hot, black coffee.

The lights in the house were on, and a few more trucks were parked by a squat building.

He'd never been to a slaughterhouse, but he assumed that small structure was where the condemned were taken.

Next to it was a long building where the pigs were kept, or so he thought.

The truck pulled to a stop in front of the house. Davey opened the door and grabbed his coffee cup. He hoped the ad was right and that lunch was included. He hadn't eaten much the day before, and he could use a solid meal. But from what Brett and Wayne told him, he wasn't expecting much.

Davey slammed the door of his battered truck a little harder than intended. Rocks crunched under his feet as he walked up the old steps leading to the house's front door.

He knocked and sipped his coffee.

A silhouette moved inside the house, and he could tell it was a woman. And a shapely one at that.

He remembered what Brett and Wayne said about the farm owner. Sometimes, when she was short on cash, she'd pay with other means.

Davey was a man who thoroughly enjoyed other means. He loved cash, but pussy or a good blow job would certainly go a long way. As long as he could keep his bitch of a probation officer off his ass, that was all that mattered. He certainly didn't want to go to jail.

Peering through the old door curtain, he saw the woman stop and check her hair. He plastered on a smile that had dropped dozens of panties, and hoped it might drop another pair soon.

2

It was a make-or-break day for the farm.

The slaughter finally arrived; Beulah had gambled and pushed it off long enough.

Other farms in the area had already gone to slaughter, but she held out, hoping the demand would rise and her meat would fetch top dollar. With the amount of calls she received, and the down payments submitted on carcasses already, her luck was turning around.

When the old truck came bouncing down the driveway, she didn't know who it was. Then, she remembered the new guy she hired over the phone. He had little experience, but she didn't need a seasoned farmhand, just someone to help Ralph, Wayne, and Brett. They'd show the new guy around and make sure he didn't fuck up too badly. And if she was lucky, she could short him on his pay in lieu of sucking his cock. That was always a plus in her mind. She didn't like marinated nut sack in her face, especially after a long day's work, but the stench of dirty balls and the taste of cum that was born of a poor diet were better than shelling out a lot of cash.

Beulah turned at the sound of approaching footsteps.

Hattie walked into the kitchen with her mask tied around her deformed face.

She hoped her daughter wouldn't be there when the new guy arrived. Beulah wasn't stupid, and knew the deformed girl could be quite off-putting to look at, especially with the mask on.

"What are you doing?" Beulah asked.

The new guy knocked on the door.

"Iss the day of the slaugher," Hattie replied.

Beulah put her hand on her hip. "Yes, I know that. A very important day for us, which is why everything has to be perfect."

Having the deformed girl meet the new guy was less than ideal.

He knocked again.

Beulah could see him through the curtains, and she knew he could also see her. Leaving him outside wasn't the best start to his new position. She hoped Hattie would get the hint, but the girl didn't budge, and Beulah opened the door.

He stood there looking like he'd stepped out of a magazine. His dark eyes were the shape of almonds. A light beard framed his face, matching the dark hair on his head. His forearms were bare and covered in tattoos.

Beulah hadn't seen a man as sexy as Davey since

her modeling days in New York. "Hi, I'm Beulah." She extended her hand. "And you must be Davey." She could feel his eyes on her as she took his hand.

Davey didn't hide that he was checking her out, and Beulah didn't mind it. She knew she could still turn heads, but impressing the locals or the farmhands wasn't difficult. Getting the attention of a man with the attractiveness of a male model, now *that* excited her. She hoped he'd take a pay cut for pussy. Beulah might even offer it anyway. Almost all her orgasms had been self-induced over the last few years, but she had a feeling this stud might change that.

"Yes, ma'am," Davey said as he entered the house. He inhaled sharply as if he'd seen something shocking.

Hattie.

"Helwo, I'm Hattie." She stepped forward and extended a scarred hand.

Davey, save for the initial shock at seeing the girl, responded perfectly. There was no shock or disdain on his face, but a smile. "Nice to meet you, Miss Hattie."

Even with the mask on her face, Beulah knew her daughter was smiling.

"*Ahem.* Davey needs to get to work, Hattie. If there's time, I'm sure he'll join us for lunch."

Davey let the girl's hand go, much to her displeasure. "Well, I'm ready to work."

"Great. Follow me. I'll show you to the slaughterhouse."

Davey turned and walked out.

Before she left, Beulah looked back at her

daughter with a sneer.

3

Hattie watched them walk away with a stab of jealousy.

Her mother and Davey laughed, and she even saw her mother put a hand on his shoulder. It wasn't casual; there was something behind it. There was always something behind her mother's moves.

Some would consider Beulah dumb just because she owned a farm, but they'd be wrong. Hattie knew how much of a calculating bitch she could be.

She wanted to follow them to be around Davey, but she wouldn't. Hattie didn't want to see Wayne again. *Ever* again. She was still sore from his violation of her virgin body. The blood had finally stopped, but the pain, both physical and emotional, still lingered.

But not with Davey. There was something about him that Hattie felt. It was almost like a calming sensation, which was odd considering she only just met him. She didn't know if it was pure physical attraction, but there was a connection already.

If she gave herself to him, he'd be gentle. He'd be caring, making sure to be nice to her. Maybe he'd even pleasure her like she'd done to herself many times. He wouldn't ram himself in, but gently slide into her, maybe kissing her neck or breasts.

She grew slick with lust at the thought. Her body was confusing her. Less than twenty-four hours earlier, she'd had the worst experience of her life, and now she was thinking about letting another man inside her tender sex.

Deep down, she knew it would never happen; her mother wouldn't allow it.

Beulah wouldn't let her have something nice or even be loved. She needed that control over her daughter.

Hattie knew her mother hated her. Even if she never said it aloud, Hattie knew. She knew her mother blamed her for ending her career and forcing her back to the miserable life on the farm.

It was a life that Hattie hated also, but not one she could easily escape. And after the assault on her body by Wayne, it would only get worse.

She knew what her mother did for the men to keep the farm running, but now Hattie was expected to follow suit.

That wasn't her. That wasn't a life she wanted, nor was she that type of person. But what choice did she have?

There wasn't much hope of escape. *Except…*

Her mind wandered back down to the basement. Could that be the key to saving her life and starting anew? Hattie didn't know, and that was a dangerous thought. But her life had just become even more perilous.

Hattie walked outside and could smell the stench of the animals in the row.

On the wind came the screams of the pigs.

The slaughter had begun.

4

The air was thick with the smell of fear. One by one,

the pigs were led into the abattoir. Most people thought pigs to be dumb animals, but they are quite smart—smart enough to know when death was looming.

Davey hadn't slept well the night before, but he found himself holding an electric stunner with a disgusting amount of glee. It resembled large tongs with electricity running through them.

He had many jobs in the past, but working on a farm was new to him. Not just the farm work, but slaughtering. There were a few menial farm jobs in the past, but they were mostly during the harvest of crops and such. Never had he held a job like the Winslow Farm.

"It's easy," Wayne said. "Ralph will herd them into the chute, and Brett will secure them. When they're secured and squeal'n, smack 'em in the head with the buzzers. The electric shock will knock them out. Then, just wrap the rope around their back legs and hit this button." He showed Davey a small remote on a long wire. "This will hoist them up and send them back to me." Wayne drew a long knife from his belt. "I'll be waiting for them with this bad boy to open their throats and bellies. I've gotten damn quick with gutting them, but I might need some help. Doubtful, but you might have to help dump some entrails with me. Each pig is marked, and then they'll be given to the buyer to do with it what they will."

It sounded easy enough to Davey.

But when the first pigs came into the chute, he wasn't sure of himself. He wasn't an animal lover by any means, but they all just seemed so helpless.

The buzzers gave off a hum in his hands.

The pig ran itself right into a smaller chute that closed behind it. It squealed and thrashed, but was held firm, with only its head sticking through.

Knowing he had to hurry to get over his nerves, Davey stepped forward and clamped the buzzers around the pig's head.

The smell of animals was quickly replaced with the metallic tinge of ozone as the connection was made.

Once lively eyes went blank as the pig collapsed unconscious.

Davey pulled the lever, opening the chute, and set the buzzers down. He wrapped a rope loop around the pig's back legs and pressed a button to hoist it into the air.

The unconscious beast flopped as it was pulled toward the ceiling and moved on a track.

Wayne waited with his blade. With a practiced hand, he opened the pig's throat under a torrent of blood. He pushed the carcass on the track, which led to another part of the slaughterhouse.

Davey stared in awe at the practiced brutality of it all. He snapped out of his reverie at the sound of another pig crashing into the chute.

Again, he grabbed the buzzers and went to work.

5

The trucks had all been loaded, and the carcasses waiting for more buyers were stored in a large walk-in cooler.

Gallons of blood had been washed away, but the

stink of copper hung in the air.

Spilled guts and fear lingered with the scent of blood, and Davey didn't know if he'd ever get the smell out of his nose. He had to figure something out, because tomorrow was another day of killing. More pigs had dates with death and the buyers were ready to collect.

Beulah waited on the house's front steps with envelopes full of cash. Each of them had a name written on it. She hoped they didn't count the money before leaving.

The slaughter had gone well, and the buyers were happy with the hogs.

She couldn't quite breathe a sigh of relief as there was another day of killing ahead, but having money always made her feel better.

Dusk was settling on the farm, and Beulah watched as her employees turned off the lights at the slaughterhouse. She could hear them talking, but couldn't make out what they were saying. Either way, it sounded happy, like they were getting along, which was a plus.

She wanted to keep Davey around for a little while, at least until she fucked him. If he were a good lay, and could work the farm, she'd be happy to keep him on full time.

"Great work today, boys," Beulah said to them. "The buyers were all happy and paid on time. Which means," she held out the envelopes, "you get paid on time."

Each man took their envelope, and Beulah felt a moment of fear when she thought they were going to open them. She didn't short them by much, but a few bucks among four guys could add up.

Feeling the heft of the envelopes, all of them stuffed them in their pockets.

"That was certainly a good haul, B," Wayne said. He patted his shirt pocket containing the cash. "Hopefully, tomorrow is just as good."

Beulah cocked her hips, looking at Davey. She didn't care what Wayne thought, only that he'd return the next day. He was old news to her, and since she'd let him violate her daughter, she could hardly stand to look at him.

"What about you, new fella?" she asked.

Davey pulled the envelope out of his pocket and smacked it on his palm. He looked up at her with dusky eyes that made her pussy hot.

She could feel the stubble of his beard on her thighs already.

"Not bad. Not bad at all. I've done worse for less money."

She grinned. "Well, this is only your first day. I'm sure there are worse things we can arrange."

Smiling at her, Davey licked his lips. "I'm sure."

Brett grabbed him and Wayne, pulling the three of them together. "Let's hit the bar and spend some of this blood money."

They all smelled like death, but Beulah knew Davey could stink like he'd bathed in a septic tank and still get laid.

"You read my mind," Wayne said. "Ralphy, care to join us?"

The older farmhand looked at them and shook his head. "Nah, not tonight. I'm going to splurge with the missus." He sniffed at his shirt. "After I take a shower and change. You boys have fun, but not too much. We still have work to do in the morning."

"Eh, you don't have to worry about us," Wayne said. "We're pros." He smacked Brett and Davey in the chest. "Come on. This money is burning a hole in my pocket."

They all turned and began walking to their trucks.

The front door of the house banged open, causing the men to jump and turn.

Hattie stood behind her mother. Her mask was on, but her hair was up like she tried styling it.

Wayne and Brett said something low between themselves, laughed, and kept walking to their vehicles.

"Dabey," Hattie said.

Beulah looked back at her daughter with a sneer. "Yeah?"

"Hattie, don't bother Davey. He's off the clock and wants to get home."

"No, no. It's okay," Davey said, smiling at the girl.

Hattie looked up at her mother, her breath raspy behind the mask. She turned her attention back to Davey. "Are ooo comin ba themarrow?"

"I plan on sticking around until your mother gets rid of me." He gave her a slight nod. "Have a good night, Miss Hattie." Davey turned and walked to his truck.

The old rust bucket struggled to start, finally catching with a puff of smoke.

Beulah snapped at her daughter. "I can't with you, Hattie. Don't bother the workers. They need to rest and stay focused." She stormed off into the house, slamming the door behind her.

Hattie didn't move; she just stood watching Davey as he drove away.

6

JD and Rich sat at the small table playing checkers. Neither of them was very good at it, nor were they trying.

All four of them did their best to kill time until the tire was ready.

They decided to explore the property a little earlier in the day. There wasn't much else to do in the dusty cabin, and the weather was decent.

After stumbling upon a deep stream, they took a short rest.

"You know, if it wasn't for the freak, and the fact the air around us smells like shit, this would be pretty nice," Rich said. He sat on the soft moss around the water.

"Very nice," Danielle said, sitting next to him. "If it wasn't for this place, we would've been fucked. Our entire budget would've been blown on a hotel, and that would've been the end of our summer trip."

A loud squeal tore through the calm sound of the stream.

All four of them looked toward the farm.

"That didn't sound good," JD said.

The others nodded in agreement.

Another cry of fear sounded.

And another.

"What the fuck?" asked Ari. She, like the others,

was sitting near the water, but after hearing the cries of agony, she jumped to her feet.

"Sounds like they're killing them," Rich said. He snapped his fingers. "Of course. It's a fucking slaughterhouse. Must be their time." He stood and wrapped his arms around Danielle, who also had gotten up. "Maybe they'll have some fresh bacon for us." He nuzzled her neck, but she spun away.

"Stop. That's fucked up. Those pigs are living creatures."

"Yeah, but they're delicious," Rich said as he licked his lips. He was doubling down on the levity, hoping his girlfriend would turn her emotions around. If not, he knew his chances of getting pussy were reduced.

It didn't work.

"Yeah, well, I don't care. I'm not saying I won't eat meat, but hearing it doesn't make things any easier."

Rich nodded but said nothing. He slowed it down with the jokes, hoping to save the miserable time at the cabin. "Look, maybe we can use the cell phone and get a ride out of here? We'll call the tow guy and see about the tire and maybe get a ride into town. I doubt there's a booming metropolis around here, but it's worth a shot."

"Metropolis?" Ari asked. "That's a big word for you."

They all laughed, including Rich. If she hadn't been dating his friend, he would've kissed her for bringing an actual joke to the situation.

"Yeah, well, I am top of my barber class."

Rich never intended to go to college like JD and

Ari, but he wanted something more for himself. He was always obsessed with his hair, so attending a barber college was the most logical choice. There were quite a few shops in his hometown, and he knew most of the owners. Finding a job and getting experience wouldn't be an issue for him, but that was only until he saved enough to open his own place. He already had the name picked out: *Rich and Stylish*.

Danielle thought it was corny, but he liked it. She was going to a community college close to his school.

Even though they were young, they already had their futures on the brain.

She would get a degree in business management and finance. There were plenty of opportunities for her, and the fact she was attractive helped.

Once they gathered enough real-world experience, they'd go into business for themselves. It was on track.

Thinking about their future, Rich smiled. Again, he wrapped his arms around his girlfriend, who he'd, someday, make his wife. This time, she didn't push him away.

"I think heading into town sounds like a great idea." He kissed her neck, which she allowed, and even leaned in. "Maybe later we can do a little skinny dipping."

Danielle turned with a shocked look. "My ass isn't getting into that cold water. Hell no."

Rich shrugged. "I guess I'll have to get you naked in the cabin, then."

Ari cleared her throat. "About the cell phone?"

"Oh, yeah. Let's go back and make the call. Get

away from those sounds and smells for the day. And, hopefully, have our asses back on the road tomorrow."

Rich and Danielle led the way back toward the cabin, talking amongst themselves.

JD followed, but realized Ari hadn't moved; she was just staring into the thick trees around the stream. "You see something?"

She didn't know. After she caught the pig girl spying on her, Ari couldn't help but feel uneasy. The sounds and smells were unsettling, but something else about the property had her shaken. Being gawked at didn't help, but that was something she could look past. Something just didn't feel right. It was like the air before a storm, charged to the brim with electricity, ready to explode.

"Nah, probably just a deer or something." She turned and laced her arm through his.

JD pulled her close and kissed her on the head. "Yeah, you're probably right. I'm sure that girl freaked you out. I know I would've shit if I saw her with that fucking mask looking at me."

"Just weird, but then again, we're not in New York anymore. Although we have plenty of weirdos by us." She squeezed him tighter and lifted her lips toward his ear. "You know, I'm not afraid of a little cold water."

JD had a confused look on his face until it hit him.

Skinny dipping!

He smiled. "Well, at least we have something to look forward to tonight."

They followed their friends back to the cabin,

hoping for a ride away from the sounds of death.

CHAPTER 10

1

The bar wasn't busy, but more people were there than the night before.

Davey had showered before heading out. It wasn't to strengthen his chance of getting laid—he needed no help with that. No, it was the fact that, for once, he couldn't stand his smell. Body odor didn't bother him; sometimes, he thought a faint musk drove the women wild. But the smell of pig shit and unwashed swine did bother him.

When he was in the thick of it at the farm, his sense of smell quickly became used to it. But the stink was overwhelming once he arrived back at his meager apartment.

He sat at the bar sipping a beer. The last of the barfly's money had bought his drink, and he'd have to use some of his hard-earned cash to get his next round.

Most of the women in the place had a guy with them, and none of them were hot enough to fight over. So, unless someone new came in and wanted a shot at fucking him, he was on his own.

A cool breeze wafted in, smelling faintly of farm and cheap cologne.

Wayne and Brett entered. They scanned the crowd, finding him. Both of them worked their way past a few couples before reaching him.

"Did you check your pay?" Wayne asked.

Davey hadn't. The envelope felt thick enough for him. Besides, he wanted to fuck Beulah, and bitching about a few missing bucks could hurt his chances. Doubtful, but he didn't want to start off on the wrong foot. He couldn't make waves if he was going to keep the job and exploit the fringe benefits. At least, not yet.

If he was fired, his probation officer would have a field day. The last thing he wanted was to find himself back in jail.

"Nah, it felt good to me."

Brett and Wayne pulled out stools beside him and ordered a round of beers.

At least my next drink is taken care of, Davey thought.

"Well, you should have. That fucking bitch stiffed us again," Brett said, drinking almost half his beer in one gulp. "And it's not the first time. That was a damn good slaughter. The buyers practically came in their pants when they saw the quality of the hogs." He lit a cigarette and grabbed an ashtray.

"You mind?" Davey asked, gesturing toward the pack of smokes.

"Help yourself."

Davey lit up, letting the chemicals in the cigarette mix with the alcohol in his bloodstream.

"I'm done with her. I fucking mean it. I want to take my ass over there right fucking now and get the rest of my cash," Wayne said. He chugged his beer and ordered another, paired with a shot.

The shot glass barely hit the table before he threw it back. He grimaced and chased it with his beer. "If I didn't need the money, I'd fucking quit right now and no-show tomorrow. Let that cunt and her freak daughter kill the pigs. I'm sure that twat never even got her hands dirty. Unless they were wrapped around a filthy cock."

Wayne and Brett continued to drink, slamming shots and beers one after another.

The conversation drifted away from work, becoming light, but Davey could see the lingering anger hidden in Wayne's eyes.

His new friends hadn't bought him any more drinks, and he didn't splurge too much, only drinking a few more beers.

Then, the inevitable happened.

Wayne tipped back his last beer and slammed the glass on the bar, garnering a few nasty looks. "Fuck this. I'm going over there and getting my money." He threw a few crumpled dollar bills on the bar and stood. "Come on, Brett. This bitch isn't getting away with this shit anymore. If she won't pay, we'll take it. And if she wants us back tomorrow, she'll fucking pay."

Davey didn't try talking them out of it. He didn't have a moral high ground. The fact of the matter was that he didn't care. People cheated other people. It was human nature. He'd done it dozens, if not hundreds, of times, and he'd do it again.

"Well, we might see you tomorrow," Brett said as he grabbed his cigarettes. He offered a final one to Davey, who took it, along with a light. "For your sake, you'd better hope she pays up. The slaughter with only two guys is going to be a bitch. I know she'll lose money with less crew. And she does, too, so let's hope this goes our way."

Wayne was already on his way to the front door before Brett realized he was alone.

With both of them gone, Davey quickly swiped the few bucks on the bar. It wasn't much, but it would be enough to get him another beer before he called it a night.

2

Hattie stood nude. She'd never seen another naked woman besides her mother until that night. Watching the other girl shower excited her. She didn't know if it was sexual or something else, but she'd changed.

The other girl was pretty. Her face was clear and symmetrical. Her body was smooth, not riddled with scars. Even her lady parts looked nice. The girl's private hair was short and trimmed, unlike Hattie's, who never dared use scissors near such sensitive areas.

She ran her hands over her chest, caressing her nipples. They stood hard and firm, sensitive to her touch. She lifted her breasts, which were bigger and hung less than the girl's. It felt good to touch herself.

Slowly, her hands wandered lower, parting the thick hair. She winced in pain. For a few moments, she'd been able to push away Wayne's violation upon her body. While she did her best to forget, her body still remembered.

What was once so sensitive and a source of pleasure, throbbed with a dull ache. She didn't know if all men were as large as Wayne, but if they were, she didn't think sex was something she wanted much of in the future.

According to her mother, sex was fun. She certainly wasn't shy about telling her daughter about it, and Hattie had even caught her a few times in the act with various men. She never appeared to be in pain. Quite the opposite. Her mother always had a look of pleasure on her face, even if sometimes it looked fake.

Hattie didn't know if she'd ever feel such pleasure. What man would ever love her? A freak, a monster. She was doomed to be seen as a lesser person, one to poke fun at and abuse. That was the life her mother left her with.

No, there was one man who could love her. A man she hardly knew, yet felt a connection with. A man her mother kept locked in the basement of the old house which was once his.

Her grandfather wasn't perfect, at least according to her mother, but he was blood. He wouldn't let the other men hurt her, unlike her mother.

Hattie heard something through the open window.

Besides the crickets and other night bugs, something else stirred. The pigs were quiet, except for the occasional grunt or squeal, but something else was moving in the night.

Turning off her light and moving to the open window, Hattie saw a truck was driving down the moonlit driveway. Even with the headlights off, she knew the vehicle.

Wayne!

What is he doing at the farm so late at night?

And why are his lights off? Could it be a midnight meeting with Mother? Could the lady of the house have a late-night desire that needed fulfilling? Hattie didn't know.

In the darkness, her hand wandered back down to her wounded sex. She plunged her fingers inside, wincing, letting the pain rekindle the memories burned into her mind.

Could he be here for me? The thought hit her like the buzzers hitting the brain of a sow. She didn't think so, but why else would he be driving up with his lights off? If he was there to meet her mother, he'd drive right up without a problem.

Hattie's chest felt tight. Her breathing was ragged, and for a second, she thought she'd pass out. The pain felt fresh not only in her mind, but in her body. She wouldn't let him hurt her again, not for the farm or her mother.

She knew what had to be done. The fear remained, but the pain dwindled. She had a plan, and she needed help.

Dressing quickly, Hattie grabbed her mask before she left her room.

Then, she headed toward the basement.

3

Wayne felt as if his feet were made of lopsided stone.

The house was dark, and the porch light had blown out years ago.

As quietly as he could, he stepped onto the old wooden slats. His boots sounded loud in his drunken ears. Slowly, he walked up each stair.

A step behind him, Brett lacked any stealth ability.

"Shh," Wayne hissed.

Brett put his hands up in mock surrender.

Wayne watched his friend make faces behind his back in the reflection of the glass door. They'd have a nice conversation about following orders on the ride back into town once they found the money.

Beulah could be forgetful from time to time, leaving the door unlocked.

Unfortunately, this wasn't one of those times. The door was locked and even dead bolted.

Wayne peered through the glass into the empty kitchen.

Nothing moved.

Slowly, he crouched down and lifted the chipped ceramic toad Beulah kept out front. It was a shitty hiding place for a key, but there wasn't much need to hide it well.

The sound of the tumblers shifting echoed in Wayne's ears as he slid the key into the lock. His pulse raced and, for a moment, he considered giving up the whole operation.

Low-level crimes didn't bother him, but this was something different. Breaking and entering was a serious crime. He and Brett would both lose their jobs and get arrested if they were caught. They might avoid jail time, but he didn't want to take the risk.

"What's the problem?" Brett slurred. "Let's get this fucking money and get out."

His drunk friend was right. Beulah owed them, and they were going to get it—one way or another.

He turned the handle on the door.

A sound tore through the night.

Someone turned on one of the saws in the slaughterhouse.

Both men froze and snapped their heads to the brick building.

The pigs were in a frenzy.

"What the fuck?" Wayne asked. "Is she in the slaughterhouse?"

"Why would she be out there? It's late; you know she hasn't gotten her hands dirty in years. She only goes out there to check in on us."

Wayne nodded, but something wasn't sitting right with him. Who turned on the saw if she wasn't in the slaughterhouse? It hadn't been running when they pulled up, and the damned thing didn't just turn on by itself.

"Fuck," Wayne said. He pulled the door closed with a gentle click. "That fucking thing is going to wake her up if it hasn't already. We need to shut it off and give it a few minutes. Just like deer hunting, make all the noise on the way in, then let the woods settle before first light."

Brett looked at him. His brow glistened even though the night air was fairly cool. "B-but who's in the slaughterhouse?"

"I don't know. Maybe one of the hogs found their way in looking for their dead buddy and knocked into it. Or maybe it's the ghosts of all the pigs whose throats we cut. I don't fucking care. All I know is that if we don't shut that shit off, we're not getting paid."

Wayne walked down the steps louder than he'd gone up. He pushed past Brett, who looked like he was having second thoughts about the situation.

The moon was high and bright, giving them enough light to go to the house of death.

Wayne's balls pulled tight against his body. He'd been in the slaughterhouse thousands of times, but never at night. There was something different, almost primal, about the dark. His lizard brain told him to run, but greed pushed him further into the abattoir.

He felt like a child sneaking out of the house. His yard and swings had been his haven in the daytime, but the old tree had looked evil at night, like a monster poised to attack and pluck him into its hard branches.

His hand inched toward the lights, but Brett spoke.

"What are you doing? You'll blow our cover."

Wayne's hand hung in the air.

In moments, their resolve had flip-flopped. The terror Brett exuded at the doorway took root in Wayne's belly.

"You're right," Wayne said, letting his hand drop. He wished he had a flashlight to help guide him to the running saw.

The room was dark, save for the moonbeams which found their way through the dirty glass.

Machines stood silent.

Large chutes and conveyors gleamed with cleanliness.

A giant counter took up most of one wall. Its surface was covered with white cutting boards the size of dinner tables.

Above the counter was a magnetic strip, which

glistened with knives and cleavers.

Wayne looked at them all. Each blade had spilled swine blood many times over. His eyes stopped, and his heart raced.

"What is it?" Brett asked, standing at his side.

"My knife; my throat slitting knife is missing," Wayne said. His armpits were stained with cold sweat.

Brett walked up beside him looking at the knives. "So what? You probably left it out somewhere."

Wayne shook his head. "No, man. I put it away. I know I did."

Something moved in the darkness, shuffling across the concrete floor.

"What the fuck was that? One of the hogs?"

Swallowing hard, Wayne strained his eyes trying to find what moved in the darkness. "No, it wasn't a hog." His face split into a grin. "Maybe it was the freak."

Brett scrunched his brows, then it hit him. "Oh, the girl with the mask, Hattie."

"Yeah. Tight pussy on that young thing, and a set of tits like I've never seen before. It's too bad her face doesn't look as good as her mother's, or she'd have a chance at life. She'll be cursed to live here, probably getting hooked up with another retard and having retard babies. Hey, I think it's our duty, no, owed to us, to show her a good time. Our little fuck session the other day was fun, but brief. You know, not because of me, but because I had to get back to work. And she wouldn't stop fucking screaming. If you fill her mouth and I fill her pussy, she won't be able to scream now, will she?"

Brett nodded. "That bitch'd better not bite my cock. I'll fucking kill her if she does."

"Easy, tiger. We ain't killing no one. If we get to blow loads, that'll cool our heads, and maybe we can give Beulah a chance to make the money right."

The shape moved again.

This time, both men had a better view as it moved along.

Hattie was a tall girl, and her coat made her look much bulkier than she was. But the silhouette of the pig mask was obvious, even in the dark.

"Hattie, it's your two buddies, Wayne and Brett. Stop playing with the saw and come see us. We won't hurt you, promise," Wayne said. His cock was already swelling in anticipation of entering the girl again.

"Yeah, we just want to have a little fun is all."

The duo moved through the slaughterhouse like prowlers.

Streams of moonlight created bars of silver through the windows.

More movement ahead.

"Come on, girl. Don't make us chase you around here. We don't like playing games."

They moved deeper and paused.

The silhouette of the figure stood just outside of the moonlight. Raspy breathing could be heard from it, but it was facing away from them.

"Jackpot," Wayne said, tapping Brett on the chest. Then, to the shape, "Atta girl, Hattie. This time will be different, I promise. Brett is gonna join. You'll see, it'll be twice as fun."

They moved closer.

Wayne was within arm's reach of her when he stopped.

Hattie's mask covered just her face, not the back of her head. Her hair should be visible in the weak light.

The back of the mask looked real, like genuine, living swine flesh.

His eyes went wide as Wayne found his missing knife—it was clutched firmly in the creature's hand in front of them.

The monster turned and stepped into the moonlight. It was a beast ripped from a nightmare. The head of the creature was part man, part pig. The face had the eyes of a man, but the snout of a swine. Fat yellow, cracked tusks poked up and down from the hellish maw. Old scars were visible, and the creature looked like a crude hand had sewn it together. The ears were wide and floppy, cut straight from a pig and attached to the beast.

What Wayne thought was a coat was layers of muscle, barely contained by an old, tattered work shirt. One arm ended in a black, cloven hoof, while the other was a man's hand. That hand was the one holding the sharp, curved knife. The legs were thick, full of muscle, and covered in tight pants.

The monster opened its mouth and squealed. It wasn't a shriek of fear, but anger.

Wayne stepped back as the monster swiped at his belly with the blade. He felt the tug as the knife passed through his shirt, narrowly missing his gut. He grabbed Brett and threw him at the beast as he ran toward the door.

4

Motherfucker! Brett thought as he stumbled toward the monster. Wayne betrayed him, which wasn't a shock, but caught him off guard.

The beast jabbed Brett in the face with its hoof-tipped arm, breaking his nose.

Brett's hands came up in an attempt to stem the flow of blood rushing from his face. He didn't even have a chance to defend himself as the beast lunged forward.

The blade they'd used to open many throats entered Brett's chest under his ribcage. Thin steel slid through meat and organs, finding his pulsing heart.

Face to face with terror, Brett tasted blood and could smell the stench coming from the monster's mouth.

With a squelch, the beast pulled the blade free and struck again. Warm blood ran down Brett's stomach and over the hand of the pig creature.

His energy was fading, but Brett still tried to fight. He clawed at the face of the beast. His fingers sought the soft, human-like eyes, but found the hellish mouth instead.

The monstrosity opened wide, unleashing another torrent of rotten breath into his face as it bit down.

Brett shrieked and blood sprayed from his mouth as his right hand was pulverized under the blunt teeth of the beast.

It ripped and tore, taking his hand off at the

wrist.

Brett could only watch as blood pumped from the ragged, bony stump.

In two crunching bites, the creature swallowed his mangled hand. It twisted the knife, burrowing it deeper into Brett's shredded viscera.

The pain was leaving his body as his life followed suit. A vile mixture of gut fluid sloshed on the floor with each movement of the blade.

Brett was collapsing, but the pig monster kept him up as he pulled the steel from his belly. With a final stab, the wet fist of the beast slammed into Brett before letting him drop, leaving him for dead.

5

Wayne slammed into the door expecting it to fly open, but it didn't budge.

It wasn't locked, but something was keeping it from opening.

"Fuck!" he yelled, turning to face the bloody beast stalking him. Wayne looked around for a weapon to defend himself. He wished he'd grabbed a blade from the rack, but his drunken, scared mind was only bent on escape. Now, his focus was on survival.

He felt the slightest twinge of guilt for throwing Brett to the monster, but it bought him some time which he'd hoped to use to escape, but the obstructed door prevented that.

His friend lay dead on the floor, a blooming puddle of gore leaking from the holes in his gut.

A metal snow shovel was propped against the

wall. They'd use it to scrape up any bits of offal or shit left by the pigs on their way to the slaughter. Now, it was Wayne's only hope.

He wobbled as he grabbed it.

In the movies, a traumatic situation always sobered up the hero, but not in real life.

His head was spinning, and he thought he was going to puke.

The monster rushed him.

Wayne could see the horrors of the beast as it moved through the light of the moon with each window it passed.

Brett lay in a lifeless heap in a puddle of light and blood. His eyes were open, locked in abject horror. The pig creature was the last thing he saw before he died.

"Come on, you fucker!" Wayne yelled, doing his best to find some courage in his fear.

The beast roared and charged with its head down like a boar. Its yellowed tusks looked much too sharp and deadly.

Wayne knew he had to time his strike or be impaled on the horrid teeth.

As the creature rushed closer, Wayne pulled the shovel back. Even drunk, he still thought he had a good chance of taking out the monster that killed his friend.

He swung and connected. The thin blade of the shovel caught the mutant in the forehead just as Wayne sidestepped the tusks. A vibration ran up his arms, reminding him of hitting a baseball off the end of a bat. He wished he had a bat and not a shitty snow shovel, but he used what he had.

The grotesque thing roared and shook off the blow. It turned and charged again, much faster than Wayne expected.

He didn't know if it was the booze that slowed him down, but Wayne knew he was fucked. His hip slammed into a table as he tried to run.

With a mighty swipe of its gigantic head, the pig creature gored Wayne in the flank with its tusks.

Screaming, Wayne turned, further tearing his flesh.

The beast's head was still down, level with his belly. It thrust forward again, this time finding Wayne's soft gut.

His legs went out from under him as the creature drove him onto the hard ground.

The shovel clattered away, sliding out of reach under a bench.

Wayne punched and gouged at the monster as it thrashed, tearing his soft flesh open.

Loops of intestines and bile flung through the air with every violent motion of the tusks.

Wayne struggled, but was powerless against the monster.

The man-beast pulled its head back. Its horrid face was slick with internal fluids and gore. It chewed a chunk of Wayne's intestine, squeezing a glob of shit from the ropy organ.

The putrid lump landed on Wayne's face, one last little bit of indignity before it finished the macabre feast.

6

Hattie stood outside the slaughterhouse door and smiled. She held the key for the lock that secured the chain around the handle, keeping the two men locked with her grandfather. With her back against the wall of the building, she slowly lowered herself to the earth. She pulled the stifling mask from her face and took in the night's beauty.

Bugs called to one another, and the bats responded by eating their fill.

As she listened to wet sounds coming from the slaughterhouse, Hattie's mutilated face split into a grin. She laughed listening to her grandfather feed and squeal with glee.

After minutes went by, the sounds stopped, and Hattie stood and pulled the mask back over her face. She took the key from her pocket and undid the lock, letting the chain fall to the dirt.

Shep Winslow stood on the threshold. His clothing dripped with blood and shit. He smelled awful, but he looked wonderful. Just like Hattie, he was a freak—a freak created by the same person.

Beckoning him to her, she put her hand out.

The pig beast, her grandfather, slid the gory knife into his pants. His piggish face morphed into a grin not all that dissimilar to hers.

She took his hand, feeling the tacky gore, and they walked away, using the moonlight to guide them.

7

Beulah's eyes snapped open, and she let out a small shriek. She sat up in bed, her body slick with sweat. The nightmare was fading away, but she still felt dirty. Her body odor was so pungent she could smell herself. She was tempted to jump in the shower and freshen up, but couldn't be bothered. Her bed had been lonely for years, and she had no one to impress in the middle of the night.

Even with the nightmare ebbing away, she still felt uneasy, like something was wrong. Doing her best to shake the feeling of dread that lay over her like a wet blanket, she climbed out of bed.

The sounds of the night crept through the house.

Beulah unlocked her window and opened it, letting fresh air enter the stale room.

Something was wrong; she could feel it. Her gut never failed her before, even though she ignored it in her younger years.

Bugs and night creatures sang their songs, but another sound rode the calm breeze.

There was a faint moan coming from the slaughterhouse. It almost sounded like that of passion, but she didn't know who'd be fucking in the brick building unless it was the kids she rented the hunting cabin to. But why would they walk to the farm to fuck when they could just stay in the cabin and go at it?

No, this was something else. It wasn't a sexual moaning she heard. It was more feral, but as quickly as the sound came, it was gone.

It had gone, but not before triggering a host of

memories of times past when she was at her lowest and most vulnerable, a time in her life she tried and tried to repress.

It was no use. Like trying to hold back the tide, the memories overwhelmed her, taking her back to those dark days.

1991

CHAPTER 11

1

Beulah looked at the shot glass full of pig semen and threw it back neat. She swallowed, doing her best to control her gorge as the slime ran down her throat.

If she puked up the pig spunk, there was a good chance they were going to make her slurp it, and the rest of her stomach contents, off the dirty floor. That, or she wouldn't get paid, and that was even worse.

She put a fist to her mouth and held it back. The spunk slid down and settled in her belly. Beulah opened her empty mouth, showing it to the camera.

Mike stood behind the camera with a look of glee on his face.

The camcorder whirled as it recorded Beulah's shame, and she knew it was only going to get worse.

Waving, Mike signaled the pig cum had been consumed, and the rest of the scene was good to go.

The hay spread out on the studio floor was irritating her knees. Beulah was warm, but not because her boss had turned the heat up. A rash had broken out all over her body.

As a girl on the farm, she couldn't stand dealing with hay. It would often give her an allergic reaction, leaving her soaking in an oatmeal bath. She learned that wearing long sleeves and gloves was the only way to combat it. Sweating for a few hours was better than itching. Still, that did nothing for her eyes and nose, which constantly ran.

Beulah adjusted her knees, trying to find a comfortable spot, but couldn't. The plastic pig nose over her face was annoying, but not as bad as the hay. She knew she'd have a mark around her nose when the scene was over. If the guys weren't gentle, she'd have more marks than just the one left by the pig nose.

And they almost never were.

Two men walked into the small studio wearing cheap farmer costumes. Each wore a floppy, wide-brimmed hat, and had a piece of straw hanging from their mouths.

"This damn swine is acting up again, ain't she?" the farmer in the red hat said.

His southern drawl, paired with his stereotypical New York accent, almost made Beulah laugh.

"Yah, I reckon she is," the farmer in the blue hat said. His bastardization of the southern accent was just as bad. "I think she needs to go on the rotisserie."

Again, Beulah held it in.

Mike liked to get all of his movies in one shot, which was part of his film branding.

She didn't understand why, considering movies could be edited, but it was what his customers had grown to love. And something she'd grown to hate.

Beulah never met the men and women who consumed Mike's filth, and prayed she never would. Their depraved requests were things she never thought possible.

That was, until she was recruited by Mike.

2

Hattie had been born just as Beulah feared—a freak. The baby's face was cleft and horribly malformed. Her small body was covered in cuts, thanks to Beulah's botched abortion in the tub, which almost cost them their lives.

Each of them spent some time in the hospital, which thrust Beulah deep into debt and depression.

When they were finally released, she considered dropping the swaddled infant into one of the many rivers in New York City. Standing on the bridge, looking down at the frigid water, she knew she couldn't. Hattie was her daughter and, as far as she was concerned, the only family she had left.

There was no point in looking for the father. She fucked more guys than she could remember, and knew the number she didn't remember was probably greater.

Beulah considered adoption for her daughter, but the horror stories of the state-run services left her terrified. She might not provide the best life for the child, but it had to be better than leaving her in the clutches of the state.

She was still making good money with her acting gigs, and she could keep that going.

Beulah was wrong. She was old news to the execs, and with the baby weight clinging to her, she received more rejections than acceptances.

The meager savings she did not put up her nose was running out. Diapers, baby clothes, and formula were killing her.

Social Services were almost no help, just giving

her enough to keep her from drowning.

She had to figure out how to make money, and fast.

One rainy night, almost three years after Hattie was born, Beulah was walking back to her apartment after being rejected again. The rain sluiced down, making her cheap makeup run. That, and the tears burning in her eyes.

That gig was supposed to be *the one*. She was perfect and knew it, but she was still rejected by the studio.

The pilot for the show was pretty much the life she was living: farm girl leaves home and heads to the big city, makes new friends, and funny antics ensue. It was meant for her. Her age and weight didn't matter; they helped contribute to the story.

Before heading out into the rain, Beulah stood in the hallway outside the producer's office. She wasn't a God-fearing girl, but she prayed at that moment; it was her last hope at a normal life for her and Hattie. She could hear the producer talking on the phone.

His voice was low enough that she couldn't hear what was said, but a few loud laughs erupted occasionally.

The phone call ended with the sound of the handset dropping into the receiver.

"Hey, B, you can come in."

Beulah straightened her skirt. She wore nude hose over her legs, doing her best to hide the varicose veins that were a gift from her pregnancy.

If there was a classic, greaseball, Hollywood type in the dictionary, David Liebgott was it. He was thin and wore a cheap suit at least two sizes too big.

His thinning, black hair was slicked back. A pencil-thin mustache rested on his upper lip, and a filter-less cigarette hung from the corner of his mouth.

David sat on the edge of his desk. His beady eyes looked Beulah up and down as she entered.

Even wearing professional clothes, Beulah still felt like a piece of meat, nothing more than livestock. Her mind flashed back to life on the farm; it had been no different there. She seemed to always be just a piece of meat to men.

Clenching the cigarette between his middle and forefingers, David pointed at her. "Look, kid, I like ya, I really do. But the studio doesn't."

Beulah nodded slightly. Her eyes burned with tears as they welled up. She did her best to keep them back. This was it, her last shot at stardom, or even a decent fucking life for her and Hattie.

"B-but, I thought I did great. My lines were flawless; even the co-stars said I nailed it." A tear slid down her cheek.

"Ah, they're generous. You did okay, but that's not why we passed on you. It... well," he paused and took a drag on his cigarette, "it's you. There's nothing left to you, B. You need to sell the character, bring life to the role, and you don't have it anymore. It's like... like the light is gone from your eyes."

Beulah couldn't hold it in. A sob wracked her, and the tears fell.

David handed her a tissue, and she quickly put it to her face.

"But listen, it's not all bad news. I found a promising lead for you if you're interested."

She looked at the man on the desk and perked

up, but his face had changed.

The life had drained from his eyes. There was something different in them, something predatory.

"It's still in the film industry, but not quite what I do. I have an associate who makes adult films, and his stuff is hot right now. He's always looking for fresh talent, and his customers love a new girl. I told him about you, and he's interested, but he asked me to get him an audition tape."

"But you already have my tape. Did you send it to him? Well, I guess not, considering you just spoke with him."

"About that. Like I said, he's in a certain type of business. He's not looking for you to read off some lines or shit like that. He needs to see you *perform*."

Her stomach dropped.

After Hattie was born, Beulah's life took a turn. She stopped drinking, drugging, and random fucking, but there was no money. The few jobs she got here and there went into her life, and she, shamefully, was paid a few times for sex. Those were low points in her life, and she felt she was approaching another.

"I get it," she said, standing up. She wanted to turn and run out of the office after telling David to go fuck himself, but she didn't. Beulah stood planted, quivering, her mind racing.

Just leave. Tell him to fuck off and go. No, you need this. This could be the boost you need to get back on your feet. A few scenes could land you some serious money, and then you can get the fuck out of this city. But, if you can't escape, then what? No film studio will hire you if they find out you did porn.

You'll be stuck forever.

Beulah kicked the angel and demon from her shoulders and unbuttoned her shirt.

David jumped off the desk and clapped his hands together, causing his smoldering cigarette to throw ash around. He unlocked a cabinet, removed a camera and tripod, and set it up in front of his desk.

He checked the viewfinder. "Okay, we're looking good."

Walking back over to the desk, he unbuckled his belt. "This will be easy, B."

His pants fell to his ankles, pulled by the weight of the belt.

"Just give me a blowjob." David dropped his briefs and began playing with his flaccid penis. "That's it." His eyes wandered to her chest.

Beulah wanted to cover herself from his repulsive glare.

Before giving birth, she wasn't shy of her body at all. But after Hattie was born, Beulah's body changed. Her once perky breasts hung a little lower. Thin, jagged stretch marks ran down her smooth flesh. She knew her chest was still desirable and attractive, but it was changed.

"My, oh my, I've dreamed of those beautiful tits," David said, working his cock to a semi-erection. "Tell you what, I won't bust in your mouth. Let me cover you with my load. That'll look better on camera anyway." David pointed to the ground before him, beckoning her like a dog.

As Beulah walked over to him, her demeanor changed. She was an actress, and this was just a gig—a gig that could, hopefully, start a new future for her and Hattie.

She steeled her nerves, pushing the self-loathing from her mind. As much as she hated herself, and David, at that moment, she was an actress. Beulah looked over at the camera and heard the tape spinning inside.

Her attention snapped back to David, pulling her into the scene. "So, you want me to suck your cock?" Beulah rubbed his chest.

David shuddered. His member went from semi to rock hard in an instant.

Beulah took her hands from his chest and placed them on hers. She lifted her heavy breasts, pulling her nipples taut.

David swallowed and licked his lips. He nodded slightly and removed his hand from his shaft.

"Fine, but only if you promise to blow your fat load on these tits." She pressed her chest together, then descended to her knees.

Even though David's crotch was a little musty, she would much rather give him head than fuck him. She didn't think he'd wear a condom, and if she asked him to, her shot could be blown; the perverts who consumed porn wanted to see everything. She wasn't on any form of birth control, and sure as fuck couldn't afford to get pregnant again.

Beulah greased David's shaft with the clear pearl of pre-cum clinging to the tip of his cock. She lifted his member and kissed his balls. Gently, she sucked the skin of one nut into her mouth, letting the oblong gland fill her.

David whimpered like a baby, afraid he would blow before she even put his dick to her lips.

Knowing her luck, he wouldn't warn her and his cum would end up in her hair.

Beulah let his nut fall from her mouth. She ran her tongue along the seam in his sack, then worked her way up his shaft. When she reached his tip, she kissed gently, but didn't take him into her mouth. She looked up at him with wide eyes full of faked lust.

Just as David was about to speak, Beulah took him into her throat.

"Fuck," David groaned. He gathered her blonde hair in his right hand.

Moaning on his cock, Beulah took it as far as she dared. Spit and precum drooled from her mouth, making a puddle on the floor. She rubbed her chin, wetting her left hand, then reached under David's cock and cradled his balls. Her wet index finger played with his asshole as she sucked him. He was writhing, and she knew it wouldn't be long.

Faster, she sucked.

Deeper, his cock went, filling her throat.

"Fuck, now," David said, pulling her hair to get his cock free from her mouth.

Beulah pushed her tits together and smiled at him. She didn't flinch when his load exploded onto her.

The first shot landed in the hollow of her neck, for which she was grateful. No one liked a cumshot in the eye.

David's following spurts were guided by his hand as he jerked his load onto her tits.

Rubbing herself, Beulah smeared his spunk over her nipples. She blew him a kiss before standing up and grabbing a box of tissues.

Leaning against his desk, David stood panting like he'd just run a marathon. His eyes were closed, and his knees were shaking.

Beulah cleaned the cum from her chest and tossed the wet tissues in the garbage, then picked up her top.

"How was that?" She buttoned her shirt and ran her fingers through her hair. She needed a mirror to see how bad her lipstick was, but she'd stop in the ladies' room on her way out.

"Holy shit," David said, finally opening his eyes. With his pants and underwear around his ankles, he penguin walked to the camera and stopped the recording. "If this guy doesn't hire you based on that, there's no justice in the world."

For women like me, there's never any fucking justice. The words sat on the tip of her tongue, where his cock had been moments earlier. Beulah cleared her throat, swallowing the remnants of David's salty discharge and her words.

"I'm gonna copy this tape," David said. He pulled his pants up, but left the belt undone. "I'll send it to him, but I need to keep one for myself."

Beulah shrugged. "Whatever you need. So, when should I expect to hear something?" She hoped it didn't come out as needy, but she couldn't feed herself and Hattie on promises and hopes.

3

It was raining the day Beulah met Mike. She handed the cabbie a five-dollar bill, but didn't get any change. She waited momentarily, but the driver closed the divider between them.

The rain fell in sheets, sluicing away the grime of the city streets. Trash and assorted filth ran down the gutters, draining into the sewer.

She stood in the downpour, watching as garbage flowed freely. Beulah knew that feeling, being out of control and along for the ride; it was her life. From an early age, she had almost no say in what happened to her. Whether it was her father, modeling execs, or scummy producers, Beulah felt like trash.

Standing outside of an old warehouse as the cab drove away into the storm, Beulah broke her trance on the refuse and pulled her raincoat tight. She jogged, skipping over the river of filth.

Under the awning, she pulled a sodden paper from her pocket. The ink was smeared, but not badly enough to make it illegible.

"Well, this is it," she said, steeling her nerves for what was next.

The metal door was locked tight.

She pulled on it, but nothing would budge.

Just turn around. Try to hail another cab and get the fuck out of there. No good can come of this.

Coward.

This is your only shot. You know this shit will pay, and hell, you've done worse for free.

Make your money and move on.

Beulah made a fist and pounded on the door.

What felt like an eternity crept by before she heard footsteps approaching.

A half-dozen locks clicked, then the door opened.

A tall, gaunt man stood on the threshold. His

face was marked with acne scars, and black eyes glared at her.

Instinctively, she pulled her jacket tighter, shielding herself from what felt like an evil man.

"Can I help you?"

"I…ah… I'm here to see Mike." Her voice was as soft as the squeak of a mouse.

The man pulled a cigarette from his pants pocket and lit it. Thick smoke rose to his dark eyes, but he didn't flinch. "Beulah, right?"

She nodded. "Yeah."

He pulled the door open the rest of the way. "I'm Sally."

She walked into the warehouse as he closed the door behind her, then followed Sally through the dark warehouse.

Overhead lamps shone on the floor, providing pools of light as they walked.

His dress shoes clicked with every step, echoing off the walls.

More lights shone ahead, and Beulah could see a small room in the middle of the warehouse. There were no windows, just a sliver of light under the door.

When a man walked out of the room, brightness poured into the darkness.

Beulah looked into the room for just a second, glimpsing nude bodies. She couldn't tell if they were male or female before the door swung shut.

"Ah, this must be the new girl," the man said, walking toward her and Sally. He had a slight belly and close-cropped dark hair. His nose was large and round.

Adjusting her purse to her left shoulder, Beulah extended her right hand. "Hi, I'm Beulah."

"Mike," he said, shaking her hand.

His palm was wet, and Beulah had to fight the urge to wipe her hand on her pants.

Mike took a step back and looked her up and down. "Yeah, you'll do just fine." He took a cigarette from his jacket pocket.

Sally already had his lighter in hand, bringing the flame to life and pressing it to the end of the smoke.

"Well, let's get started, shall we?"

4

Beulah grunted around the cock in her mouth. It wasn't intentional, but the one in her ass went deeper than she expected.

The scene was simple: she was a bad piggy, and the two farmers put her on a spit roast. Instead of a metal bar impaling her, it was two dicks—one in her mouth and one in her ass.

She arrived for her scene just as they were bringing the pig in. Her heart stopped, thinking they were going to make her fuck it, but it was just for show.

Unfortunately, the glass of pig cum wasn't just a prop.

All Beulah could do was hope the men finished quickly. Her knees and palms were raw and itchy from resting on the hay.

The pig in the corner squealed watching the performance. It let out a long stream of acrid piss that made the room smell even worse.

As she watched the puddle of vile urine soak through the hay, moving toward her, the taste of the animal's jizz lingered in the back of Beulah's throat, mixed with the pre-cum of the farmer fucking her mouth.

"Yeehaw!" the one fucking her ass yelled. Without warning, he pulled his cock from her ass.

A stream of shit and lube ran down her crack, coating her pussy lips and legs. A thick load landed on her back.

Beulah gagged as the farmer on her face thrust his fat shaft down her throat. She did her best to hold her vomit, but the violation was too much.

He pulled out just as her gorge overflowed.

Her nostrils and throat burned as puke erupted onto the floor. She was ashamed and mortified as his load landed in her hair, and Beulah kept her head down, praying Mike would end the scene and not make her eat the mess.

The twin cum shots were cooling as Mike spoke. "Cut."

Beulah looked over at the camera. Her face was red, and her mouth tasted like hell, but Mike was smiling. A wave of relief washed over her as he turned the camera off.

On shaky legs, she stood and removed the pig nose. Her asshole was on fire, and remnants of shit and cum slid down her body.

"Damn, girl. That was a hell of a fuck," the farmer with the shitty dick said. His hairy belly glistened with sweat. "I haven't had a nut like that in a while." He touched his wilting erection and put his fingers to his nose. "I'll need a hot shower to get your shit off me, but it was worth it."

Mike walked in front of the camera with a cigarette in his mouth and a robe in his hand. He did his best to avoid the mess of shit, cum, lube, vomit, and animal urine. "Great scene, B," he said, handing her the robe.

Beulah took it and put it on. The cooling liquids felt even colder under the fabric, but she was happy to cover herself. Her face had marks from the fake snout, which she felt as she brushed away a tear and forced a smile.

"Thanks." She looked over her shoulder toward the exit. "I'm gonna shower before I leave, if that's okay."

"Sure, sure," Mike said, waving his cigarette to dismiss her. "Get cleaned up. We have another scene tomorrow night, so get some rest."

Still shaky, she walked past the nude men and pig and left the studio, but didn't close the door behind her.

The laughter of the men followed her out.

Even the pig grunted in humor.

5

The smell of shit and screaming welcomed Beulah home. She walked into her dark apartment and recoiled from the odor.

"Goddamnit." She turned the small entry light on and hung her keys on a hook.

A garbled cry came from the bedroom. Wails of, "Mama," screamed through a misshapen mouth.

"I'm home, Hattie. Mama's here." She didn't bother kicking off her shoes as she stormed into the bedroom.

The old dog crate was on its side. A mixture of water, food, shit, and piss ran from the bars of the locked cage.

Hattie's eyes were red and swollen. Snot ran down her face, dripping into her cleft mouth. The toddler was covered in the same mess that decorated the floor of the cheap apartment.

Beulah righted the crate, flipping her messy daughter with it.

This elicited more cries from the frightened girl, and sloshed more foul mess onto the floor.

"Shh, mama's here." Beulah unlocked the cage, and Hattie scurried out.

The girl's Barney pajamas were a mess, clinging to her little body. She'd outgrown the diapers she wore months ago, but Beulah didn't have the money to get the next size up. Hattie was growing like a weed and would soon outgrow diapers altogether. Not that they did much good when the girl was left for hours on end.

Beulah allowed her daughter to crawl into her arms, once again soiling her with feces.

The child sobbed into her mother's freshly-washed hair. Her body quivered with fear and relief, and snot ran down Beulah's neck as Hattie buried her face against the flesh.

"Come on, let's get you cleaned up and in bed."

Together, they walked into the bathroom; and together, they showered and cried.

6

Hattie was finally asleep. It had taken Beulah a while to calm her down, but the girl succumbed to exhaustion.

Beulah wished she could do the same. She sat on her threadbare couch with a smoldering cigarette in her hand. A snake of gray ash hung from it, but the smoke had been forgotten. For the second time that night, Beulah had showered, but even under the lukewarm water, she felt unclean. Her body had been scrubbed, washing away the human fluids and waste, but it wasn't her flesh that was dirty, it was her soul.

The ash fell onto the couch.

"Shit." She brushed it off, leaving a gray smear. Beulah took a final drag, which was mostly filter, and crushed the butt into the ashtray. Opening her purse, she pulled out the thin envelope of money from the sick movie she just made.

It wasn't much, but it would support them for a little while if she could keep herself from snorting it away.

She and Hattie hadn't had a decent meal in weeks, resorting to canned or packaged garbage from the corner store.

Beulah rubbed her nose with the back of her hand; the thought of cocaine was calling to her. She tried to kick the habit after Hattie was born, but found quitting almost impossible. Even with barely enough money to keep them afloat, Beulah had to resist the temptation to get high.

Now that she had money coming in, keeping the drug away was impossible. The potent narcotic had become part of her. It kept her going even as her life collapsed. She never thought the drug was to blame for her woes. No, it was needed.

If Mike needed her for a scene tomorrow, she knew she'd have to get high, but it was late, and Hattie wouldn't sleep long.

Beulah grabbed her phone and clutched it to her chest. She felt her heart racing through the receiver.

Another girl from Mike's, Simone, introduced her to The Snowman, as she called him. He was grimy, as were most drug dealers, but took payment in cash or pussy.

Since Beulah only had that little bit of money to keep her going, the slit between her legs was good enough, at least for the time being.

Without another thought, she called the dealer.

He answered on the second ring and told her he'd be right over.

Something caught Beulah's eye: a blinking *'1'* flashed red on her answering machine. She never would've spent money on it, but Mike insisted his girls had a machine at home.

Her finger hovered over the button, but she knew who left the message. She pressed it, and the tape whirled as it prepared to play.

"Beulah, it's Daddy. I'm just checking in…again. I wish you'd call me back. Darlin', whatever you're into, I can help. Hell, *I* need *your* help. The farm isn't the same without you. We have a full stock of swine ready for slaughter. I-I sure could use you here. Anyway, please call me."

Beulah's eyes stung with tears. She deleted the message, as she had all the others he'd left.

Her father didn't need her; he *wanted* her. Just like everyone else, he wanted to use her whether it was for free labor, or to be his whore so he didn't have to pay horny farmhands.

There was no love there, and there never would be. That man had stripped her of every dream she ever had, and would do so until the day he died.

He laughed when she told him she wanted to be a veterinarian and save animals, not kill them. He told her she was too stupid to be a doctor. He told her the world had too many smart people already. They didn't need brains on the farm, only a strong back and hard work ethic. What he didn't tell her was the hard work she'd be performing was to pleasure disgusting men to clear his debt.

The thought of becoming a veterinarian was still a dream of hers. So much so, Beulah bought herself a second-hand animal anatomy textbook from the thrift store. She'd only opened it a few times, but it fascinated her the way animals differed from humans, and the unique qualities they all possessed. It was a subject she could lose herself in. But the world she lived in swallowed her whole, eliminating every hope and dream.

A light knock pulled her from her reverie. She dashed over to the door so he wouldn't knock again. She couldn't have Hattie waking up, considering how she was about to pay for her coke.

"The Snowman has arrived," the dealer said with a sly grin, looking her up and down.

Beulah wore a baggy sweatshirt with no bra and equally baggy pants. Her hair was wet and tossed up in a messy ponytail. All the makeup had been scrubbed from her face. She was tired and felt the onset of a few pimples forming. Even though she didn't look like much, she still felt like a piece of meat under his glare.

"So," he leaned in the doorway, "how are we paying? Ass or cash?"

She wanted to puke. Was this what her life had become? Performing one disgusting act after another just to keep going? If she said she hadn't considered suicide many times, she'd be lying.

"You know how. Now get in here, bust your nut, and give me the shit before my kid wakes up." She pulled him into the apartment, quietly closing the door behind them, then took a condom from her purse and handed it to him.

"Alright, alright. I get it," he said.

The apartment still smelled like shit, but he didn't say a word. She figured a man in his profession had smelled worse.

The Snowman handed her a baggie of white powder.

It looked smaller than the last bag she purchased, but Beulah wasn't in the mood to argue. She just wanted him to cum and leave. She opened the baggie and dumped half of the contents onto the webbing of her hand, and snorted it as he pulled his pants down.

"Ah, a little help here." The nub of his flaccid penis poked out from a tangled nest of pubic hair.

Beulah snorted again, driving the narcotics deep into her bloodstream. She dropped to her knees, getting a whiff of his vile crotch and ass, and sucked him until he was hard enough to get the rubber on.

"Good?" she asked.

He stroked himself, bringing a little more rigidity to his cock. "Eh, that'll do. Now, bend over that couch. I got places to be."

Beulah looked at the bedroom door, which was still closed. She walked over to the couch, buzzing from the drugs in her system, and pulled her pants down before resting her arms on the back of the sofa.

The dealer stood behind her and spread her ass.

For a second, she feared he might try to stick his prick in her already abused anus. He'd never done it before, but he was unpredictable.

"Damn girl, who blew out your O ring?" he asked as he ran his dirty fingers over her pussy and ass.

She didn't answer, and he didn't ask again.

The dry condom, and her lack of arousal, elicited a small shriek when he plunged into her vagina.

The Snowman must've thought her reaction was from pleasure, not pain. "Yeah, girl, take that dick," he grunted as he bucked with his pathetic cock.

Beulah looked out the window at the city below her. How many others were doing the same thing? Paying for numbness to escape the misery of their lives.

She was so entranced in her thoughts, willing herself to be anywhere but there, Beulah didn't hear the bedroom door open.

Hattie stood watching, a stuffed Barney toy clutched to her chest, as her mother grunted with each thrust.

1994

CHAPTER 12

1

Beulah balanced the plates of food on her arms. It had taken her a few weeks to learn the skill, but her early life on the farm taught her how to multi-task. She swerved around a mother and child as they passed her, heading toward the bathroom.

"And here we go," Beulah said, unloading the plates at a table. "Silver Dollar pancakes for you."

A little girl held a fork and knife like a cartoon character, anxiously awaiting her breakfast.

"A Western Omelet for you."

The little girl's father wasn't so focused on the greasy food in front of him; rather, his eyes were on Beulah's chest.

"And a waffle for you."

The matriarch of the family glanced at her husband and cleared her throat, snapping the man out of his sexual fantasy.

His cheeks bloomed red as he picked up a half-empty ketchup bottle. "Ah, could we get a fresh bottle? I like to lay it on heavy."

Beulah smiled, knowing the guy was in trouble with his wife who hadn't taken her eyes off him. "Sure." She took the bottle, carefully avoiding touching him. She had a feeling his gaze would affect her tip, even if she'd done nothing wrong. Beulah set a stack of extra napkins in the middle of the table.

"Can I get you folks anything else?"

The woman at the table finally broke her death glare from her husband's head and turned to her.

She wasn't that old, and quite attractive, but Beulah could see the hurt in her eyes. She'd seen it many times before, and sometimes in the mirror. The dad/husband may have portrayed a nice guy with his smile and how he interacted with the little girl, but he'd hurt the woman. Whether it was with a remark, or he cheated, he'd done something to her.

"No, I think we're good," the woman said, trying to force a fake smile.

Beulah softly clapped her hands and smiled, looking at the perfect little girl stuffing huge pancake chunks in her mouth—her pristine, normal mouth— and her mind wandered to Hattie.

Hattie would never have a perfect mouth. Even with all the money in the world, nothing could be done to eliminate the cleft that split her face.

Even so, Beulah knew her life, and her daughter's life, was better on that day than it had been years before.

After Beulah's last movie with Mike, one in which she was forced to give a guy a rimjob after he shit on her tits, she knew her life was spiraling out of control. Her nose bled almost constantly from coke use, and her daughter hadn't had a decent meal in months.

Mike paid her well, but her addiction was killing her.

As much as she thought Hattie was a curse, her motherly love for the girl grew daily. She felt horrible about the dog crate, but it was a necessity to keep the girl safe. Beulah did her best to get home early to avoid cleaning shit and piss, but oftentimes, the girl would still mess herself.

It was after that film, with the taste and smell of shit clinging to her, she knew her life had to change; and she was glad she did.

The diner wasn't much, but with no skills or schooling, it was the best Beulah could do. It was hard leaving that money, but the life she was living would put her in an early grave. And without her, she knew her daughter wouldn't be far behind.

The state would take the deformed girl and stuff her into foster care.

Beulah knew Hattie wouldn't fare well, and couldn't fathom what would happen to her child.

A year into working at the Starline Diner, with rent always late and leftover food as their main source of nutrition, Beulah learned what happened to Mike and his crew.

It was a bloodbath.

One of his performers, a girl named Talia, killed them all.

From what Beulah heard, it was a massacre. Mike, Sally, another performer named Ingrid, some of his lackeys, and even the big boss, were slaughtered like animals by Talia's cool, powder-dry hands.

If Beulah said she didn't smile the day she heard the news, she'd be lying. Mike and his people were the worst of the worst, and she could only imagine how bad things got after her departure.

She knew how it was to be under his thumb. Before a few of her scenes, she saw what she thought was blood on the set. High and needing money, Beulah pushed the image from her mind, praying her blood wouldn't spill. But, if that was what the movie called for, she didn't know if she had it in her to turn it down.

Pushing those thoughts from her mind, Beulah walked behind the counter. She pulled her pad from her apron and began tallying up a few bills.

"Got time for a twenty?" a voice said from behind her as a hand squeezed her ass.

Beulah tensed at the smell of Preston's cheap cologne and firm grip.

Preston Kinsley was the manager at the Starline Diner, and a bona fide creep.

It seemed no matter what Beulah did, she couldn't outrun shitty men. She had to wonder if they were everywhere.

2

It wasn't long after Beulah began her job at the diner that her boss started hitting on her. He wasn't the most subtle of men, and she thought he might have seen a few of her movies. After telling him about her daughter and her financial situation, Beulah hoped she'd get sympathy and pick up more shifts. She was wrong. What she received, instead, was the offer to give him a blowjob for twenty bucks. So, before long, *time for a twenty,* became their key phrase.

Each time she got on her knees in his office, she felt her old life creeping back in. But she knew this was different. For a few quick minutes, she could make what she'd make in tips in an hour. It didn't make her proud—far from it—but Beulah was a survivor, and twenty bucks could go a long way.

Beulah looked at her tables. They were all good, at least for the few minutes it would take her to suck him off.

Preston's erection poked her in the ass. If he was already hard, he would blow even quicker.

One time, after he dumped a load down her throat, he told her he and his wife rarely fucked. And if they did, it was out of pity. Preston was put on a clock, and Brenda urged him to cum as quickly as possible. And blowjobs? He laughed when he told her the last time his cock had been in his wife's mouth was on their honeymoon.

With how quickly he busted, Beulah believed him.

His skin had an oily sheen developed over years of working in the diner. The smell of his cologne mingled with the scent of grease was strong. It even overwhelmed the odor of whatever product he used in his thinning hair.

"I can make that happen," she said. Beulah looked around, making sure no one was watching, before grabbing his crotch.

Preston shuddered, and she thought he might blow right there. "Meet me in the office in two minutes." He disappeared, but his scent lingered.

Beulah grabbed the coffee pot and made a quick round, topping her tables off before walking to the office.

A few of the cooks gave her a wink, but said nothing.

The other waitress, Shan, didn't look at her, and

for that, Beulah was grateful.

Preston's pants were already off as he quickly ushered her into the office so as not to be seen.

A twenty-dollar bill, and a tube of bright red lipstick, sat on the messy desk.

Beulah grabbed the money, stuffing it away with the rest of her tips.

"You know I like the lipstick," Preston said as he plopped onto his battered chair. He spread his legs and stroked himself.

Using the framed photo from his promotion to manager as a crude mirror, Beulah smeared the cheap makeup onto her lips. It was a familiar feeling, even though the only time she wore makeup anymore was to suck his dick.

She adjusted her ponytail and kneeled in front of him.

Preston shuddered from only thirty seconds of her blowing him. He grabbed the back of her head and forced her further onto his cock as he came.

Beulah tightened her lips around the base of his shaft, smearing the lipstick. He liked it, and if it meant another twenty in the future, she'd do it.

Preston's head was back, and his eyes closed. "Damn, that might have been a record."

She swallowed his salty load and stood. The blowjob had been so quick, the lipstick didn't even smear. For a second, she considered leaving it on, but didn't. She was sure she wasn't the first girl he had, and she didn't need any more rumors flying. Beulah dipped a napkin in an old glass of water on his desk, then scrubbed at her lips, removing the garish red.

"I gotta check my tables. They should be done

soon."

Preston looked at her with relief in his eyes. His chair groaned and his cock softened as he stood. "Yeah, best we go out separately anyway."

Beulah opened the door a sliver, slipping back out into the dining room, leaving her boss nude from the waist down.

3

Beulah walked into her apartment and was greeted by the sound of cartoons. She took a quick whiff of the air and didn't smell smoke or shit, so that was a big plus.

"Mama," Hattie yelled. The girl came running in from the living room, barreling into Beulah. Her cleft mouth split further into a grin as she smiled at her mother. "I mithed you."

Rubbing her daughter's head, Beulah showed her the bag of food she brought home. "I brought you some pancakes. Chocolate chip."

Hattie let out a little squeal and took the bag. She dashed into the kitchen, and there was a rattle of cheap cutlery before the girl ran back into the living room.

Beulah hung her purse and sweater on the hook near the door. She kicked her shoes off and wished she had someone to rub her aching feet. "So, what have you been doing all day?" she asked as she leaned on the wall leading to the living room.

Hattie crammed another large bite of pancake into her mouth. Her lips and face were already smeared with melted chocolate. "Nuffin' mush. Just washing TB." She swallowed and looked up as if in thought. "Oh, Mith Janey came over and played Candyland with me." She took another bite and went back to watching her show.

Jane was their next-door neighbor. She was in her early sixties and already a widow. She was a sweet woman at heart, but sometimes, she could be a bitch.

When Beulah started taking more hours at work, she asked the elderly neighbor to pop in and check on Hattie. Beulah would have rather had an actual babysitter, but she couldn't afford it. This was a better option, albeit not the safest. It beat using the dog crate, though, which Beulah had thrown out when they moved from their old place. It was only a matter of time before she was caught keeping her daughter locked away, and she knew what that meant: jail time and Hattie going into foster care.

"Well, that's good. Did you win?"

Hattie turned and looked at her with a mischievous grin, bits of food showing between her crooked teeth. "Uh huh. I kicked her butt."

"That's good, baby." Beulah moved into the small kitchen, shut the open silverware drawer, and picked up a stack of mail. It was the same stuff: bills and junk.

She'd done pretty well in tips at work. Even the table with the wife shooting her daggers gave her a decent tip, which she didn't expect.

"Oh!" Hattie yelled from the other room. "Grandpa called."

Beulah froze, letting the paper fall from her hands. It had been years since she talked to her father, even though he insisted on calling. Each call was the same. He'd put on a show, telling her he loved her and that no matter what, she always had a home on the farm.

"Did he leave a message?" It was the only thing Beulah could muster, praying her daughter hadn't answered the phone. As many times as she changed her number, her father always found it.

"No, I talthed to him. He wath very nice."

Rage burned through Beulah's chest, and before she could control it, her hand slapped Hattie's face.

The flesh-on-flesh smack was loud, even more so than the cartoons.

Half-chewed pancake flew from the child's deformed mouth, landing on the floor. A red handprint and a fresh crop of tears sprouted up immediately. The violence was so fast, Hattie still had a deformed smile on her face before the pain and shock registered.

"Oh, baby," Beulah said, the regret instant. She dropped to her knees, narrowly avoiding the mush from her daughter's mouth. "I'm so sorry." She pulled Hattie into her chest, doing her best to stifle the tears before they worsened.

Hattie shuddered, but kept her crying at bay.

It was something that Beulah noticed her daughter had become good at. She didn't know if it was a good or bad thing.

"Grandpa isn't a good man, sweetheart." She pushed Hattie away from her so she could look at her. "He's not like the grandpas you see on your shows, baby. He's mean. He was mean to mommy when she was little, and I'm sure he hasn't changed a bit."

Hattie's eyes were red, but the tears didn't fall.

"So, ith he wike you? You're mean."

The wind rushed out of Beulah. It seemed like the tears meant for her daughter found her. Her eyes stung as she rose to her feet. She wanted to tell her daughter she was nothing like her father, but feared opening her mouth would unleash a torrent of emotions. Turning away from her daughter, Beulah walked back into the kitchen and took a few calming breaths.

She picked up a large textbook buried under the mail. It was almost due back to the library, so she only had a few days left. Reading was the last thing she felt like doing, but it was an excuse to remove herself from the situation.

"Mommy has to study," Beulah said when she returned to the living room. Her voice was shaky, but she maintained her composure.

Rubbing the raised lettering of the animal anatomy book, she thought of all the fingers that had done the same. Even though it felt like climbing a mountain, Beulah still hoped she would, one day, make it to college. And what better way to progress quickly than to study the material you love beforehand.

"Ottay, mama," Hattie said without taking her eyes from the TV. It seemed the slap was all but forgotten.

Beulah clutched the book to her chest. Back in the kitchen, she noticed a message on the machine. She wondered how many times her father called before Hattie answered. Her finger hovered over the play button, tempting her to press it and hear his voice. She hesitated and deleted the message without listening.

In her room, Beulah removed her work clothes. She tossed them into the overflowing hamper, threw on a pair of sweats and an old t-shirt, then collapsed on her bed and opened the book. It was hard to read with tears in her eyes.

4

The bell above the door jingled as Beulah walked in for her shift. It was her longer day, and she was ready to make money. It seemed like every time she paid the bills, they were due again. But the lunch/dinner shift was always a good money-maker, especially on a Friday night.

Shan was wiping down a table and loading plates into a bus bin on the bench seat. She stuffed the rag into her apron and lifted the heavy bin overflowing with dirty dishes.

"Hey Shan," Beulah said, catching the eye of the older woman.

Shan glared at her. She was never the friendliest person, but was never rude to Beulah.

They worked well together for a while, but something had changed.

"Preston needs to see you in his office." Shan pushed past Beulah, bumping her with the dishes.

"Oh, okay. Let me put my things away and get my stuff se—"

"No. He said he needed to see you immediately." Shan's voice had venom as she kicked the kitchen door open before disappearing.

Beulah felt sick and could see the side-eye glances from the few customers. Their conversations had stopped, and Beulah itched to tell them to mind their fucking business. She pulled her purse closer to her body, comforting her as she walked to his office door.

How often had she been in that office for a twenty? Enough times she'd lost count.

He never called her in to suck his cock at the beginning of the shift. Usually, it was random, but it was almost always mid-shift.

And the way Shan looked at her made her stomach roll. No, this wasn't just for a suck job.

Beulah knocked on the door. She heard his chair squeak as he rose, and wondered if that would be the last time she heard the sound.

Preston looked like shit. His face was drawn and unshaven. Even his shirt, which was usually neat and pressed, was messy and wrinkled. "Come in," he said, ushering her through the door before closing it behind him.

Returning to his chair behind his desk, he put his head in his hands for a moment before looking up. "She found out."

"Who found out what?" Beulah asked in shock.

"My fucking wife. She found out about us."

Beulah wanted to tell him there was no *'us,'* only an agreement where she was his whore for a measly twenty bucks. She wanted to tell him she had no interest in him, and if she saw him on the street or in a bar, she'd not look twice. That sucking him off was the low point of her days, and sometimes, she cried herself to sleep with shame.

It was a part of her old life she couldn't escape. She'd been given certain gifts that were no good for her soul, but things she did to survive in the shit world.

"For once, she wanted to fuck. And I was so damn thrilled she was horny." He put his head in his hands again before looking back at her. "I forgot to shower. It didn't take a genius to notice the red lipstick on my dick." He rubbed his cheeks; he was crying. "I-I broke down and told her everything. She might divorce me."

Beulah didn't give a fuck about his marriage and never had. That was his commitment, not hers. She cared about making sure she and Hattie were taken care of.

"I have to let you go." He took an envelope from a drawer and put it on the desk. "Your last check and a little extra." He slid it forward. "I'm sorry, Beulah."

Anger. That was it. That was all she felt. Once again, she'd been used and discarded by a fucking man.

"How can you do this to me? I didn't come to you; you came to me. You whined and bitched about your fucking life and bitch wife."

Preston put his hands up. "Now, that's unnecessary."

"Fuck you," she said, snatching the envelope off the desk. She held it in front of his face. "*This* is it? My parting gift for my work. All because you couldn't keep your dick in your pants?" She was yelling and could see the fear on his face as he looked past her at the closed door leading to the restaurant. "Oh, what? You don't want them to hear me?"

Beulah threw the door open and stormed out.

"Beulah, wait." He chased after her, which was what she wanted.

Beulah stopped in the dining room, drawing the attention of the diners. "So, *you*, the fucking *boss*, used your power to get me to *suck your cock*!"

A collective gasp rose from the customers and employees alike.

Raising his hands, Preston forced a smile at the disturbed faces in the restaurant. "Sorry about that, folks. Just enjoy your meals, please."

"No. They should know what kind of piece of shit runs this place." Beulah looked at the crowd, watching them. "This man, the *boss*, has made me give him blowjobs since I've worked here. He told me I'd get fired if I didn't." She didn't care about the lie; it made Preston look even worse. "And now, he was caught by his wife and is firing me. Fuck you. I hope you and your wife are happy with each other."

Kids were crying, and families gathered their belongings to remove themselves from the establishment quickly.

"Please, sit back down, folks." Preston was sweating.

Beulah wanted to rip the envelope in half and throw it in his face, but she needed the money. Instead, she turned on her heel and stormed out the door. She held it open for the outpouring of angry diners.

5

Even though she wanted to, Beulah didn't head

straight home. She hefted her purse, which was heavy with library books, and walked.

The weight pulled her down. It wasn't just the weight of the books, but of her shame. It was hard, but she'd been putting some money away, hoping she could attend school. Nothing crazy, but a few night classes here and there would help. Becoming a veterinarian was her life goal, and that wasn't possible without college.

College.

That word was rarely spoken in her life. But Beulah was resilient. When she went to school, she did well, but deep down, she knew her father would never allow her higher learning.

After leaving home, she thought there might be a chance if she could save enough money modeling. But the high life of society, especially after being sheltered, was too alluring. Now that she was older, and hopefully wiser, she thought it might be time.

Things were going well for her at the diner until that day. And, once again, she had to start at the bottom.

The library was huge and one of her favorite places.

She wanted to check out a few fiction books, something more mundane to occupy her mind, but didn't. Wandering through the stacks, touching the books, her mind drifted as much as her fingers. Telling Hattie things were about to get rough was like a pit of worms burrowing in her gut.

Finding a new job could be tough, especially one that paid well. There were plenty of restaurants in the city, so she could always start there. Deep down, she feared she wouldn't be successful, that a new employer would know Preston and find out what she'd done. She was sure the weasel of a man would, somehow, blame her. Even more so, Beulah feared falling back into her old life.

The money she made from porn was much more than she'd ever make waiting tables. Mike and his guys were gone, but getting in with someone else didn't take a genius. But who? And what would they make her do? It was bad enough that there were films of her in the world, but she was trying to be a good mom now, and couldn't imagine putting new disgusting videos into the wild.

A few years back, she could've found an escort agency, something safer than walking the streets, but she didn't know if that was possible anymore. Beulah was still attractive, but the men who paid top dollar for company weren't looking for a mother in her thirties. They wanted young girls; she knew how fucking perverted they were.

Dancing was an option, but she knew where that would lead. Before long, she'd be getting fucked behind the club by some drunk asshole for a few bucks. Her mind would decay like it had once before, and drugs would be the only thing to numb her.

Beulah grabbed a few books she hadn't read before and wrapped her arms around them.

She headed home, trying to strategize her and Hattie's next step, trying to stay ahead of an eviction.

The sound of cartoons welcomed Beulah as she entered their small apartment.

"Mama?" Hattie asked curiously. The girl poked her head around the corner with apprehension in her eyes.

Beulah wasn't due home until that night, and Jane wouldn't check on the girl for a few hours still, so Hattie was right to be concerned about who was walking in the door.

Hattie smiled at seeing her mother home early.

"Mr. Preston gave me the day off," Beulah said. Her eyes stung with tears, but she smiled them away like she'd done so many times in her life.

Hattie's cheeks scrunched up, adding to the crooked appearance of her already deformed face. It was a grin Beulah had seen before.

Guilt.

"Mama, I haf oo ell oo somefin."

Setting her bag down, Beulah's eyes immediately flashed to the telephone.

A light was blinking on the answering machine.

"Grandpa called. Buh I dinen an'er it."

Beulah rubbed Hattie's cheeks, seeing the innocence in her.

"It's okay, baby. Thank you for telling me and keeping your promise." She crouched down to eye level with the girl. "Why don't you get changed and we'll go to the park."

Hattie smiled and ran into her room.

6

They had a good day together. The park wasn't crowded, which was a plus. Kids could be so fucking mean. Even though Hattie pretended not to hear, Beulah knew the sneers hurt her.

There was nothing worse than watching her

daughter play alone when the others shunned her. What was even more heartbreaking was seeing how the other parents treated Hattie.

Beulah sprung for a cheap dinner of fried rice and egg rolls, which they ate at home.

When Hattie went to bed, Beulah was left with her thoughts. Her small TV was low, and she stared at the pages of the book on her lap. The words jumbled together in a mess. She couldn't focus no matter how hard she tried. The problems of her life kept racing around her brain like a hamster on meth.

She looked into the kitchen where the answering machine still blinked with a new message. Beulah bit her nail, something she thought she'd outgrown. She spat the sliver of white into her palm and set it on the coffee table.

Next to the discarded nail sat her bills.

Looking them over, she prioritized the most important ones. The cold pit of despair grew colder as she leafed through them. Then, she tried to lose herself in her studies, but even that couldn't pull her from her funk.

At that point, it all felt for naught. What would studying get her? She wasn't in school, and with the loss of her job, it didn't seem like an obtainable goal. Beulah slammed the book shut and tossed it on the couch. She stood with tears in her eyes and marched into the kitchen.

The blinking light taunted her, flashing in the darkness.

Beulah put her gnawed finger in her mouth and bit down, drawing blood from her cuticle.

Don't do it. Nothing good can come from him.

That life is behind you. You're down right now, but you always find a way to bounce back. And do you want Hattie living that life? Even if you have to scrape and beg, you'll find a way out.

She wanted to believe what she told herself but couldn't. Over the years, one disaster after another made Beulah feel like a failure. It wasn't as bad when she was alone, but she had a child relying on her.

Could her father have changed? Doubtful.

Thoughts of her battered childhood lived rent free in her mind. The nights of abuse from him, and other men, would never go away.

People always say not to live in the past, but her past forged her present and future.

Could she let her and Hattie live on the streets, or worse yet, in a city-run shelter? She heard the horrors of those places, even if they were built with the best intentions. And how was she supposed to find work if she couldn't watch over her child? There was no way she would leave her there. She might be able to get away with it during the school year, but that was only six hours a day, five days a week.

Again, the sting of tears burned her eyes. Beulah wiped them away and looked toward her daughter's bedroom. Maybe she'd get another shot if she worked on the farm for a few years.

She experienced life and all the pitfalls. The farm was the biggest money maker, and it would give her and Hattie a roof over their heads and food in their bellies. The money she would make could go a long way to get her a place of her own for good.

Maybe she would even get lucky and her scumbag father would die and leave it all to her. The land alone had to be worth a hefty sum.

Beulah stared at the flashing light again, then pressed the button.

2003

CHAPTER 13

1

The cab was a far cry from those in New York, but they arrived safely back at the cabin.

"Here," JD said, handing the driver a ten-dollar bill.

The brusque man behind the wheel grunted at him and stuffed the money in his pocket behind a pack of cigarettes.

The ride was only five bucks, but it was clear the driver had no intention of giving any change.

Ari, Danielle, Rich, and JD climbed out of the smelly car, happy to have the fresh air filling their lungs. The stench of death was still on the night breeze, but it was faint compared to earlier.

The cab's tires crunched on the earth as it drove away into the gloom.

"Well, he was certainly pleasant," Ari said. Normally, she would've rubbed her arms for warmth, but it was warmer than expected. It also helped she was drunk. Not fall-down, hammered, but the booze had been flowing.

Rich threw his arm around Danielle's shoulders and kissed her neck. "I can't believe they didn't card us. There's no fucking way any of us look old enough to drink."

"I told you these backwoods places don't give a shit. They just want money. And since they knew we didn't drive, there was no harm in serving us," JD said, taking Ari's hand.

A dim light shone from the windows of the cabin in the distance. The moon was full, bathing the path in silver.

"Who would've guessed a night out in the sticks could be so much fun?" Danielle said. She snaked her arm around Rich's waist.

"Oh, it's going to be much more fun in a few minutes." Rich kissed her neck as they walked.

JD and Ari looked at each other and rolled their eyes. Even in their jest, they were feeling the same way.

Their detour to the cabin had started as a nightmare, but they were making the best of it. And as hard pressed as they may be to admit it, they were all having fun. There was something to be said about the charm of the little cabin, especially the opportunity to fuck in a new location.

Most of their sex had to be secretive. JD and Ari rarely had the chance to fuck in relaxation. It was a quick, passionate session, half clothed in a bedroom, usually with Ari wearing a pair of torn pajama pants. Or the awkward, risky fucks in the backseat of the car.

With the cabin to themselves, it was finally a night to truly explore each other unabated.

The cabin still had the musty smell they'd become familiar with. It hit them as they walked in, but none of them cared, especially Rich and Danielle.

The two of them drank the most, and almost had to be separated in the bar to stop them from fucking on the tabletop. They wasted no time when they walked into the cabin.

Rich grabbed his girlfriend's face and nearly inhaled her.

Their lips and tongues met in a wet fury as they crossed the threshold. Without thinking of their other friends, Rich thrust his hand down Danielle's pants, letting his fingers explore her.

Danielle moaned, lost in her passion.

"Okay, well, I guess you two are just going to fuck right in front of us," Ari said. She looked at JD and rolled her eyes with a grin.

Snapping out of her lustful trance, Danielle pulled Rich's hand from her pants and giggled. "Sorry. It's been a long trip."

"Yeah, it's been almost twenty-four hours since we've last fucked. And goddamn, this country air has my dick like a rock." Rich reached into his waistband and adjusted himself.

"Well, if you two are going to abuse the couch, I guess we'll take it to our room," JD said.

Ari put a hand on his chest and stopped him. She opened a small closet full of old blankets and grabbed a stack. "How about you and I take a little walk? Maybe head down to the stream? I think we talked about skinny dipping or something." She kissed him on the nose and then the mouth.

JD smiled and took the blankets from her. They smelled of mothballs, but he didn't care. "Okay, you crazy kids. We're going on a little walk. We'll knock before we come back in."

Rich and Danielle weren't paying attention to him. They dropped onto the couch and resumed making out.

"Let's go before we see something we can't unsee," Ari said.

JD wouldn't mind staying a minute longer, as Danielle was about to take her shirt off, but Ari yanked his arm, leading him back outside.

2

Rich helped Danielle out of her shirt. He kissed the hollow of her throat as she moaned. With passion, his lips worked down to her chest. He pressed her tits together, kissing the smooth skin.

Danielle grabbed the back of his head, playing with the nape of his neck. She released him and reached behind to unclasp her bra.

As many times as Rich tried, he could never master the art of removing a bra.

The lacy cups loosened, and Rich pulled the garment free. His mouth never left her body as he took her left nipple into his mouth.

Whimpering, Danielle pushed the back of his head, pressing her hard nub against his teeth.

Rich let her nipple pop from his mouth, kissing under her areola as he did. "Lay back," he ordered.

She smiled and scooted on the couch with her feet on the floor.

Rich stood in front of her and took his shirt off. He threw it aimlessly and kneeled between her legs.

Danielle already had her pants unfastened as Rich pulled at her zipper. She lifted her ass as he yanked her pants and underwear off in a few tugs. They fell in a heap, inside out. His aggression only led to her further arousal.

She pulled her heels onto the edge of the couch, bending her knees and spreading her legs.

Rich stared at the wet slit, waiting for him. Giving Danielle head was one of his favorite things, and he knew if he could get her off with his mouth, she'd cum again when he fucked her.

Kissing her inner thigh, he savored her smell. Some men were turned off if pussy had any kind of scent to it, but Rich considered it extra seasoning.

His tongue slithered along her flesh, causing another whimper to escape. He knew the whimpers would turn into moans, which would turn into screams as she came. Rich breathed her in before his tongue caressed the moist opening calling to him.

"Fuck!" Danielle shouted. She reached down and grabbed his hair.

"Oh, watch the hair," Rich said, pulling his wet face from between her legs with a grin. He didn't care at that moment, but it was a running joke between them.

Danielle smiled at him. "Yes, sir. I'm sure I can find a better use for them anyway." She took her hands from his head and began playing with her tits.

Rich went back to work, letting his tongue explore her. He wrapped his arms around her legs, knowing she'd squirm as she got close to climaxing. Which, by the way she was grinding her clit into his face, wouldn't be very long.

Arching her back, Danielle rubbed her pelvis in his face. Try as she might, she couldn't writhe away from the grasp Rich had on her legs. Her eyes rolled back, and she pulled at her nipples. A howl of ecstasy erupted from her lips as her body pulsed with pleasure.

Savoring her as she came, Rich accepted the nectar dripping down his chin. He teased her clit one last time, just to get a giggle out of her, before looking up. His face was soaked and split in a wide grin.

"Fuck me like it's our last day on earth," Danielle said, looking down at her lover. Her face was flushed, and she continued to knead her breasts.

Rich stood and pulled his pants down.

His cock sprung out, seeking the wetness his mouth had devoured.

He collapsed forward, kissing her, their bodies pressed together.

Her taste was shared between them, and it only seemed to make Danielle want him even more. Her ass rose off the couch as if her pussy were searching for him, begging to be fucked.

"It's yours, babe. Just grab it and put it in," he breathed, their lips barely touching.

Danielle grabbed his throbbing member and pulled him forward. Her body welcomed his as they slid together in a wet union, praying the night would never end.

3

Hattie masturbated furiously outside the window. Her hand was stuffed down her pants as she watched the couple fuck. She grunted along with them, her breath ragged behind the mask. A wave of pleasure and warmth rode over her in a cascade as she orgasmed. Her knees went weak, and she leaned against the side of the cabin. She removed her hand from her crotch and pressed her wet fingers to her misshapen nose.

A low rumble came from the darkness of the trees behind her.

She wasn't alone.

The mutated creature that was once her grandfather stepped out into the moonlight. In his one human hand was a knife, one that had opened the throats of many swine.

The monstrosity walked toward the door.

Hattie touched his chest, still tacky with the blood of the farm hands. "No, noth yeth."

The deformed pig's head turned to the side, like a dog hearing a shrill whistle.

"Follow me," Hattie said, leaving the two lovers in the cabin.

Together, they melted into the darkness, heading toward the stream.

4

Ari wasn't the type of girl who dipped her toes in the water before jumping in. It just wasn't her. If she wanted to do something, she did. That was just the person she was, even as a child. Unfortunately for her, that cavalier attitude resulted in a few youthful hospital trips.

As she carefully walked into the chill water of the stream, she wished she'd taken the time, at least this once. But it was too damn picturesque—nude, bathed in the moonlight—to tippy-toe in. Her skin was covered in goosebumps, but she didn't stop.

Without looking back, she knew JD was staring at her nakedness. The lapping water reached her thighs, and she looked over her shoulder at her boyfriend. Her hair was down, and she knew it was kinky and curled just as JD liked it. Part of her face was obscured by her locks, but not her smile or eyes.

"Come on, before I change my mind." Her breasts were mostly under the water, but just enough were exposed to give JD a peek.

JD threw his pants on the blankets, which he took the time to spread out, and joined her in the water. "Fuck, this is colder than I expected," he said as he swam over to her.

Ari welcomed him with open arms. "Well, I guess we'll have to warm each other up." She pulled him to her, relishing in the warmth of his body heat.

They kissed with the moon as their only witness.

Even in the frigid water, JD's cock was hard. His throbbing erection pressed against her stomach, and Ari's desire rose.

Warmth blossomed inside of her, and she drove her tongue deeper into his mouth.

JD returned the passion of her kiss and lifted her. The tip of his penis grazed her opening, yearning to enter the softness beyond.

Adjusting her hips, Ari let his erection caress her clit. She shuddered as JD allowed her to put her feet back on the silty streambed.

They didn't speak, just looked at each other. The stream babbled and spoke, but they didn't. At that moment, they were the only things in the world.

JD sighed and broke his stare. "I'm scared, Ari."

She kissed his nose. "I'm sure there's nothing in

here that will bite that worm of yours."

He looked at her with feigned annoyance. "Worm? Come on, give me a snake or something."

Ari's lips grazed his. "Oh baby, it's a snake. A big, thick one." She grabbed his cock under the water.

"You know what I mean. I'm certainly not worried about river creatures. I-I'm worried about us. About not having nights like this again. Sure, we have the rest of the summer, and I'll cherish each day we spend together, but what then? College is a big step for both of us, and you know how long distances work for people."

She stroked his hair and stared into his eyes.

His hands played along her back and the top of her ass, but not sexually. It was a loving way that showed he cared.

"Look, we love each other. And tonight, we're together. I can't tell you what the future holds, only that for right now, life is perfect." She kissed him, pressing her body tight against his.

JD's shaft split her cleft, and she ground her already-electrified clit against him.

They broke the kiss but stayed close.

Ari gently gyrated her hips against him, relishing in the sensation on her sex. "I think I'm ready to get out."

JD smiled. "Me too." He took her hand and led them out of the cold water.

Grabbing two old blankets, he turned to give one to Ari, but she knocked it from his hands and kissed him. It wasn't a soft, sensual kiss, it was filled to the brim with passion.

Their teeth clicked together in hunger to consume the carnal desire.

Ari pushed the thoughts of the future from her mind, letting herself solely enjoy the present. She was hungry for him and needed him. It was like an itch she waited all day to scratch, and it was time. She stroked him to a hardness she felt was almost impossible.

Moans escaped JD's mouth and entered hers. She didn't mind. She knew he'd stay hard if he came right then and there, but he was far from a minute man. Then again, she had a desire to make him cum, to show him she was in charge. There were plenty of times during sex when he'd take charge, and she loved them. But when she did it, it was something special.

Without warning, Ari dropped to her knees in front of him.

JD didn't even get a word out before she took him in her mouth.

It wasn't a slow, teasing blowjob. Ari was on a mission. Her right hand joined her mouth, stroking as she sucked, while her left played with his heavy balls.

"Holy shit, Ari. You're gonna make me cum," JD breathed. His fingers were in her hair, pulling it taut.

The pleasure of the gentle pain only fueled her. Ari took him as deep as she dared, tasting him the entire way down her throat.

"Fuck, fuck." JD squirmed and rose on his toes.

Ari looked up at him with her dark, doe eyes and didn't even blink as he came.

Hot, salty cum shot into her mouth, but she kept eye contact.

JD thrust deeper, depositing his seed into her throat.

She welcomed it, letting it coat the back of her tongue. A gentle moan escaped her mouth, the vibrations only enhancing his pleasure.

After the deluge of spunk slowed, Ari took her mouth off him.

JD stared at her as she swallowed his load before licking a pearl of cum off his tip. His knees were shaking, and she didn't even have to tell him to lie down. He looked at her with hunger in his eyes, and his cock lay against his belly, still as hard as before.

Ari stood over him, letting him see her full nudity in the silvery moonlight, then lowered herself to the ground, straddling him. She took his cock in her hand, rubbed his slick helmet against her clit, and slid it inside her pussy. It was her turn to gasp.

He filled her, and she accepted every inch.

Back and forth, she ground her pelvis slowly, as to not orgasm immediately.

JD sat up, pressing their chests together again. His tongue plunged into her mouth, and the taste of saliva and semen was shared. He pulled her hair, taking her mouth from his, exposing her neck.

Her nails dug into his back as he nipped at her.

He knew her all too well; it was one of her trigger points—an area of her body that drove her wild, especially during sex.

Faster, she fucked him, her hips becoming a blur.

Their combined wetness dripped onto the

blankets.

Her nipples rubbed against his chest hair as the wave of pleasure built and rose. Ari's body was electric, and she felt like she was glowing.

JD's lips went to her ear. "Come for me, babe, and I'll come with you."

Ari's pleasure was immeasurable. Her orgasm flowed from her scalp to her toes as her sex pulsed around JD's cock.

A silent scream masked her face, and only a squeak escaped as she shook.

Grunting, JD buried his face in her neck.

The spurt of his load inside her only made her orgasm intensify, and she continued to ride him.

Finally, the oversensitivity of her clit became too much, and she slowed her rhythm.

They looked at each other and kissed with love in their eyes.

Slowly, she rose, letting his spent cock slide from her, but she didn't stand. They stayed locked in embrace as their love further wet the blanket.

Together, they giggled and kissed again.

Neither of them was aware of the monstrosity watching from the shadows.

5

JD awoke with urgency. He was still nude and could feel the warmth of Ari's flesh against his.

Her back was pressed against his chest, and their combined body heat under the blanket chased away the coolness of the night.

The smell of hair mingled with the lingering

musk of sex.

His hand was cupped over her right breast, a common position for the rare times they slept together. He caressed her nipple, bringing a gentle moan from her sleeping lips. His cock was hard, not from arousal, but from the intense urge to pee.

Gently, and reluctantly, he released her breast and slid his arm from around her. His body ached from sleeping on the ground, and he knew both of them would be sore in the morning, but it was worth it.

After his nature call, he'd be sure to press his erection against her behind in an attempt to rouse her. Cumming for a third time that night might take some rough sex, but if she was up for it, so was he.

JD didn't bother putting on any clothes, even though the night was cool. He slid his shoes on so he didn't end up cutting his foot or stubbing a toe.

The moon provided enough light to move away from their little campsite.

Leaning against a tree, JD let his urine fly. It felt good not to have to aim, especially when pissing with a hard-on.

The night was still, and the only sound he heard was his pee hitting the ground. He shook out the last few drops and paused.

Something moved in the gloom.

A copse of pine trees was visible in the dark, but their thick boughs kept the moonlight at bay.

He squinted, trying to pierce the darkness.

Something moved again, crushing the debris underfoot.

JD figured it was a deer or some other wild

animal.

What emerged was not what he expected.

The girl from the house slowly stepped into the light.

Thinking she was a monster, JD nearly screamed, but quickly remembered the girl wore a hideous mask over her face. "Fuck," he said. His heart raced almost as fast as when he and Ari fucked. "You scared the shit out of me." He realized he was still nude and reached down to cover his erection.

She moved closer to him, but didn't speak.

JD felt his skin tighten. The blood rushed from his crotch, leaving him thankfully flaccid.

"Wh-what are you doing out here?" He didn't have a watch, but figured it was early morning. The sky in the east was dark, so it was still a few hours before sunrise.

As she walked closer, the clean scent of the woods eroded with each step. Something dark was coming from her, a smell that made him sick. It was the stink of death—of the slaughterhouse. Dark splotches covered her clothing, with drops decorating her mask.

JD's brain fired, and he realized what was on her: blood.

"Hunthing," she said.

It was difficult to see her face, but he could tell she was smiling.

Another, more animalistic, smell overwhelmed him, but it wasn't coming from the girl. It was coming from behind him.

He turned. The few remaining drops of urine left in his body spurted from his penis, wetting his fingers.

A monster stared at him, a beast that was half-man, half-pig.

For a moment, JD was certain it was an elaborate mask, but the smell and dried blood had him thinking otherwise. And the knife—a wicked, curved instrument of death clutched in one deformed hand—looked very real.

The edge of the blade glinted in the light as the monster shot forward.

JD thought he'd been punched, but when he looked down, the hilt of the blade stuck in his bare gut.

The beast contorted its swine face into a hellish smile and tugged, opening the teen's belly.

Pain flooded JD's senses, and the warmth of his blood ran down his crotch. A weight seemed to leave him as his severed entrails fell onto his feet.

JD opened his mouth to scream, but the beast only drove the blade deeper.

The edge of the knife scraped bone, leaving him in agony.

He was collapsing, falling to the ground, but stopped.

The monster released its grip on the knife and grabbed his neck. Its other arm—this one ending in the dirty hoof of a pig—plunged into the gory cavity of his stomach. It fished around in JD's oozing orifice, wetting its hoof.

With a slurp, the beast pulled its hoof out from JD and sniffed the bloody limb.

A thick tongue slithered over yellowed and cracked teeth, tasting the gore of the boy.

The light was fading from JD. He looked back toward the campsite, but was too far from Ari. Just one more glimpse was all he desired before the darkness overtook him.

The moon reflected off the stream snaking through the woods, leading to his love.

"Ari," he croaked from his constricted windpipe.

With a wash of fetid breath, the monster snarled, opening its maw.

Mangled teeth were all JD could see before the creature wrapped its jaws around his face.

6

Grandpa's mouth closed over the boy's face with a crunch.

Hattie smiled at the sound.

The corpse shuddered at the brutality of the bite.

With a few violent shakes of powerful teeth, the boy's face was removed. Bones, blood, and skin were mashed into a slurry as Hattie's grandfather fed.

Together, they fell to the ground in a heap of man and monster.

Walking over, Hattie stared at them through the mask.

Blood flew and entrails were consumed, bits thrown about.

She'd have to cover the mess before the night was over.

She tapped on the deformed back of her grandfather.

He snapped and turned his face up at her. His snout was black with gore, nearly the color of his swine eyes. He chewed with his mouth open, loud snorts coming as he tried to breathe through the meat clogging his throat.

"Geth him away from here," Hattie said. "They'll be loothing fo him." She didn't know what right she had giving orders to the monster, but he listened.

Reluctantly, he stopped feeding and stood. The beast dwarfed the girl. Globs of blood and drool ran from his fiendish mouth.

Hattie feared he might turn on her, making her soft flesh his next meal, but he didn't.

The monster that was her grandfather crouched and grabbed the mangled corpse with his human hand. With not so much as a grunt of exertion, he threw the meat sack over his shoulder.

What was left of the boy's face flopped on the broad back of the beast, dripping blood down the ridges of his muscled spine.

Hattie watched as her grandfather carried the corpse into the thick pines. Then, her attention snapped back toward the area the dead boy walked from. She'd been in those woods for most of her life and knew them well.

There was a clearing not far ahead. She had spent a lot of time throwing rocks into the stream from that spot.

It didn't take long for Hattie to find the sleeping girl.

The moonlight made her pale skin glow and reflected off her dark hair.

Hattie hated and loved her all at once. She wanted to be her, and desired to kill her. The way she moved, the way she looked, everything Hattie wasn't and never would be. Hattie knew what her life would be—at least what it *would've been*—if she hadn't released her grandfather: more abuse by men and, even worse, her mother.

The violation of her body by Wayne was the worst pain she'd ever felt, but it was even more evil because of the way it transpired.

She wasn't stupid and knew people had desires, but because her mother used her, the pain was even worse. And if something didn't change, her life would be a cycle of misery until she killed herself.

Life before the farm, even for a young girl, was misery, but things had changed. What she thought was the bottom had dug deeper. If her mother used her once, she wouldn't stop. The bills would pile up, and her body would be traded for work.

Wayne wasn't gentle, but he wasn't rough. She knew things could always be worse. Men came and went, but the offer of flesh was a consistent payment. And now that she was older, her mother felt Hattie's body was included in the price of doing business.

Hattie stood over her. She exhaled deeply, tasting her foul breath.

A pile of clothes was nearby. She picked through them, taking the dead boy's garments and throwing them into the moving stream.

With that done, Hattie returned to the girl's side. Slowly, she lowered herself to the blankets. Hattie pulled the blanket back, revealing the girl's nudity beneath. She ran her crusted fingers down the girl's spine, caressing her behind. Her fingers explored until they reached the girl's vagina. Gently, Hattie probed, entering the slick opening.

The girl stirred, but didn't wake.

Hattie pulled her fingers free and raised her mask.

Shadows darkened the deformation of her cleft palate.

She put her fingers to her crooked nose and sniffed. The odor was rich and musky, smelling of lust. She put them into her mouth, tasting the salty mingling of sex.

As Hattie licked her fingers clean, she fought the urge to taste the girl at the source. As much as she wanted to, she didn't. That would undoubtedly rouse the girl, and she couldn't have that, at least not yet.

She pulled the mask off and laid it down in the dirt, then wrestled her bloody clothes off, letting the night air caress her nudity.

She pressed her body against the back of the girl, wrapping an arm around her. Hattie took one of the sleeping girl's breasts in her hand and held it tight. She pressed her deformed face, bare of the mask, against the girl's scalp and inhaled.

Slowly, her free hand ventured south. Her fingers wove through her mess of pubic hair and found the hard bump of her clit. Gently, Hattie pleasured herself, and when she came for the second time that night, her crooked teeth bit into her lip so hard she drew blood.

With her carnal desire satiated once again, Hattie kneaded the girl's breast as she slept.

The night was quiet besides the sound of their combined breathing.

That, and the sound of wet chewing coming

from the thick pine trees.

CHAPTER 14

1

Davey couldn't sleep. He tossed and turned, finding himself wrapped in the damp sheets. The window was open, but the night was still. Even nude, he couldn't seem to cool off.

He looked over at his alarm clock. It was set to ring in an hour. Getting up for work was the bane of his existence, but if he wanted to keep his ass out of jail, he had to hold down a job.

The slaughterhouse was less than ideal, but it was work. Plus, he knew there was a very good chance he'd get his dick wet sooner than later.

Beulah wasn't the best-looking woman in the world, but she was still sexy, especially for her age. Much better than the barfly he couldn't seem to keep his dick out of. He was sure Beulah had been a knockout when she was young, but age caught her, like it did everyone. And, if what Wayne and Brett said was true, she liked to fuck, so that was a plus. If Davey could bust a nut and get some cash, he was winning.

It wasn't Beulah, or even the pigs, which made him uneasy. It was the girl, Hattie. Even with the mask on, he knew she wanted him. Her body was amazing, but he could only imagine what horrors lurked behind the mask.

They were a blessing and a curse, his looks and

charm. There were plenty of girls who lusted over him. Usually, it ended with him blowing a load in their mouth, hair, or pussy, and him doing his best disappearing act.

There was something about the girl he couldn't get over. Her speech led him to believe something was wrong with her mouth like a cleft palate or missing teeth.

The missing teeth he could deal with, but a cleft? He didn't even know if he could handle that. And she might not even be legal. Not to say Davey hadn't fooled around with ladies of a questionable age before, but fucking his boss's underage daughter in a backwoods town was a recipe for disaster; even he knew that. He'd lose his job and probably be arrested with a new charge, not just a probation violation.

Davey had to play this one straight, sticking to only fucking the mom.

His eyes drifted back to the clock. The urge to sleep had left him. If he tried to close his eyes, he knew nothing would happen until it got closer to the time he needed to leave. And then, without fail, he'd drift back to sleep and miss work.

"Fuck it." Davey kicked the sheets off and put his feet on the cold floor. He stood, stretched, and scratched his bare nuts. Even when he wasn't drunk, he mostly slept nude.

In the bathroom, he turned on the yellow light and the fan above him shrieked as it came to life. He stared at himself in the mirror as he waited for the shower to warm up.

The face of his father took over his own. *I don't know why you bother. You know you'll fuck this one up too. Just quit and continue being the loser we both know you are.*

Davey took a deep breath and focused on his face in the mirror, chasing away the ghost of his dad. His eyes locked on the hair on his face, pushing the image away, but not the voice. Never the voice.

The scruff on his face was getting thicker, but still no grays. He touched his overgrown neck, and since there was time before work, decided to edge up his beard.

If Beulah wanted to fuck him before, it would be a guarantee with a trimmed beard.

The tattoos on his body were a jumbled mess, but somehow, they worked for him. They were the result of many poor decisions, the story of his life. But each one was part of him. There was no rhyme or reason to them, blending styles and colors.

He opened the medicine cabinet, grabbed a razor, filled the sink with hot water, and shaved.

Giving himself a once over, he knew fucking Beulah was all but guaranteed. Then, he showered, dressed, and jumped in his truck all before the sun rose.

For once in his life, he'd be early to work.

2

Davey wasn't the only one who couldn't sleep.

On the farm, Beulah tossed and turned. The night air did little to cool her off.

She couldn't get the sounds she heard earlier out of her mind. The noises weren't the normal grunts and groans of the pigs; they sounded like fucking.

The sounds weren't what kept her from finding her slumber. It was an overwhelming feeling of unease. During her time in New York, that sense had tried its best to keep her out of trouble. But she rarely listened to it, and often found herself in less than desirable situations.

Her mind raced. Each day felt like death row, and at the end of every night, she got a pardon, delaying her death for one more day.

Beulah threw the sheet from her and stood, listening.

The house creaked and groaned like any old building did. Those noises she was used to. There was another noise she listened for: snoring.

Hattie, due to the deformities of her face, was a horrible snorer. It had been like that since the girl was born.

Beulah stood still and listened.

Nothing.

No snoring, only the sounds of the house.

Something was wrong.

Something had happened.

Hattie wasn't in the house.

As much as Beulah blamed the complexities of her life on Hattie, and viciously tried to abort her, she loved her daughter. She hoped Hattie knew that. She hoped Hattie understood it was her time in life to pick up the slack on the farm, and not just with work, but with the men. It was a fucking sin, but to survive on the farm, things had to be done.

The girl was strong, but Beulah didn't need her strength. She needed Hattie to use what was between her legs if they were going to stay afloat.

Barefoot, Beulah left her room.

The hallway was sweltering, but quiet.

Slowly, she approached Hattie's room.

Pressing her ear against the door, Beulah listened. Nothing.

She opened the door, feeling a blast of heat and the stench of stale clothing.

The moonlight shined through the window, illuminating Hattie's empty bed.

Fuck.

Beulah walked into the room, thinking the worst; maybe Hattie had fallen out of bed and hit her head.

The room was empty.

Stopping near the window, she looked around for any sign of the girl, and did a double take.

Wayne's truck was parked outside.

Motherfucker!

It was early in the morning, and for all of his qualities, being at work before the sun rose wasn't one of them.

Were the sounds she heard earlier Wayne and Hattie? She didn't think so, but anything was possible. Maybe their impromptu fuck session in the cabin hadn't been as bad as Beulah thought. Her daughter was developed, and she'd heard the telltale sounds of masturbating coming from her room before.

Wayne's cock was formidable, even for her, and she knew it must've been unbearable for her virgin daughter. But sometimes, with pain came pleasure. Maybe Hattie enjoyed it more than she let off and wanted another fuck.

No, there was no way unless Wayne was *taking* it

again. It wasn't beneath him to sneak over drunk and tell the girl he wasn't done. But there was no way they'd be able to fuck in the house without Beulah hearing.

Earlier had been a business transaction, a one-time deal to keep Wayne on the farm. But if that scumbag was back trying to collect what wasn't his? Now that was a fucking problem.

Beulah went back into her room and opened her closet. She pushed aside the clothing and grabbed a battered case.

The shotgun gleamed with an oiled death. The barrel was slick black, and the wooden pump action was worn by the many hands that had gripped it.

She hadn't used it in years, but the muscle memory came back to her as soon as she held it.

A box of shells was alongside the gun. She grabbed five of them, all buckshot, and loaded it.

The sound of the action slamming open and shut was loud, but she was the only one in the house.

With the gun over her shoulder, Beulah rushed downstairs. She passed by a door—one with many locks on it—and froze.

The locks are open!

Her blood ran cold. Suddenly, the house felt like a refrigerator, not a sauna.

She'd often walk down to the door at night, quietly opening it before throwing piles of garbage and fetid meat into the maw. But now, the locks were undone.

Panic set in when she touched the door. It was ajar.

Beulah's mouth was dry, and her armpits wet. She

pointed the big gun at the door, steadying it with one hand. Slowly, she opened the door fully, seeing nothing but darkness. Shaking, she reached into the gloom, searching for the light switch.

He's going to be there waiting. He'll grab me and yank me in. And then I'll pay for my sins. All of them. In the darkness, I'll have to face him again.

She found the nub of plastic. Her heart thumped, and she thought it would explode.

Beulah flicked on the light.

A dim bulb lit the stairs and erased some of the darkness at the bottom of the steps.

Nothing moved.

The smell of animal and unwashed human flesh rose from the chasm, but nothing else. There was no movement or sound besides her ragged breath.

He's out.

And then, it clicked.

Hattie found him and let him out.

She thought back to Wayne and the sounds she heard. It wasn't the sound of fucking she heard earlier, but chewing and ripping.

Her legs went weak. She leaned against the wall, cradling the shotgun in her arms. Slowly, she slid down the rough plaster until she reached the ground.

Shep Winslow, her father, the monster of a man, the man she'd made into a monster, was free.

Beulah's eyes drifted toward the front of the house, to the east, and noticed the sky turning pink on the horizon.

She nearly dropped the gun as the phone rang. Beulah's eyes snapped to the phone on the wall, with the old answering machine attached to it. She ignored the shrill sound of the bells until they stopped. The machine clicked on as a tired voice spoke.

"Beulah, it's Ralph. Sorry for calling so late, but I'm not going to be at work tomorrow. Well, I guess it's, technically, today. The missus fell down the stairs and broke her ankle. We're on our way to the hospital now, but I can't leave her alone. I know we have work to do, and I'll do my best to make it the following day." He hung up without another word.

Losing Ralph would set them back, but the farm was the least of her worries at that point.

Davey and the others would arrive soon, but at least she didn't have to worry about Ralph.

She did her best to calm herself, pushing the phone call from her mind, but couldn't. There was a bigger problem besides the lack of one worker. Another one of her choices was coming back to haunt her, and this one wasn't an old fling or drug addiction. It was a monster—one she created in that very house.

1999

CHAPTER 15

1

Summers on the farm were horrible, but winters were the worst. It was a time of harsh work and even worse conditions.

At least during the summer, Beulah could soak up the sun when she wasn't knee-deep in pig shit. The winter was a time of misery for her.

The piglets were getting older, losing the cuteness of their infancy. They were slowly introduced to the rest of the swine and, of course, there were accidents. Some pigs, even the females, would harass the little ones, sometimes killing them. Each dead piglet was money lost, and losing money wasn't something Shep tolerated on his farm.

Money made from the summer slaughter was dwindling, and other forms of income were needed to keep the farm afloat.

Shep was always resourceful; whether it was pimping his daughter or scamming people, he was a survivor. But now that Beulah was grown, and with a child of her own, his control over her waned.

He had to come up with something fresh and new in the years she was gone. He'd never been one for pomp and circumstance, even if he pushed it on his daughter. But, after nearly losing the farm a handful of times, he shifted gears.

Raising a few of his better-looking animals as

show pigs was lucrative. The money didn't come at the shows—though some of them paid—but the notoriety. His farm would receive sponsorship when he entered a sow into the show. The Winslow Farm would be out there to everyone, and the name would spread if he won. That bit of help kept the farm afloat throughout the years.

The small pen he constructed for the show pigs wasn't anything grand, more like a glorified shed with some fencing around it. It resembled a dog kennel modified for pigs.

The cold air bit Shep's face as he unlatched the door.

He'd grown used to the smell of the animals over the years. The acrid stench of piss, shit, and dirty animal didn't even phase him. To him, it was the smell of his livelihood.

Peaches lay in a pile of hay. She twitched, rising from her slumber when the door opened. Beady, black eyes were set deep in pink flesh. She looked at Shep and struggled to rise. Hay gave her little traction on the wooden floor as she skittered to her hoofs. It was feeding time, and she knew it.

"There's my girl," Shep said.

He unshouldered a bag of grain, which was slightly better quality than what he fed the meat animals. Laying the bag in her trough, he slit it open with his knife; the same motion he used thousands of times to open throats.

A mix of corn and barley poured out as he watched the trough fill. When there was enough, but not too much, he put the bag on the floor and tied it with a piece of wire.

Peaches waddled over, excited to feast.

Shep took a gallon-sized plastic bag from his coat pocket. He upended the bag's contents—leftovers from dinner—into the grain.

The big sow fed as he stroked her head.

Normally, he'd show no affection to the pigs. It was never something he did. First of all, they weren't pets; they were products. There was no room for affection, and he hadn't seen the pigs as pets until he started raising them for show. Even then, once they lost their value and stopped winning, or a better one took their place, they went to the slaughter.

Peaches was different. Something about her separated her from the other pigs in the past. She had a self-awareness about her he hadn't seen in other animals.

She lifted her dirty snout and nuzzled his hand.

Rubbing the wet, grainy snout of the beast, he smiled. He would never be confused for a man with a heart, but even he didn't know if Peaches would ever go to slaughter.

"Good girl." Shep took his hand from her snout and placed it on her head between her ears.

The pig snorted in happiness and put her face back into the food.

The door creaked behind him and Shep turned.

Beulah and Hattie stood in the doorway.

"Sorry we're a little late," Beulah said.

When she returned to the farm, she had little in the way of work clothes. Even five years later, her clothes were still hand-me-downs from him and some old clothes she could squeeze into.

Hattie, in her early teens, stood close to her

mother. Her clothes were even more awkward. The jacket was patched and three sizes too big. Her boots were a pair of Beulah's from her youth, and seemed to fit better than her jacket. But it wasn't her clothes that caused Shep to scowl; it was the mask.

Halloween had come and gone, and even in their small town, trick-or-treating was popular. After one of the farm shows, the sponsor gave away novelty pig masks. Shep thought they were silly, but his granddaughter gravitated to the cheap plastic. She lived in it until the holiday. But after the pumpkins had been smashed, and candy eaten, the girl hadn't taken it off. She was rarely seen without it.

Shep walked over to his granddaughter, a child he didn't think he'd have any connection with until the day he met her. He crouched down, wincing as his knees popped. "Hattie, why are you still wearing that silly mask?" He touched it with calloused fingers, sliding it up, exposing her deformed face. "You're a beautiful girl, and grandpa loves to see you." He rubbed her cheek with his smelly hand.

Hattie's mangled mouth split into a wet grin. "Tank ooo," she mumbled.

His hand slid down her cheek and onto her shoulder. He pulled her in and kissed her on the corner of the mouth. "You're developing into a fine young lady." His eyes slowly drifted down her body. "But, if the mask makes you feel better," he stood to another volley of cracking joints, "then who am I to say anything?"

Beulah pulled her daughter closer and looked at her father. "She likes it. She says it makes her feel safe, especially around the workers."

"Bah, they're harmless. You've known most of them since you were a girl." Shep waved at her with both hands, dismissing the statement.

"Exactly," Beulah snapped. Her eyes met Shep's in a quick stare down, which she lost. "Anyway, what needs to get done this morning?"

"The same as every day. Feed 'em and clean 'em. Let me know if there are any holes in the pens or any major injuries. That should take up the better part of the morning. A few guys are coming by for a half day to help install the new chute."

Beulah nodded. "Come on, Hattie. If we get done quickly, I'll let you bottle-feed some piglets."

Hattie clapped her hands. "Yay, they're tho cuth."

Mother and daughter turned and walked away.

Hattie's jacket may have been too big, but Shep noticed her jeans fit her *just* right.

The door slammed behind them, and he went back to tending to his prized pig.

2

Five years ago, Beulah made the difficult decision to return to the Winslow Farm. This time, she wasn't alone. She dragged her young daughter along for the ride, and now, she was trapped.

Stuck in a meaningless existence, with nowhere to turn, Beulah abandoned life on her own and went home. Once again, she fell for the lies fed to her by a man. But this wasn't just some guy looking to get his dick wet. No, this was her father, the man who was supposed to be her protector and guardian.

The messages he left for her over the years had grown increasingly desperate. And like a fucking sucker, Beulah fell for it.

Like every lie she'd ever been fed, she ate it up. Out of desperation and trust, she went home.

Things started great, as every relationship does. Her father had been thrilled to see her, and seemingly fell in love with his granddaughter.

The two of them were inseparable. Oftentimes, Shep went out of his way for the young girl.

Beulah couldn't help but feel a twinge of jealousy, but knew it was his way of making up for the years of shitty parenting. She'd never tell her daughter that, but her father knew; it was like a code amongst shitty parents.

The first year they were there, the slaughter was one of the best. With two extra hands working for free, Shep saw his biggest profit yet. Not nearly enough to pay his debt, but more than enough to allow him to gamble it away and not worry.

The first card game he had after Beulah's return made her sick. She thought back to those games when she was younger, and the nasty comments and horrid things she'd done to *'help'* her father.

Even when Shep tried to get her to come down and say hi to everyone, Beulah forcefully declined. It was easier to do since she had Hattie to take care of. The excuses weren't far-fetched, and she thought they worked, until she walked into the kitchen after thinking the game ended.

Shep and a new guy, Max, drank beers at the table. Everyone else had gone, and the two of them were fucked up.

She didn't know how they kept quiet as long as they did, but they did.

Beulah, only dressed in shorts and a t-shirt, covered her braless breasts when she realized the two men were there.

"There she is," her father slurred. His eyes were glassy and droopy. "This here is Max." He patted the young man on the shoulder.

Max was younger than her father, probably close to her age. But he had the eyes of an old man.

She didn't know how to describe it, but they looked *off*.

He wasn't fat or thin, just average. And if it wasn't for the lack of emotion and strange eyes, he could've passed for attractive in their small town.

"Max is somewhat new in town, and a hell of a card player."

Turn around and run. This isn't going to end well for you. RUN!

She looked up at the ceiling, which was below Hattie's room.

"This kid is so damn good, Beulah, but I thought I had him." Shep shook his head. "Fucker baited me." He laughed and slapped Max on the shoulder like it was a big joke.

"D-did you lose the money from the slaughter?" *Here it goes again. Drunk and stupid, he lost it all. And with the winter looming, things will be tough, once again.*

"Ah, some of it. But I knew I had something more valuable in my pocket."

Max smiled at her, but the lupine grin never reached his eyes. He held up the condom pinched

253

between his middle and forefinger.

Rage bubbled up from Beulah's gut. The twin smiles on her father's and Max's faces made her seethe. Nothing had changed, and she felt like a fucking fool for thinking so.

"Fuck you," she spat, then looked at her father. "And fuck you too. I'm not a fucking kid anymore that will do what you demand. Pay your fucking bills."

Her eyes stung with tears. She couldn't believe she fell for his shit again.

Shep would never change; he was a user—a man who took what he wanted and cared little about who he hurt. Even if the person he hurt was his only living blood relative.

"Whelp, I guess that's that," Max said. "Pay up, old man."

She slowed. Of course, her father had lost money, but how much? How much was she worth to him? A few hundred? Or had he fucked up and bet more? Her father was an asshole, but could he have bet away the profits made from the slaughter? She stood at the base of the steps, but didn't look back at them.

"Fuck," Shep said.

Beulah wasn't looking at him, but from the sound of his voice, he was facing her direction.

"Can I give you half now and half in a month or so?"

"Nah, no can do, old timer. A bet is a bet. You shouldn't have had such rich blood in you if you didn't have the cash in your pocket."

Fuck you, Dad. Fuck you for everything.

Beulah knew she could walk away and head back to bed. The sun would rise in a few hours, and work would continue. But for how long? If her father blew their money, things wouldn't take long to unravel.

The finances didn't get to her as much when she was a girl. Her father shielded her from things like that, using her to pay his shitty debts with her body. It made her feel worthless, but thinking back, she realized he would've lost the farm long ago if she hadn't done those things.

What bothered her was that he'd been able to keep the farm afloat while she was gone, meaning he could control himself when needed. But if she were around, he was loose with his money, counting on the horny men he played with. Knowing he had an attractive daughter who'd do what was necessary to save the farm was his ace in the hole.

Beulah felt like she was on autopilot. "How much?" She turned and looked back at them.

As she'd suspected, her father was looking right at her. That shitty grin never left his face.

"All of it. Every red cent made from the pigs would be wiped out." He opened both hands like he was giving mass. "The farm would be finished."

She didn't know if she believed him or not.

It wasn't beneath him to gamble it all away, especially if he thought Beulah would bail him out.

Her mind raced. That life, the one he was trying to pull her back into, was behind her—a mark on her life she'd never erase, and had forged her.

She wanted to get dressed and leave, but wasn't alone anymore. Even from the base of the stairs, she could hear the gentle snores coming from Hattie's room.

Beulah sighed and stomped back into the kitchen. "Fuck you," she said to her father. "Fuck the both of you."

Her eyes drifted to Max, who still had the condom in his hand. She stared at the hard eyes of the man who'd won the bet. "This will wipe out his debt?"

Max ran his pointer finger over his heart. "Cross my heart and hope to die."

I wish you would. I wish you'd drop dead right now, you sick fuck.

"Get out," she said to her father.

Shep was slow to move, and for a second, he remained still. His eyes wandered to her chest.

Beulah felt dirty as he gazed at her nipples. She wanted to cover herself again, but wouldn't give him the satisfaction of knowing it bothered her.

Finally, Shep pushed his chair back; the wood groaned on the floor.

"I was calling it a night, anyway." He downed his drink and took his cigarettes from the table. He sparked one up before heading upstairs.

Max stood as well. He was rubbing his cock through his jeans. "Wanna go somewhere more private?"

"Fuck you," she spat. "No, you're gonna put that thing on," she pointed at the condom in his hand, "and bust your pathetic nut as fast as humanly possible. Then, you're going to leave and never come back." The tears stung, but she wasn't sad. She was pissed.

"Awe, come on, darlin'. It doesn't have to be that way." He reached out to grab one of her breasts.

Beulah swatted his hand away. "Don't fucking touch me."

The smile on Max's face melted away. Rage overtook him, and the tendons in his hand creaked as he made a fist.

His hand shot forward quicker than anything Beulah had experienced. It was more like the strike of a serpent rather than a man. He didn't punch her, but grabbed her hair, pulling her face close to his.

His breath was a vile mixture of beer, cigarettes, and unbrushed teeth. "Don't you ever put your fucking hands on me again."

She shrieked, but kept her voice as low as possible. She stared at him, locking her eyes to his. She'd dealt with worse men before. "You have five minutes."

Max let go of her hair and pushed her.

Her hip hit the counter, but her hands slowed her enough to not cause any damage. She had her back to Max, which was the only way she could think about fucking him. She looked over her shoulder as he unbuckled his pants.

With the condom in his teeth, Max dropped his pants and underwear to his knees. His flaccid cock peeked out of a tangled nest of pubic hair.

Even soft, she knew he was small. Much smaller than average. Now it made sense why he was such an angry prick. An involuntary laugh escaped her mouth.

Max, who was playing with himself in an effort to get hard, looked up at her. Rage boiled in his eyes.

"Max? You should change your name to Minimum," she joked.

"Fuh yoo," he said with the condom in his mouth giving him a lisp. Max pulled at his cock, but it wouldn't respond. It almost seemed to shrink away from his aggressive tugs.

"Clock's ticking, Min," she said. Beulah turned and pressed her back against the counter. She couldn't help but watch as this once-tough guy panicked while he did his best to will his dick into any semblance of an erection.

Max looked down, the condom still in his mouth. He pulled and slapped his cock around, but no blood would flow. It was all trapped in his red face.

Even though it was funny to her, Beulah knew a sexually frustrated man, especially an embarrassed one, was dangerous. She eyed the butcher block and slid down the counter toward it.

"Come over here and suck it," Max said after spitting out the condom.

Beulah shook her head. "Sorry, I don't like baby mushrooms."

That was it.

That was his breaking point.

Even with his pants around his ankles, Max was fast. He lunged across the kitchen and grabbed her neck. His first punch hit her in the gut, doubling her over. The punch was made even worse because she was just starting to laugh at him again.

Max threw an uppercut, catching Beulah in the eye, and forced her up again. His grip around her neck was tight, like a band of iron.

Their eyes were locked, and they were nose to nose.

Beulah reached out to grab a knife. She plucked a small blade from the block and pressed the tip against the root of his soft member.

His grip loosened immediately.

"I'll jam this fucker so deep into you, you'll never have to worry about fucking again." Her voice was wheezy, but strong.

Max let her go and backed away, but Beulah held the knife. Defeated, he pulled his pants up. "I don't want to fuck a nasty skank like you anyway." He hocked back and spat.

His thick glob of spit hit Beulah's stomach, but she didn't flinch. Her grip on the knife was unwavering.

Storming out, Max slammed the door behind him.

Beulah followed, throwing the lock as she watched the taillights glow red on his truck.

A rooster tail of dirt battered the house as he sped away.

The knife fell from her hand, narrowly missing her bare feet.

Her eye throbbed, and her stomach ached, and her legs couldn't hold her anymore. She slowly fell to the floor and wept.

3

Word must've traveled quickly, because that was the last time her father gambled with her body. He knew she was no longer a bargaining chip and had to play to his limits.

Shep never said anything, but Beulah knew he resented her for that, and she was happy he did. She wasn't his, no matter what backwoods shit he believed.

The pig pens were cold, but warmer than it was outside. The combined body heat of the animals kept them alive. That, and the layers of fat they naturally possessed.

Beulah shoveled shit into wheelbarrows. Once full, she pushed them outside and dumped them into piles. She didn't think pig shit was the best fertilizer, but her father found someone to buy the waste.

Hattie sat on the ground in a separate area. She grunted with delight as the piglets swarmed her. The girl did her best to feed each of them, but the rambunctious babies fought for every drop of milk. Still, she ensured they all ate.

They worked for hours feeding and cleaning the animals, until it was finally time for lunch.

4

Shep sat at the kitchen table smoking a cigarette. He'd finished prepping Peaches for the upcoming season of shows. With any luck, he would win a few and get some cash.

Money wasn't always easy to come by on the farm. He made a little to help keep him afloat selling the pig shit, but more likely than not, he'd gamble it away.

There was a poker game scheduled that night.

Alan Sinkmore was supposed to pick up his load

of pig shit in a few hours, giving Shep a couple of bucks to play with, but it wouldn't be enough. And after his crazy daughter almost took out Max's manhood with a paring knife, he knew she was out of the picture.

Smoke rose past his face as the door opened.

Hattie and Beulah kicked off their boots, leaving them on an old piece of carpet by the back door.

"I'm going upstairs to wash up and use the bathroom. Wash your hands and get the cold cuts out," Beulah said as they entered the kitchen.

Beulah disappeared up the stairs.

Shep listened to her footsteps as she entered the upstairs bathroom.

Hattie stood at the sink. She'd taken her mask off and set it on the counter.

He stared at her—*really* stared at her. Even though she was barely a teenager, Shep couldn't keep his eyes off her.

She was built like her mother. Her jeans were tight, but there was no money to get her new ones. At least, not money he'd spend on them.

Over the past few months, puberty struck her like a ton of bricks. She shot up a few inches, and a few cup sizes. Like her mother, Hattie's breasts developed early, leaving her with a woman's body when she was still interested in playing with dolls.

After drying her hands on a towel and wiping her face, Hattie put her mask back on.

"Come over here, Miss Hattie." Shep adjusted in the chair, offering his knee to her. He patted his thigh, ensuring the girl knew exactly where to put her behind.

Hattie walked over and sat.

Shep adjusted her, pulling her butt closer to his hardening crotch.

If the girl felt anything, she didn't say a word.

"Say, how would you like to hang out with grandpa and his friends tonight?" Shep wrapped one arm around her shoulder, his fingers dangerously close to one of her breasts.

Hattie looked at him. Her breath was muffled from behind the mask. She looked at him and nodded. "At ood be fun."

"Good girl. It'll be lots of fun. You'll get to meet my friends, and you can even be my good luck charm. But there is one thing I need from you, and it's very important, okay?"

Hattie nodded.

Even behind the mask, he knew the girl was smiling.

She wiggled her hips, trying to face him better.

Shep grunted at the tightness of her young body against his manhood. "You can't tell mommy. It has to be our secret. So, I'm giving you permission to stay up late tonight. When your clock says eleven, you can come down. But be super quiet. Just like a spy."

"Wath's a sthpy?"

At the sound of Beulah marching across the upstairs floor, he pushed Hattie from his lap and stood.

Shamelessly, he adjusted his erection, tucking it into his waistband. "That's someone who keeps secrets." He put his index finger to his pursed lips and smiled.

Hattie returned the gesture, touching her finger to the plastic snout of the pig mask, and giggled. She pulled the fridge open and removed the cold cuts.

Beulah looked at her daughter, who did her best not to make eye contact.

Shep looked back and forth at the two of them. He wanted to tell the little freak to act normal, but couldn't.

"What's so funny?" Beulah asked. There was humor in her voice, thinly veiled with suspicion.

"Nuffin," Hattie said, grabbing a bottle of barbeque sauce from the fridge.

"Barbeque sauce?" Shep asked. "Put that away. Barbeque sauce is disgusting." He looked at his daughter, hoping to change the topic. "Oh, Alan Sinkmore is coming by later for his load of shit."

"Language, please," Beulah said. She pulled three plates from the cabinet.

He waved her off. "The girl works on a farm. And I'm sure she's heard worse from you over the years."

Shep didn't want to argue with his daughter, but he'd take it if it got her attention off Hattie.

He couldn't help but sneak glances at his granddaughter as she made a sandwich.

After all those years, he finally had a new bargaining chip.

5

Beulah was uneasy. She didn't know if it was the microwave dinner they'd eaten or something else, but she couldn't sleep. Her body was tired from the day's work, but she had things to do.

She sat at her little desk with a stack of paper in front of her, looking over her financial aid application one final time before placing it into the envelope.

Even though she was back on the farm, she hadn't lost hope of one day getting out for good. She had almost no discernible skills for the real world, but her love of animals and anatomy had grown.

Before returning home, she purchased a stack of second-hand textbooks on veterinary science. It took her a while to understand some of the complexities of animals, but after years of self-teaching, she felt ready.

Her plan was simple, but as she often found, the easier, the better. Going away to college wasn't something she ever thought possible, especially with Hattie. But there was another option: remote schooling.

Beulah researched the program and found she could take her classes from home. The teacher would mail her a week's worth of work, which she'd do at night and send back. After years of studying already, Beulah knew she'd advance quickly in the program, hoping her grades would allow her to skip ahead.

Once she received a tech certification, she could find a *real* job and get Hattie away from her father. She'd need much more schooling before earning a degree to work as an actual veterinarian, but she figured with a tech license, she could get a job and freelance at some of the local farms.

The plan was far from perfect, and hinged on her getting money from the state to attend. Without financial aid, she'd be sunk. Even though the course wasn't expensive, she had almost nothing to her name. Her father controlled the finances, telling her the money made was rolled back into the farm.

She knew that was bullshit. The extra money went into beer, cigarettes, and gambling. But there was nothing she could do. A few times, she considered turning tricks again to make a few bucks. It wasn't as if the people in town didn't know her and what happened in that house. But Beulah was determined to leave that life behind. Those were past mistakes, and what she'd done in the house were propositions made by her father, not her.

It was either the right way, or not at all.

Beulah placed a stamp—one she'd stolen from her father's desk the day before—on the letter and set it down.

A textbook lay open on her desk and her eyes drifted toward it.

She wanted to get some sleep, but was in the middle of a fascinating chapter about feline circulatory systems.

The radio was on low, the sound of music providing background noise.

Her father was having one of his many card games downstairs. It was quieter than normal, which was a blessing. He'd woken her and Hattie up many times before, and when they could hardly work in the morning, he agreed to keep it down. It wasn't so they could sleep peacefully, but so he could work them while he slept off a hangover.

She tapped a pencil against the book as she read. Another noise caused her to pause, leaving the pencil in the air.

Hattie's door opened.

It wasn't uncommon for the girl to use the bathroom in the middle of the night, but what *was* unusual was she didn't slam her door. As often as Beulah told her to leave her door open when going to the bathroom, the teen would often throw the door closed; but not that time.

Beulah turned the radio off and listened.

Soft footsteps padded across the hall.

Maybe she finally listened, Beulah thought.

There was no sound of the bathroom door closing either—another door she tended to slam, especially in the middle of the night.

She strained her ears, trying to pick up any sound of her daughter returning to her room.

Maybe she needed to poop. I'll give her privacy, at least for a few minutes, before checking on her.

Beulah went back to studying, but was having difficulty focusing on her work. She knew what was happening downstairs, and could never let Hattie be a part of it.

She began tapping the pencil again, never hearing the creaking sound of her daughter going down the steps.

6

Hattie was cold. Her bare feet felt like blocks of ice on the ground. Even her chest was cold, making her nipples hard.

The bras she had hurt her, and she hated wearing them. It was so freeing to take it off at night.

The smell of smoke found its way into her nose through her mask. Downstairs smelled bad—like armpits, beer, and cigarettes—but grandpa told her it would be a good time. She guessed everyone had different versions of fun.

Hattie rounded the corner of the steps and saw the game.

A bunch of men, some she recognized from deliveries and pickups on the farm, sat around the kitchen table. Smoke hung in the air, making them look weird.

Her grandfather laughed and chugged from a beer can. He looked strange. Something was different about him, something scary, but she couldn't put her finger on it.

And then, he saw her.

"There she is," her grandfather yelled. "There's my sweet Hattie girl."

Her heart was racing, but there was no turning back.

"Come over here," Grandpa said. He turned in his chair and positioned his knee like earlier in the day.

When she was little, Hattie liked sitting with Grandpa. He'd bounce her on his knee, and she'd giggle and laugh. But recently, she started not to like it as much. She didn't know why, but something felt weird about it.

He didn't bounce her as much. After sitting on his knee for a little while, he'd pull her back into his lap.

She didn't know if she was getting too heavy, but he'd only wiggle his hips, not bounce.

The men all looked at her as she walked toward them.

Her mask covered her face, and she was glad for that, because she was blushing.

Their eyes looked weird and glassy, like stuffed animals. And they were all on her chest.

Self-conscious, Hattie crossed her arms, covering herself. She sat on her grandfather's knee, doing her best to stay on the bony edge, even if it was uncomfortable.

He put his hands around her waist and pulled her back. It wasn't gentle, like normal, but rough, making her yelp.

She wasn't wearing thick jeans, only pajamas. He had something hard in his pants, poking her in the butt.

"There, that's much better," he said. His breath smelled worse than usual.

"So, Shep, I see you have more to bet now," one of the men said.

Hattie turned and looked at him.

His eyes were glued to her.

She didn't know how to play cards, but her grandfather had fewer colorful chips in front of him than the other players.

A calloused hand rubbed her thigh.

"Yeah, I think I do. I know you boys love a good gamble, and I could sure as shit use the extra money."

The man laughed. "You sure breed 'em well. Thick, just how I like 'em."

She didn't know what they were talking about, but felt uneasy. Hattie's body was cold in some parts and sweaty in others. She wished she was back in bed, snuggled up and warm.

Her grandpa wiggled under her again, and she felt something wet on her butt.

"I'm sure we can arrange something if the bet is big enough," Grandpa said.

"This one's a little more damaged than the last one, so maybe not as big." The man was playing with a stack of his chips. "But I'm sure we could work something out."

"What the fuck is going on?" Mommy yelled from the base of the steps.

Hattie's eyes, misty with tears, snapped toward her. She didn't know why she was crying. Nothing had happened. Grandpa loved her and was just playing a game, but it felt wrong. And she felt dirty like after rolling around with the piglets.

"Get your fucking hands off her." Beulah stormed across the room and yanked Hattie from her father's lap.

It hurt, but Hattie was thankful.

"Go upstairs," Beulah told her daughter.

"Buth the game, I wanth oo pway."

"Hattie, go!"

Her mother didn't yell much anymore, so Hattie recoiled in shock. She walked away, but didn't go upstairs. Standing just around the corner, Hattie waited and listened.

"If you ever touch her, any of you, I'll fucking kill you. I'll burn your fucking houses to the ground, but not before telling your family what pieces of shit you are."

Hattie had never heard her mother so angry and was scared she would get yelled at next.

"Calm down," her grandfather said. "We were just letting her watch."

"Yeah, right. Just like you *let me watch* when I was nearly her age. Touch her again and I'll kill you."

"Whoa, someone is on their period," one of the men said.

"Fuck you."

Hattie rushed up the stairs when she heard her mother storming toward her.

7

Beulah listened to Hattie's door close. She was shaking with rage and took a few breaths before continuing. She hated herself; she hated the fact she was forced back into the hell hole of her childhood with the devil himself. And it wasn't out of bad luck or misfortune, but her own doing. If it weren't for her decisions, she and Hattie could have a better life. It wouldn't have been luxurious, but work at the diner was steady and going well.

As Hattie aged, Beulah knew college could've become a real thing, not just a dream. But her greed and lust drove that reality away, like it had done before.

She stood at the landing and looked down the hallway. Her bedroom door was the only one open.

Her eyes drifted to her father's room.

It was where the monster slept, where he resided and thought of the evil he perpetrated on others.

She didn't know how much more she could take.

Hattie was still a little girl when they first arrived

home. But now, she was growing, and growing fast. Just like her mother, Hattie's body developed early. She would soon learn the horrors of the world, and the thoughts of men. Unfortunately, the only man in her life who should be their protector was the worst.

Beulah's mind raced. She didn't know what to do, but she knew something had to change. She had to protect her daughter. And she prayed she would never be like her father.

That was what bothered her the most; that one day, she would be him. She hated herself for thinking that way, but knew it was true. In her past life, she'd used people to get what she wanted. Whether it was with her body, or her brain, she manipulated and blackmailed men and women, bending them to her will.

But could she ever do something like that to her daughter?

Her mind flashed back to the early years and the dog crate. Beulah could've found the money for a sitter, but chose not to. She decided to save the money, locking her infant in a disgusting cage while she fucked and got high.

Without realizing she'd been walking, Beulah arrived outside her father's room.

The doorknob was warm, like it was alive, even though the house was cold.

She turned the knob and flinched as the door squealed in the darkness.

The room breathed his noxious scent into her face.

Even as a girl, she wasn't in his room often, which was a blessing. It felt like walking into a lion's den.

Turning on the light, she moved with a purpose.

When she was a girl, a few pigs got into a nasty fight. One of the animals was attacked by a few others, leaving it bloody and broken.

Rather than spending the money on a vet, or trying to scavenge the meat, her father had another idea. He sent Beulah to the very room she was standing in to grab his shotgun.

The gun was heavy and terrifying in her little arms, but she lugged it down the steps and gave it to her father. She didn't ask questions, but it must've been on her face.

Her father threw his cigarette in the mud and chambered a shell. "Why would I use a big, loud gun when I can simply slit her throat?" He separated the injured sow, but kept her close to the others. "Well, this will set an example. Pigs are smart creatures, but you already know that. Weakness, even against overwhelming odds, is not tolerated."

Without warning, he turned, pointed the big gun at the wounded animal, and fired.

The blast caught her off guard, releasing a fearful squirt of urine into her pants.

Beulah never forgot that day. She never forgot the sound of the other pigs squealing in fear, or the frantic death throes of the mangled pig as it dug furrows in the earth while its nerves slowly died.

The big gun scared her as a girl, but now it called to her.

She opened his closet and pulled the string to turn on the light. The bulb was dead, but she didn't need it.

Reaching into the gloom, her hand touched cold steel and wood. She pulled the shotgun out of the dark and into the light. A shock of fear rushed through her, not from the unknown of what her father would use the gun for, but fear of what she would do.

Beulah hid the gun in her room and steadied her nerves. Then, gently, she knocked on Hattie's door.

8

Beulah was seething. She finally got Hattie to sleep, but explaining why she couldn't hang out with her grandfather was interesting.

"Listen, baby. Grandpa isn't a good man. I know you love him, but don't think for a second that he loves you or me."

Hattie looked at her with the forlorn gaze of youth.

It killed Beulah to know how much her daughter loved Shep Winslow.

He was not a good man, and that didn't just include his family. He cheated buyers, his workers, and the other women who came and went in his miserable life. But worst of all, he was a user. If you could give him something, he'd take it. Your life and feelings meant little to nothing to him. His only concern was himself.

With Hattie being as sheltered as she was, that was hard to explain.

Hattie didn't argue, and that was for the best.

Beulah figured the girl heard more than she should have when she yelled at the men, which was fine by her. She wanted her daughter to know how upset she was with them.

She left her door open, something she never did. Even as an adult, she didn't like seeing the black pit of the hallway staring at her.

Knowing sleep wouldn't come until the sun pinkened the sky, she put her time to good use rather than let herself stew on her father's shortcomings.

A litany of used books were spread on her bed. She read them, focusing as hard as she could on the text. Lost in her studies, Beulah finally pushed the thoughts of her father from her mind.

She jumped at the sound of car doors slamming. Beulah slid from her bed and walked over to her window.

The card game was finally over.

Sweat broke out over her body, fighting the coolness of her room.

Shep stood outside as the taillights from the other men disappeared into the night. He lit up a smoke and zippered his jacket. The old man rocked on his heels as the smoke created a cloud above his head.

Taking a final drag, he tossed the butt onto the frozen ground. Instead of walking back into the house, he started toward Peaches's enclosure.

"What the fuck?" Beulah muttered.

He disappeared into the small building, then emerged soon after with the show pig in tow. He'd wrapped a length of rope around her neck as he led her toward the slaughterhouse.

Beulah didn't know how the night would end, but she knew how it started. She grabbed the shotgun, ensured it was loaded, and left her room.

9

The breeding chute was narrow by design. It wasn't just for insemination, but was also helpful with holding the pigs still for vet check-ups or inspections.

"Atta girl," Shep said as he led Peaches into the chute. He placed a pile of food on the ground by her head, keeping her occupied while he secured her.

Shit and filth were caked on the pig's ass.

As hard as he tried to keep her pen clean, she was still an animal.

And so was he.

Shep wiped away the globs of shit from the animal's rear, letting his finger caress the puffy opening of the pig's vagina.

Peaches ate, content with her position, but Shep knew her attitude would change soon.

He double-checked the restraints, ensuring they were tight. The last thing he needed was a hoof in the balls. "Oh, Peaches, you're the only steady thing in my life."

Shep unbuckled his pants, letting them fall to the ground. He took a plastic bag filled with old bacon grease from his shirt pocket and opened it.

The rancid fat stunk, but the odor helped turn him on. It was the scent of the only fucking he'd done in years. And, if he was honest with himself, some of the best pussy he'd ever had.

With a palm slathered in grease, Shep rubbed Peaches's vagina. He slipped two fingers into the animal, eliciting a squeal from the beast.

"Now, hush. You know the drill for our dates.

Eat your food and keep quiet." Shep felt his old cock swelling with arousal. He took the remnants of the congealed fat and stroked himself, working up a full-blown erection, or at least what passed as an erection at his age.

Shep ambled closer, using one hand to control the pig's behind and the other to guide his greasy pecker.

Peaches's squeal tore through the night.

10

It sounded like he was killing the pig.

Beulah stood outside the slaughterhouse with the gun in her hand.

From inside, Peaches howled something fierce. She wasn't being killed; she was being tortured.

Beulah's thoughts raced as to what could be occurring behind the doors. Something vile and sick permeated her mind, but the thought was unspeakable. Surely even her father wouldn't stoop that low, would he?

She pushed the door open using the barrel of the shotgun.

Her father stood with his back to the door. His bare ass was bright white in the dim lighting of the slaughterhouse. He thrust forward, each time eliciting another squeal from Peaches.

Beulah wanted to rack the action on the shotgun for effect, but doing so would eject the live shell she already inserted. "I knew you were a sick fuck for the things you let your friends do to me, but this is downright vile."

Her mind flashed back to the porno she made years ago that opened with her drinking a shot of pig cum. Somehow, she justified that, but vilified what he was doing.

Shep turned, his greasy penis in hand.

Peaches settled down and began sniffing at the ground. With the violation of her body over, she returned to searching for food.

Beulah couldn't help but look at her father's penis. It was still hard, but beginning to deflate. A disgusting sheen covered it.

He bent down and pulled his pants up. The look of anger and shame shone bright red on his ruddy cheeks. "What the fuck are you doing out here?" He buckled his pants. For a moment, he stared at her, not realizing she carried his big gun. "And what the fuck are you doing with my shotgun? Come to kill Peaches? Are you jealous my cock is in her and not you? I know all about the so-called life you had before coming back here. I've even seen some of the movies."

She felt her gorge rise. Beulah was sickened by the fact he'd seen her nude and violated. But what bothered her more was that he insinuated watching more than one.

Beulah stepped forward and put the shotgun to her shoulder like he taught her. Something snapped inside of her, something that frayed years ago.

When she saw Hattie with him and his friends, she knew what her only option was. It was the pig tonight, but how long would it take for it to be Hattie? The image of his saggy ass thrusting as he fucked the girl drove her mad.

During the walk down to the slaughterhouse, Beulah had a cinematic speech planned about how he fucked her life up and destroyed everything beautiful she could've been, and how she wouldn't let him do the same thing to Hattie. That all went out the window as she stared at his face through the crude bead sight of the shotgun.

The safety clicked off with an audible *snick* sound.

"Wai—" Shep yelled with his hands out.

The gun roared. Flame licked the muzzle like a hungry dog as the buckshot spat into Shep's face. The plastic wadding kept the pellets close together, and from that range, they all hit their mark.

Shep's face, from the top of his upper lip and above, disappeared instantly.

Wet gore mixed with bone and brain hit Peaches like macabre confetti.

The pig thrashed in fear, doing her best to escape the pen. Her pink skin was speckled with bits of the monster who just finished assaulting her.

As her ears rang from the blast, Beulah didn't even hear the wet slap of her father's body hitting the ground.

Peaches continued to thrash.

Beulah didn't hate the animal, but what it represented. It was love. Even if it was a perverse love, it was a love her father shared with the pig, and never her. The fracture in her psyche grew, becoming a chasm.

Blood pumped from the jellied stump of Shep's head.

"Where's your love now? Huh? Where the fuck

is it now?"

She set the shotgun down on the floor. Her hearing was returning, but a slight *buzz* was still present.

A low hum was bothering her. She thought it was coming from her damaged ears, but the longer she listened, the more she realized it wasn't. She looked at the ceiling and found the source of the noise.

Hanging from a hook were the buzzers—the two electrodes used by the farm hands to stun the pigs before cutting their throats. A pulley and track system had been installed years ago, allowing access to the buzzers anywhere in the slaughterhouse.

Beulah picked up the shotgun and used it to knock the buzzers from the hook.

They fell, landing in front of her.

She put the gun down and picked up the electric probes. They vibrated in her hands, but she didn't get shocked.

"Fuck you!" She clamped the buzzers against Shep's corpse.

His body became rigid as the power surged through him.

She watched and thought, *Is there still life left in him? Could he still be here somewhere, in whatever hell he was in?*

Peaches was licking the floor, seeking out any remnants of food she may have missed. The pig looked up at Beulah, who held the buzzers over her.

Beulah's reflection shone in the pig's black eyes as she clamped the buzzers around its head, sending a current of electricity through her brain.

Peaches fell to the ground with a *thump*.

Beulah set the buzzers down and dragged her father's body next to the unconscious pig. She set one end of the buzzers on Shep's chest and the other on Peaches's head, completing the circuit.

Both forms seemed to vibrate with electricity.

From the wall, Beulah removed the long, wicked knife used to slaughter. She pressed the blade against the pig's throat, and could feel its pulse through the steel as she drew it across.

Blood poured from the swine's neck, rushing across the floor like a crimson tidal wave.

There was no time to waste. Beulah didn't know if what she was about to attempt was possible, but she had to try; she didn't study anatomy for nothing.

2003

CHAPTER 16

1

A sick sense of dèjà vu washed over Beulah as she walked toward the slaughterhouse with the shotgun in hand.

Her mind wandered back to the fateful day four years in the past. After her experiment with her father and Peaches, things were touch and go.

Lying to Hattie was easy. The girl believed the story about her grandfather running away with one of his friends.

While Hattie came off as slow, Beulah knew there was a different level of intelligence behind those eyes. Even after installing multiple locks on the basement door, Hattie didn't raise any questions. It was as if the locks had been there forever.

Shep's friends and buyers were another story.

Beulah simply told them he left without warning. No note or anything, just gone. Some of them were weary, smelling the bullshit she fed them, but a few fucks or blowjobs helped change their attitudes. It wasn't the highlight of her life, but she'd always been a survivor. The others didn't care who they dealt with as long as their pork was delivered on time, which, for a while, was.

Standing outside the slaughterhouse, nausea washed over her at the thought of what she might find. Would Hattie be dead, mutilated, and raped by the beast? Or would Wayne be having another go at the girl?

She steeled her nerves and opened the door.

Beulah had seen countless pigs slaughtered over the years. As brutal as it was, the process was relatively humane and clean. It was a business. Just like a mechanic got dirty, so did butchers.

The carnage she faced when she opened the door was nothing like she'd ever seen before.

A mangled corpse lay in front of her.

She thought it was Wayne, but the body looked partially eaten. Entrails were thrown about, and chunks of flesh were gouged with brutal teeth marks. The smell of an open human gut was distinctly different than that of a swine.

With the gun in one hand, Beulah used the other to cover her mouth. She backed away from the mutilated meat, but saw something farther inside the slaughterhouse.

Another body lay prone. A pool of blood surrounded it, but even from a distance, Beulah could tell the legs were that of a man.

She prayed she'd find the mutated, hell-born corpse of her monster father, but she didn't.

It was Brett. Well, what was left of Brett anyway. His body suffered a fate similar to Wayne's.

Beulah snapped the gun to her shoulder, suddenly remembering who—no *what*—caused the carnage. Her father was out there somewhere, and with him was her daughter. Like she'd seen in countless movies, Beulah began to search the slaughterhouse.

The pigs were outside in the row, but they were

mostly quiet.

She didn't know if that was a good or bad sign.

The muzzle of the gun wavered as she moved, but she saw nothing. She was alone except for the corpses of her farmhands.

"Fuck, fuck, fuck," she muttered. Beulah leaned against a piece of machinery and set the gun at her side. She was stuck.

Davey would be arriving soon, and there was no excuse she could come up with. Besides, she had two dead bodies to deal with. She wasn't much of a body disposal expert. If she'd still been in New York, she was sure she could call Mike if he weren't dead.

Outside, some of the pigs awoke. Soon, the entire bunch of them were up and vocal. They knew she was in the slaughterhouse, and in their minds, that meant it was time to eat.

And they'd eat anything.

"No, no. There's no way that would work," she said.

But it could work.

She'd seen pigs gorge themselves on just about anything. And with the corpses of Brett and Wayne already partially eaten, she assumed human flesh wouldn't be a bad meal.

It would've been easier to dismember the bodies, but Beulah didn't have that kind of time on her hands. She looked around and found a tarp.

It would have to work.

Doing her best to keep the gore from her clothes, Beulah rolled Wayne's body onto the tarp.

Blood sloshed from his many wounds, but it stayed contained on the plastic.

Gritting her teeth, Beulah dragged him, sliding his body toward the pig pens.

The beasts were whipped into a frenzy. They squealed and jumped on one another trying to get closer to where she walked.

Beulah rolled Wayne's body onto the ground.

Wet snouts poked through the bars. Gnashing teeth, broken and yellow, dripped with spit as wet tongues tasted blood in the air. The black eyes of the swine were maddened with hunger, even though they'd eaten less than twelve hours ago.

Carefully, Beulah pushed Wayne's body toward the animals. One of his legs inched closer and closer.

A large sow, who would probably be under the knife if she weren't pregnant, grabbed Wayne's foot. She yanked, using her fat-covered muscles.

The corpse was like a rag doll as it whipped across the floor and into the maelstrom of hogs.

Ripping, squealing, grunting, and crying erupted from the pigs as they fed. Clothes, meat, and bone were eaten as one. The herd of swine turned red, and the smell of their already ripe environment worsened with the odor of human shit.

Beulah stood hypnotized by the carnage, but knew her job wasn't done. She still had Brett to deal with.

2

The driver's side window was cracked, and the radio was on low. A thin stream of smoke was sucked out of the truck from the cigarette clenched between Davey's fingers.

He took a drag as the vehicle bumped along the dirt road leading to the slaughterhouse.

The sun shined its bright rays into his eyes, casting a golden hue on the farm in front of him. It would've been a picturesque sight to the layman—an old farmhouse standing after almost one hundred years, the rolling hills, and the forest surrounding the house. Even the slaughterhouse with pig pens attached to it had charm.

To Davey, it was nothing special. It was just another job, albeit a violent and disgusting one. But that was nothing new to him. He'd had his fair share of disgusting, shitty jobs.

He rolled down the window the rest of the way and tossed the cigarette butt. Rounding a bend in the road, he headed toward the slaughterhouse.

Wayne and Brett wouldn't be in for another hour, but if Davey could get a head start, he might be able to have lunch early.

Maybe he'd test their theory about the boss, Beulah, and her wild side.

"No shit," Davey said. He looked at the clock in the dashboard and back at Wayne's truck parked outside the slaughterhouse.

The brakes squealed as he brought the truck to a halt near Wayne's.

The main door to the slaughterhouse was ajar.

He hopped out and put another cigarette in his mouth.

"Damn, you cocksuckers really love the smell of pig shit, dontcha?" Davey asked as he entered the slaughterhouse. "Oh damn, I'm sorry."

Beulah was looking over her shoulder at him.

She had a hose in her hand and was spraying the floor.

Rivulets of blood ran into the drains.

She looked tired, like she'd been up all night, but there was an allure to her. Her hair was up in a messy ponytail, with a good portion falling out. Her rubber boots were old and stained with a plethora of fluids and gunk. Even her overalls looked beat up, especially against the black shirt underneath.

"So, you don't like the smell of pig shit?" Beulah asked with a smile. She let the water trickle and stop as she released the handle.

Davey took a drag on his cigarette, trying to find the words. No, shit and viscera wasn't quite the bouquet he was looking for, but it wasn't the worst.

"Eh, I've smelled worse." He smiled at her, but not before letting his eyes wander over her body.

The old clothes did nothing to flatter her figure. Except for the bulges of her breasts, which were nearly impossible to hide, the rest of her attire was loose and drab. Still, that didn't stop Davey from wondering.

Beulah laughed. "I'm sure you have." She handed him the hose. "I've been at it half the night. I'm gonna shower and lie down for a bit."

He took the hose, but didn't spray. "Where is Wayne?" He looked around but didn't see the other farmhand.

Beulah tapped her head like she forgot something. "We had a late order. Or I guess it would be better to call it an early order. A very impatient buyer insisted on having a fresh pig sent to him this morning. I called Brett and Wayne, knowing those derelicts would be together, to come in and get it done. They took the farm truck to deliver it, but I'm not sure if they'll be back for the rest of the day."

Davey nodded. "And Ralph?"

A brief look of panic flashed on her face and then calmed. "He called me in the middle of the night. His wife fell and broke her ankle, so he's not coming in today. With as big as she is, I'm surprised it didn't happen sooner."

He was glad he didn't get called in the middle of the night, but knew he'd, more than likely, be working alone for the day.

"Now, finish cleaning up here and muck the pens. I already fed the pigs, so don't worry about that until later." Beulah put her hands on her hips and cocked her head. "Any more questions, or can I go?"

Under his boss's seductive, joking glare, he felt color rising on his cheeks. "No ma'am," Davey said with a grin. He made a point to look her up and down before he started spraying the jet of water at the blood.

3

Hattie awoke with the sun. She was warm and felt a body against her flesh. Her eyes fluttered open. There was hair in her crooked mouth.

She panicked when she realized she wasn't in her bed, nor was it her hair in her mouth. Her arm was numb and her hand sweaty as it still cupped the supple breast of the girl. Slowly, she removed it, risking one last caress of the soft nipple.

The girl let out a low groan and shifted, but

didn't wake.

Cool air licked at Hattie's nude flesh as she stood in the dim light of the morning and adjusted her mask and grabbed her clothes.

Memories of the night before came back to her. She looked around but didn't see her grandfather anywhere. That was good, but could be bad. If he killed the others without her, she'd be pissed. But she didn't think he did. She didn't know why; it was something she felt. Or was it the slimy feeling of his pig eyes on her from somewhere in the woods?

She looked in the dark trees for him, but didn't see his hulking form.

The girl moved and muttered, rolling to her other side. Her closed eyes were aimed right at Hattie, and if she awoke right then and there, it would be trouble.

Silently, and nude, Hattie walked into the woods. She didn't want to go back home, but she had to. If her mother realized she was missing, along with her grandfather, it would raise problems Hattie wasn't ready to deal with just yet.

After putting her bloody clothes back on, she started for the house. She didn't see her pig-mutant grandfather on her trek back, but she could feel him watching and waiting.

He just needed to lay low for one more day.

The house was in sight, and she saw her mother in a bedroom window looking down at her. Her heart fluttered, but not from the sight of her mother.

Davey was there; he came back.

The slick lust she felt the night before, as she touched herself outside of the cabin, returned. A musky heat rose from between her legs.

She raised her face and smiled, hidden by the mask.

4

Beulah breathed a sigh of relief when she saw Hattie emerge from the woods. The girl looked unharmed, but something was off. She was alone, and Beulah scanned the trees to see if there was any sign of her father. But Hattie was, blessedly, alone. Beulah didn't know if that was a problem or a relief.

If Hattie didn't have the beast in tow, where was he?

Her mind flashed back to the kids in the cabin. If her father found them, it would be a massacre. Explaining the disappearance of two farmhands, who habitually skipped town, could be done. But telling the authorities four teens went missing on her property would raise a whole host of issues.

She desperately needed a shower, but it would have to wait. As she heard the front door open, she darted out of her room and stood waiting.

A barrage of questions flew from Beulah's mouth when Hattie mounted the steps. "Where the fuck is he? Where were you?" She realized her daughter was covered in dried blood. "Are you hurt?"

Slowly, Hattie walked up the steps. She raised her masked face to her mother, but didn't speak.

"Hattie, answer me!"

"Heth's safe. I'm safe," the girl grunted. She didn't utter another word before disappearing into the bathroom and locking the door.

Beulah heard the water turn on and tried the knob for good measure. It looked like her shower would have to wait a little longer.

CHAPTER 17

1

Ari woke to the sound of yelling. She rolled over, feeling the warmth of the other side of the blanket, but the spot was unoccupied. Her eyes fluttered open, and she realized she was naked.

"I hope you two are decent," Danielle yelled as she moved through the woods.

Far from decent, Ari sat up and rubbed her face. The brisk morning air made her want to crawl back under the blankets, but she didn't want her friends to find her naked. Well, she didn't want Rich to see her like that. Danielle had often seen her in her birthday suit, but she thought Rich's head might explode if he did.

She scrambled to her feet and threw her clothes on, and had just buttoned her shorts when they entered the clearing.

"There you are," Danielle said. "Nice sex hair."

Ari blushed and ran her fingers through her tangled locks. She desperately needed a shower and a brush. And something to eat; her stomach rumbled at the thought of food.

Rich looked around. "And where is Loverboy?"

They all looked as if JD was hiding somewhere, but he was nowhere to be seen.

"Not sure," Ari said. "The blankets were still

warm when I woke up, and his clothes were gone. He's probably taking a walk or something."

"More than likely out there taking a dump far away. And I'm grateful for that. I've been in the stall next to him many times, and let me tell you, that's not an experience you want."

"How romantic," Danielle said to her boyfriend. "I'm starving, but we didn't want to eat without you two."

"Yeah, we burned some serious calories last night," Rich said, wrapping his arm around Danielle's waist.

"And some this morning," Danielle said as she kissed him.

"Oh yes, how could I forget." He smiled and kissed her back, letting his tongue explore her mouth.

Ari looked around for her boyfriend.

The sun wasn't fully up, and the woods still had some gloom.

"I could eat, but I don't want to leave JD out there alone."

"Bah," Rich said, dismissing her with a wave. "JD was a Boy Scout. He'll be just fine." He cupped his hands around his mouth. "Hey, JD, clip that dump off, and let's go! We're hungry!"

They all listened, but there was no yell in response.

"There. Now he knows. Let's go back and see what we can whip up with the things we grabbed."

Arm in arm, Rich and Danielle started back toward the cabin.

The mingled scents of her and JD wafted up toward Ari's nose as she gathered the blankets. She inhaled the smell of her shampoo, but JD's essence was gone. On his side of the blankets was another smell, something more animalistic.

"Ari, come on!" Danielle yelled.

She dismissed the smell, chalking it up to the lingering odor of the old blankets from years past. With the fabric in her arms, she rushed to catch up with her friends.

2

Sweat dripped down Davey's back, and he knew it would only get hotter throughout the day. He stepped out of the slaughterhouse and into the fresh air, and took off his gloves, stuffing them in his pocket.

Outside wasn't much better, but at least there was a breeze.

Davey put a hand to his eyes and looked at the sun. He didn't have a watch, but figured it had to be close to noon.

A hose hung limp from the side of the building. He turned the water on and let it run until it was cool. Greedily, he drank, relishing the feeling of the water sloshing around his belly. He wet his head and slicked his hair back, letting the cold water run down his back and chest.

He took his shirt off, exposing his tattoos to the sun, then wet the shirt, wringing it out before draping it over his shoulders.

With Wayne and Brett gone for the day, it was the perfect time to see if Beulah would live up to her reputation.

Davey wasn't dumb, especially when it came to

women. And when it came to older, single women, he was pretty much kryptonite.

Drops of water slithered down his hard chest, following the channels of his abs. He walked toward the house knowing he was being watched.

When Davey opened the back door, he was pleasantly surprised by what he saw.

Beulah was bent over in the fridge. She'd changed out of her overalls, and wore a sundress at least two sizes too small. The flowery material was just about see-through. She smelled clean, unlike him, who had the pungent odor of pig and sweat.

"Perfect timing," Beulah said, turning from the fridge with a bowl in her hands. "I was just about to come get you." She set the bowl on the table and grabbed a loaf of bread.

The cold air of the fridge caused her nipples to stiffen, pressing against the fabric of the dress.

He drank in her curves, following her chest up to her lithe neck.

She wore light makeup, and her hair was thrown up in a messy bun.

Davey hung his wet shirt on the back of the chair and sat. He leaned back, spreading his legs, inviting her eyes to his swelling crotch.

"Smells good in here. I feel like I could eat for days." Quickly, and almost imperceptibly, he licked his lips. But his eyes weren't on the food, they were on Beulah.

"Well, there's plenty without the other two here." Beulah grabbed a pitcher of lemonade and two glasses from the counter. "Hattie is still asleep, so it'll only be us." She sat and rested her chin in her hands, leaning forward.

He couldn't keep his eyes off her chest. He wanted to bury his face between her tits and suck her nipples until she begged him to stop.

"Here, let me," Beulah said, grabbing the loaf of bread and tuna salad. "So, how's it going? I know it must be slow work without the others, but hopefully they'll return soon." She loaded his sandwich onto a paper plate and slid it over to him.

As horny as Davey was, he was just as hungry. He took a bite of the sandwich. "Not bad. I like to work alone, so I don't mind the solitude. Just me and the piggies. I think the rest of the slaughter might have to wait a day for them to come back. That would be a pain in the ass by myself. But they're all prepped. The ones slated for slaughter are ready, and I was able to separate most of them. Just a few more to do, then I can clean up."

Beulah made her sandwich, but didn't touch it. She only stared at him.

Davey had seen that stare many times before. He'd be shocked if lunch didn't end with him blowing a load.

"I wish I had three more of you." She didn't add to that statement, but Davey knew what she meant.

Noticing the shotgun in the corner, Davey asked, "What's with the gun?"

"Oh, I, ah, heard some coyotes last night. Those little bastards can be a problem if they get too brave. I let a round off in their direction to scare them. I guess I forgot to put it away. It was a busy night, so it slipped my mind."

Davey nodded; the answer sounded reasonable

to him.

Together, they ate silently but spoke with their eyes and body language throughout the brief meal.

"Done?" Beulah asked.

He wiped his mouth with a napkin and set it on the plate. "Yeah, that was great."

Beulah slid her chair out and opened her legs just for a moment.

Davey didn't hesitate to take a peek.

For just a second, he could see her bare pussy before it disappeared again. Davey's cock was in a constant state of semi-hard the entire meal, but glimpsing her sweet cleft made him fully erect.

Beulah cleared the table and stood at the sink with her back to him.

Well, this will go one of two ways, he thought. Davey fell to his knees behind her and lifted her dress.

Gasping as he pushed her hips into the counter and spread her ass, Beulah gripped the countertop while his tongue slid into her anus.

"Oh, fuck," Beulah grunted. She arched her back and thrust her ass into his face, letting him explore her.

Davey's stubbled chin rubbed against Beulah's pussy as he tasted her asshole. His tongue played inside of her, delving deeper as she pushed against his face. He grabbed her hips and pulled her back even farther, giving his mouth access to her wet pussy. Craning his neck, he found her clit. His tongue rolled the delicate nub as he licked her front to back like he was eating a melting ice cream sandwich.

Beulah reached behind and took his thick hair in

her grasp. She shoved his face deeper into her, moaning as he licked the sweetness flooding from her.

The tight denim was crushing Davey's cock, and he thought it might explode.

Willing him to rise, Beulah pulled his hair.

Davey stood as she turned to face him.

His light beard glistened with her wetness as Beulah kissed him and licked his chin, tasting herself as she unbuttoned his jeans.

With his pants at his ankles, Davey grabbed her hips, and with almost no effort, tossed her up on the counter.

Their mouths were hungry, licking and tasting each other like rutting animals.

Beulah grabbed his swollen member and guided it into her.

Davey growled as he entered her. The tight wetness of her almost made him lose his load immediately, but he held out. He plunged into her, letting his balls slap her wet ass.

Lost in lust, neither of them heard the footsteps coming down the stairs.

3

Hattie felt reborn. She slept naked after her shower, letting the cool sheets embrace her. Her sleep was dreamless and restful, something she was happy about.

Freeing her grandfather was terrifying, but she knew it had to be done.

She'd seen too much in her short life and knew

if she didn't take control, her destiny would take her to a place she didn't want to be.

Killing Wayne and Brett was liberating. It let her know she wasn't a victim anymore. She was strong, even if others didn't see her that way.

She heard the horrible things her mother said about her grandfather, but suppressed them. Even the night he called her down to the card game was a distant memory.

Her mother wouldn't help her, only use her.

But her grandfather represented power, even if his old motives were selfish.

Hattie knew how the world worked; if she was expected to do certain things, she'd, at least, make it work for her.

Sitting in front of her mirror, still nude, Hattie looked at her face and the pink scars on her body. When she was younger, she asked her mother about them. Her face was a birth defect, but the scars were unnatural.

When asked, her mother stuttered and looked flustered. She told Hattie she took a spill through a glass table when she was a baby.

For years, Hattie believed her, but her inquisitive mind didn't take the answer for gospel. They didn't look like scars from cuts, but tears like something ripped her.

Hattie slowly brushed her hair in the mirror. She put the thick brush over her mouth, covering the wide cleft. In another life, without her monstrous mouth, she would've been beautiful. Her body was young and tight. Her chest, even with the scars, was full and perky.

Lowering the brush, she stared at the monster in the mirror. This wasn't another life; it was her life. Would she ever find love looking the way she did?

Yes, and she already had.

Davey.

The way he looked at her made her weak in the knees. They'd only known each other for days, but she knew he loved her. And she loved him. He didn't have to say it, or do anything, but she knew. The looks they shared were love. Of course, there was lust there as well—she knew he desired her body. She just needed a chance to seduce him. Unlike Wayne, she'd willingly give her body to him. She'd let him touch her, kiss her, and fuck her.

Hattie squirmed, rubbing her thighs together at the thought of Davey inside of her. Her sex still remembered the orgasm she had the night before as she watched the lovers fuck in the cabin.

She heard the back door close a few minutes earlier and knew it was him. Hattie grinned, knowing it wasn't Wayne or Brett. It was her lover. Her man.

Not bothering to wear a bra or underwear, Hattie put on a dress. She adjusted her breasts in the mirror, not that they needed it, and put on her mask.

She wanted to surprise Davey. It all played out in her mind. She would slowly make her way down the stairs and creep into the kitchen. Davey would be sitting at the table eating one of her mother's shitty sandwiches. He'd be tired from working alone all day, and miserable. And then, Hattie would appear out of nowhere. Davey would look up from his lunch and see her. The pertness of her breasts would be evident through her dress, and if the sunlight was right, he'd be able to see the outline of her pussy through the sheer material.

The daydream played out in her head, delving into how it would go that night and into the future. Hattie knew there was something special between her and Davey.

He'd never come on to her, but how he looked let her know. It was a different kind of stare, not like Wayne or Brett. They looked at her like a piece of meat. They couldn't look at her face, only her body, making her feel cheap.

Davey wasn't like that. He was different. Of course, sex would be on his mind; he was still a man, after all. But with him, it would be different. He wouldn't hurt her, physically or emotionally. Davey would take his time with her, making sure her pleasure came before his.

Hattie knew that she'd have to touch herself after lunch. She'd be too wound up waiting for him that night.

She slowed as she reached the base of the steps.

Something was wrong.

A sound echoed through the house, a sound she'd heard before.

Someone was fucking.

No, no, no.

A muffled scream—a woman's shout of pleasure—made Hattie increase her pace.

She rounded the corner just in time to see the mask of an orgasm on her mother's face.

Davey's bare ass clenched as he drove into her mother.

Beulah jammed her fist into her mouth to keep

her pleasure somewhat quiet. Then, she pulled her hand from her mouth and kissed Davey.

Their mouths were a blur, as if they were trying to eat each other.

The wet squelching of their sex reminded Hattie of the sound of murder, and at that moment, murder was the only thing on her mind.

Davey grunted into her mother's mouth as his feverish pace increased.

Beulah pulled her face from his and put her hands on the back of his head. Her fingers ran through his sweaty hair, and she smiled.

"That's it, baby. Give me that load. Bury it in me."

Davey had Beulah on her counter with her legs spread wide. His pace increased. Deeper and faster, he fucked her.

With one final plunge and grunt, Davey moaned and pushed his face into Beulah's neck.

Hattie felt tears running down her face and around the bottom of the mask. The lust she felt was gone, replaced with pure rage and hurt.

Allowing his spunk to fill Beulah, Davey sat still for a moment. He took his head from her neck, kissed her mouth, and pulled out. His cock glistened as he withdrew from her wet pussy.

Her opening drooled his white cum, leaving a drop to run down the countertop and onto the floor.

As Beulah wiped herself with a paper towel, she saw her daughter.

Hattie wanted to call out and yell at her, but her throat felt filled with hay. Her nose burned, and her eyes wouldn't stop leaking.

Davey, still coming down from the bliss of his orgasm, finally realized where Beulah was looking. He turned to face the steps, his hard cock pointing at Hattie like an accusing, veiny finger. "Oh shit," he said as he scrambled to pull his pants up.

"Hattie, wait," Beulah said as she tossed the sodden paper towel in the sink and jumped off the counter.

Hattie ran up the stairs and slammed the door behind her. She ripped her mask off and jumped face down on the bed, crying.

4

Ari stood by the cabin window, looking out into the woods. It had been almost an hour since she returned without her boyfriend. She showered and ate, but not much. Her nerves quelled her appetite, but the shower was a nice distraction.

"When do you guys want to head out?" Ari asked.

Rich and Danielle were sitting at the small table playing cards.

"Do you think we need to?" Rich asked as he put down another card. "Look, I'm sure he's fine. He is probably just clearing his head. Even though we had a little detour, this trip has been fun. I'm sure the future is weighing heavy on his mind, just like ours."

Danielle slapped a card down onto the pile and smiled at her boyfriend. She looked at Ari, who was facing them with her back to the window.

Ari locked eyes with her, willing her to join her side. She knew that if Danielle went with her, Rich would as well.

Danielle nodded. "Let us finish this game, and we'll *all* take a walk."

Rich looked up to see his girlfriend glaring at him.

Ari knew that look and loved her friend for it. Men might have strength over women, but the power of pussy was a real thing. And Ari had to admit, she'd used that power a time or two to coax JD's decisions. It was fun, a game of the sexes they always won.

"Ah, let's just go now. This shit is over." Rich tossed his cards down in defeat.

The three of them walked out into the warm morning. It was going to be a hot day, with the sun already climbing into the sky.

"So, are we supposed to yell and shit?" Rich asked as he kicked a pinecone.

Ari shrugged. "I don't know. I've never had to do this before." She scanned the woods in front of her, hoping to catch a glimpse of her love.

"How about we just go back to where you camped and start there? Maybe he's still by the creek. Could've just lost track of time."

"Sounds like a plan," Ari said.

5

Hattie couldn't stay in the house any longer. Even though Davey had gone back to work, the memory of him and her mother having sex was fresh in her mind. She didn't know where her mother was. Hattie didn't want to see her; she just wanted to leave the house.

She changed out of her dress and threw on a pair

of shorts. With the mask back on her face, Hattie quietly left her room.

The house was quiet. No sounds of fucking, or anything else for that matter.

She rushed outside without seeing another soul.

The woods called to her. They were her solace. She'd been running to them since childhood.

Something else in the woods garnered her attention: her grandfather.

Seeing him kill had done something to Hattie. It gave her strength. Even though it hadn't been her hand slicing the necks, or tearing and gnashing flesh, she knew she wielded power. It was something she planned on using, and it had only just begun.

Expertly pushing through the trees, Hattie went to the last place she'd seen her grandfather. She wasn't sure how much of his mind was his, but from the night before, she figured he had more than enough.

He was never smart, and even she knew how shrewd he was. He'd keep himself hidden in the pines if he wanted to continue the bloodshed without getting caught.

Hattie's cleft mouth drooled and smiled as she approached the copse of trees.

She stopped, her heart thumping.

Them!

Youthful voices, too loud for the quiet of the woods, sounded out as the teens from the cabin trampled the brush underfoot.

Naturally, they were looking for their missing friend.

Hattie knew that would happen, and was glad

she returned in time. She had to stop them before they found her grandfather. There would be plenty of time for them to meet the abomination, but not in the morning light. Not yet.

Sweat ran down Hattie's back as she moved, aiming to cut them off.

There!

The trio was walking along the stream.

The boy and girl she watched through the window were walking hand in hand. They didn't seem too concerned about searching for the missing teen.

The other girl, the one Hattie spent the night with, seemed different now. A genuine look of concern shone on the girl's face.

She cupped her hands and yelled. "JD!" Her sweet voice flooded the woods.

Hidden behind a tree, Hattie watched. She didn't think the kids would venture into the thick pines where she left her grandfather, but desperation made people act weird.

Hattie took a deep breath and stepped out from her hiding spot. "Are oo ooking for your fren?" she asked, doing her best to articulate through her cleft.

"Jesus Christ," the boy said. He jumped at the sound and sight of Hattie.

It was something she could never get used to.

Hattie adjusted the mask, ensuring it was snug.

The girl she slept with turned. She looked at Hattie, but there was little disgust on her face. Even after she'd been caught spying on the girl when they first arrived, there was a glimmer of hope in her eyes.

"Yes, my boyfriend. He went for a walk and

hasn't come back yet." The girl walked closer to Hattie.

She was stunning. Even disheveled and upset, she was beautiful.

A wave of lust and disgust ran through Hattie. The girl was everything Hattie wasn't. She longed to be her and longed to kill her.

Hattie didn't trust her voice, not yet, so she pointed back toward the house.

The girl grabbed her shoulders.

Feeling her skin through her clothes, Hattie shuddered.

"Did you see him? Did he go to the house?"

Hattie nodded and found her voice again. "Yeth. I thaw him walking tha way."

"C-can you take us to him? I'm really worried."

"Ari, I'm sure he's fine. Maybe he was looking for something to eat. I know I would've killed for a homemade meal instead of the slop we ate," the boy said.

Ari. What a beautiful name. Much better than Hattie. My name sounds like it belongs to an animal. A fucking pig, maybe.

"I ake oo to him," Hattie said.

Without another word, she turned and walked back toward the house. She didn't look back at them, and for a moment, they were still.

And then, she heard the tell-tale sound of old leaves crunching underfoot as they followed.

Facing away from them, Hattie smiled.

6

After getting up early and fucking during lunch, Davey's body was spent. He felt like he was aging well, but days like that made him realize Father Time came for everyone.

He stepped out of the slaughterhouse and took in the fresh air. His nose had gotten used to the smell of the animals, but the fresh air was like a sip of clean water. He drank it in and immediately grabbed his cigarettes.

Davey sat on an old chair and wiped his sweaty brow. The smoke rose into his eyes. He fanned it away faster than the air could take it. Something was stuck in his mind: Beulah. Not one to fall in love, he hadn't felt anything toward a woman in years. He didn't even know the names of most of them. And if he did, that information disappeared after he blew his load. But there was something different about his new boss. There was a strength to her he'd rarely seen before. She was a woman who knew what she liked and took it.

Sticking his tongue in her ass had been a gamble, and one that paid in spades. When she got into it, his lust was reinvigorated. For the first time in a long time, he wanted to pleasure his partner, not just turn her on only for him to bust in minutes, leaving her unsatisfied.

There was something about her hunger that drove him wild. She wasn't the first older woman he fucked. She wasn't even the oldest he fucked that week, but she was different. Maybe it was his age telling him to stop whoring and settle down.

He threw the butt on the ground and stamped it out. Davey hoped that wasn't the case. His cock didn't belong to any woman. It was his to let roam and hump as it wanted. But damn, Beulah sure could fuck.

Looking up at the house, his pulse quickened.

Beulah was outside, still wearing the same dress. She shook out a blanket that let out almost no dust or grime.

Even at a distance, Davey could tell she hadn't bothered putting on a bra after their fuck session.

She looked at him, and he raised a hand.

What the fuck are you doing? Waving like a fucking loser? Well, you are a fucking loser, so that makes sense. Whoring, drinking, smoking, and getting arrested. Yup, I'd say you're a loser.

The voice of his father always picked inopportune times to chime in.

Here's something else you'll squander. A good job, a sexy boss, fresh air. Of course, you'll fuck it up. You probably already did by sticking your dick in her. Was the nut worth it? She'll probably fire you by the end of the week for that bullshit stunt. I hope the pussy was worth it. Oh, and don't forget your PO. That bitch will send your worthless ass back to jail, or maybe prison this time. Once you're unemployed and on your ass, you'll end up behind bars. Let's see how the pretty boy does then.

Davey lowered his hand. His father's voice was insidious, burrowing into his psyche as it always did. Even thinking about the earthy taste of Beulah's ass couldn't chase away his demons.

But something else did.

Hattie popped out of the woods with three others in tow.

The girl was too far away to really see, but Davey knew she was looking at him. It was a look he'd seen before: lust. Her face was hidden behind the mask, but he'd seen enough through the holes to know something was wrong with her. That, and her speech. She was deformed worse than the scars on her flesh. But Davey, being the fucking perv he was, admired her young body. She'd gotten her mother's genes when it came to her figure.

The tell-tale swelling of an erection tightened his pants. He felt like a scumbag, but that was for a good reason—he was one.

He wondered what it would be like to fuck the mother and daughter at the same time. As badly as he wanted to see Hattie's tits, he knew he'd have to keep his eyes focused on them and not her face, or fuck her from behind, which was optimal.

The kids following Hattie quickened their pace, rushing toward the house. There were only three of them, not four.

Something was wrong.

Davey stood. He didn't run toward the house, but moved with a purpose, and arrived just as one of the girls was talking with Beulah. He took a brief second to check out her ass as she walked up the steps.

"Have you seen my boyfriend?" she asked.

Beulah laid the blanket over the railing and leaned on the wall. She was sweaty and glistening, which didn't help the swelling in Davey's pants.

Gently tugging on the neckline of her dress,

Beulah fanned her sweating bosom, drawing attention to her chest.

The boy in the group took a quick glance at the mature tits in front of him.

Davey's eyes flicked away from Beulah so as not to get caught, but it was too late.

Hattie stared at him. Her eyes locked on his from behind her mask. Like a child caught with his hand in the cookie jar, Davey looked away.

"No, sorry. I haven't seen anyone," Beulah replied. "I've been inside most of the day, and he didn't come here."

The girl rubbed her face. "Fuck. Okay, thank you." She turned back to her friends.

The boy pulled his eyes from Beulah's chest.

"Look, I'm sure he's just fucking with us," the other girl said.

"Yeah, you know he can be a dickhead like that," the boy replied. "Besides, we can't go anywhere without the car."

The first girl's face looked shocked, like she'd forgotten about their busted ride.

"The car. I forgot that was the reason we're stuck here." She looked at Beulah. "Can you give us a ride into town? Maybe the car is done."

"That would be perfect," the boy said. "If it's done, we'll bring it back, and then when JD shows up, we can get out of here. In fact, I guarantee when we get back, he'll be here. The fucker is probably hungry, and you know that boy likes to eat."

If I had a girlfriend like her, I'd be eating till I exploded, Davey thought as his eyes wandered back to the girl's ass. He didn't care about Hattie's glare.

His lizard brain was taking over again.

"Sorry, kids. I have too much goi—"

"I'll take them," Davey chimed in. "I came in early, and I'm beat. I'm headed that way anyway, so I might as well."

A twinge of jealousy shone on Beulah's face, and Davey wondered if that was a good thing or a bad thing. Jealous women were unpredictable. He'd either get his brains fucked out or bashed in.

The young, pert girls before the older woman were a threat. A threat of what, he didn't know, but he felt the scorn.

"Um, yeah, that's fine. You put in some long hours today, especially being alone," Beulah said. She flashed him an almost imperceptible smile at the word *long*.

"Let me just wash up, and we'll get going." Davey moved past the small group, taking in the scent of the younger women.

"Thank you. I'm Ari," the first girl said. "Danielle and Rich."

Davey gave them all nods, knowing his hands were flecked with pig shit. "Davey. Let me wash this crud off my hands, and we'll see about your car." He let his winning smile linger on the girls for a moment longer.

Rich threw an arm around Danielle's waist, doing his best to show she was with him.

Clever boy, but that shit rarely works. I've fucked more wives and girlfriends in skeezy bathrooms while their cuck partners sat waiting in restaurants.

Davey winked at him as he passed Hattie.

She grabbed his arm, gently rubbing his bicep. "Are oo coming bah?"

Locking eyes with her through the small holes in the mask, he said, "Well, if their car isn't done, I guess I will be. If not, I'll be here bright and early. We have another slaughter to prepare for." Gently, he shrugged her off and entered the house.

PART 3:
SCREAMS AND MOANS

CHAPTER 18

1

The leaf springs on the truck squeaked with every bump in the road. The window was down and the radio low. The only sound in the truck was that of the road and the soft country music drifting through the battered speakers.

His truck wasn't one of the fancier ones with backseats, so the four of them were crammed onto the bench seat.

Davey was hoping one of the girls would sit beside him, with her thigh pressed against his, but Rich made sure to take that seat. Davey respected that, but knew if he had a little alone time with his girlfriend, there was a good chance he'd get in her pants; it was his gift.

The younger ones and older ones were all like shooting fish in a barrel. Older women liked the attention from a younger guy, and the college girls—hell, those two might have still been in high school—thought fucking an older guy was hot. And Davey had been there many times.

Ari sat pressed against the far window, staring out of the dingy glass. She turned to the group and broke the silence. "It just isn't like him to disappear like this. I mean, he's been gone most of the day."

The clock on the dash said 3 p.m.

"I get taking a little nature walk in the morning,

but guys, you know how pissed JD gets missing a meal. And now he's missed two. No, something's wrong."

Danielle turned slightly so as not to be face-to-face with her friend. "Yeah, I'm with you. Something isn't right." She glanced back at Davey with a side eye.

He saw it, clear as day, but kept his eyes on the road.

In the crammed truck, nothing was private, but Danielle lowered her voice. "And that girl with the mask is fucking creepy. I wouldn't doubt if she did something to him. Wasn't she watching you shower the first night we got there?"

Lucky kid, Davey thought. He rolled his window down the rest of the way and hung his arm out. He needed a cigarette but was, for once, thinking of other people. If it were just him and Rich, he wouldn't care. But with the girls in the car, he thought better of it. He didn't think his chances of fucking either of them was particularly high, but lighting up would likely lower the odds.

They rolled into town, passing people out and enjoying the beautiful day.

"I'm sure he's fine. It's not cold enough to kill him, even overnight. More than likely, he got himself turned around in the woods. All he has to do is find the stream and follow it. Hell, there's even a chance he wandered his way into town. He could be waiting for us at the body shop."

Ari turned and Davey couldn't help but glance at her.

The other two occupants of the truck were looking

at him, so he fought like mad to not stare at the girl's tits.

"You think so? This is pretty far of a walk."

Davey waved a hand and put on his million-dollar smile. "Ah, he's a young kid. This shit is nothing. He probably got lost, found the stream, and realized he was closer to town than the farm. That would be a hell of a surprise if he were waiting for you. I'm sure you'd find a way to make it up to him."

Fuck, that was creepy.

"I…ah… I mean all of you."

Rich stared daggers into him, but Davey took his eyes off the kids and put them back on the road.

They were quiet again as the truck bounced into the gravel lot of the body shop.

"I don't see the car," Rich said, scanning the rows of vehicles.

"Me neither," Danielle agreed.

Davey put the truck in park and draped an arm over the headrest, looking at the kids. "We're here, kiddies."

Ari had the door open before the dust settled. She bolted away, disappearing into the shop before her friends even got out of the truck.

Danielle slid out next, and Davey took a second to admire her tight ass.

Rich wasn't looking, so Davey let his perverted gaze linger a little longer.

"Thanks for the lift," Danielle said, giving him a coy smile as she shut the door.

"Not a problem. I'll wait a second to make sure the car is ready."

The kids disappeared into the shop, and Davey

pulled his cigarettes out of his pocket. He lit one, breathing deeply, and turned up the radio.

The song ended, and a commercial started.

Hey folks, the familiar voice said through the speakers. *Are you a thirty-something-year-old loser whose only goals are to get drunk and laid? If that's the case, you're probably my son, Davey, a useless waste on society who never did a nice thing for another person in his life, including his own fucking parents.*

Davey's blood ran cold at his father's voice on the radio.

Warm air blew in from the parking lot, but his skin rose with goosebumps.

There you are having daydreams about fucking kids who could almost be your daughters, sucking down cigarettes in a truck that was new when Reagan was in office. You fucked your boss and were thinking about how her deformed daughter would look naked. A real lowlife sack of sh—

Davey punched the power button, hurting his knuckles.

"Damn, you must've hated that commercial," Rich said from the passenger window.

Startled by the presence of the boy, Davey jumped. He took a drag off his cigarette and tossed it, pushing the auditory hallucination from his mind, and did his best to go back to cool-guy mode.

"That fucking guy gives me a headache," he said with a forced smile.

"Right," Rich said, his brows furrowed. He looked in the side mirror and fixed his hair, which didn't appear to have a strand out of place. "Anyway,

JD isn't here, but the car is done. The girls are talking with the owner to see if they'll release it to us."

Davey felt the aftereffects of his dad wear away. "Unlike you and me, those two have certain *assets* that are universal with men, especially in these parts. I'm sure they won't have a problem." He winked at Rich.

Rich sucked his teeth just a little, but enough to let Davey know he didn't quite approve of his statement. "Look, we're worried about our friend. Ari is freaking out. You got her hopes up when you said JD might have been at the shop. He isn't, clearly, so she's upset. We're going to go back to the farm to look for him. I know it's not your responsibility, and you're tired, but we'd really appreciate the help."

Davey knew it was killing Rich to ask for his assistance. And he would bet his left nut that Danielle put him up to it. He was sure Rich wouldn't shed a tear if he plowed into a tree after leaving the shop.

You won't help them. You know you won't, so don't lead them on. You're as selfish as they come. His father's voice was no longer booming over the radio, but stuck in his mind where it seemed to live.

Davey had the excuse on his lips. It wasn't an excuse, but the truth. He was spent after being up half the night, working all day, and dumping a load in Beulah earlier.

The door to the shop opened, and Danielle hugged Ari, who was crying.

Yes, he thought it was hot to see their tits pressed together, but a pang of guilt overrode his lust for once. He knew the feeling of despair, of loss. It wasn't new to him, but these were just kids. And even though his mind was permanently in the gutter, he felt some responsibility to them.

He would never be confused with a man of honor, but if he could do one good deed, it might make up for some of the bad shit he'd done. "I'll help, at least until dark."

Rich patted the door. "Thank you." He looked back at the girls, made eye contact with Danielle, and nodded.

Danielle smiled as she consoled her friend.

Without another word, he trotted over to his friends.

Davey pulled another cigarette from his pack and lit it up.

The kids jumped into a small car and pulled out behind Davey's truck.

With a cloud of dust following them, they headed back to the farm.

2

A brush whisked through Hattie's hair as she tried to smooth the tangles. She stood looking in the mirror with her mask off.

She was elated and filled with hope, but the black tendril of despair wouldn't leave her. She loved Davey, but he didn't love her. At least, not yet.

Watching him and her mother fuck broke something in her. It both enraged and excited her. She couldn't help but picture her body under his, or the feeling of him thrusting inside of her, pounding. Her body would welcome him, unlike Wayne, which it rejected. He would look at her lovingly, not seeing her deformities, but *her* for who she is.

Every time she allowed herself to dream of a future together, her mind pushed the thoughts away and filled them with visions of Davey with her mother. He could never love her mother; she was unlovable. Even Hattie knew that.

Over the years, Hattie had witnessed her mother with various men. She wasn't shy, and would do anything for the good of the farm. But each and every man in her life left her. And up until recently, Hattie thought her grandfather was one of them.

One thing Hattie was certain about was this: if she couldn't have Davey, no one could.

Her mother didn't love Davey like she did. He was just another piece of the puzzle to her, someone she could use and abuse and kick down the road. Even though she'd been treated that way her entire life, Beulah wasn't above it either.

Not Hattie; Hattie loved him, and he would love her.

Once her mother was gone, they would spend their lives together on the farm and raise a family. They'd work hard during the day and make love at night.

Davey would take his time with her to start, and as she relaxed, he would ravage her, doing things to her young body she only saw in dreams.

But if he didn't see their love that way, she would end it once and for all.

It was a risk letting him leave for the night, knowing her grandfather lurked in the woods, but it would work out; fate always found a way.

There was a hard knock on her door, then it swung

open.

Her mother stood in the doorway with a mask of anger painted on her face.

Hattie set the brush down and turned to face her. She didn't don her mask, letting her mother stare at the cleft and myriad of scars on her face and neck—scars which Hattie never learned the truth about.

She pretended to believe the lie her mother fed her about the old wounds. Hattie might look different, but her mind worked just fine. Even as a young adult, Beulah never confided in her daughter as to the origin of the scars, and Hattie had a feeling she knew why.

"What the fuck did you do?" Beulah asked. Her brow was creased and her cheeks flushed.

Hattie shrugged. "Wha are oo alking abou?" The smile on her face was impossible to control.

"Did," Beulah paused and looked around like someone else was eavesdropping, "he kill the boy?"

Hattie looked down at her feet, not in shame or embarrassment, but to conceal her widening smile.

Beulah rushed across the room, catching Hattie off guard, and grabbed her wrists.

Hattie looked up at her mother. Weeks, or even days ago, she would've been scared of her, but something had changed. Something empowering overtook the girl.

"Where the fuck is he?"

Looking up, she stared her mother in the face. "Who?"

Beulah quivered and her grip tightened on Hattie's wrists. She moved her face closer, her breath sour. "Your grandfather. Where is he?"

Hattie's smirk returned.

This was power.

This was what she craved her entire life, and what she'd never relinquish, no matter who stood in her way.

A bubble of laughter rolled up from Hattie's chest and erupted in her mother's face.

Beulah, clearly caught off guard, released her daughter's wrists as the girl cackled.

The laughter wouldn't stop; Hattie couldn't help it.

A dull sound came from outside that made them both move to the window.

A cloud of dust rose into the air in the wake of two vehicles traveling down the dirt road.

Davey! You've come back to me.

"What have you done?" Beulah asked. She didn't wait for an answer as she rushed out of the room.

Hattie stood at the window as the truck and car stopped in front of the house.

The kids piled out of their car, but she wasn't watching them. Hattie stared at the truck as her love stepped out into the fading sunlight.

She smiled, put on her mask, and went down to join them.

3

Ari jumped out of the car as Beulah emerged from the house. She looked around for JD, hoping he'd found his way back while they were gone, but the owner of the farm was the only one who greeted them.

"He still hasn't come back yet?"

Beulah shook her head, looking past Ari at Davey. "No, not yet."

Rich and Danielle walked up next to her.

Danielle draped an arm around her shoulder. "Look, I'm just as nervous as you, but he's fine. I can feel it. He's probably pranking us at this point."

Ari looked at her friend and forced a smile. She knew Danielle was only trying to help, but something was wrong.

JD wasn't a prankster, and his jokes were usually pretty lame. If he was pranking them by disappearing for a whole day, he better get used to beating off for the foreseeable future.

"I hope you're right."

Davey walked past them and approached Beulah. "I told them I'd help look for the boy, but I don't know these woods very well. Maybe you could help?"

"I ow da woos," Hattie said as she burst from the front door, jumping the small set of steps. "I ow dem well."

"We'd appreciate everyone's help. These kids just want to find their friend and get on with their trip," Davey said, smiling at Hattie.

Ari watched the interaction while Danielle and Rich giggled in each other's ears.

Beulah's eyes flicked to hers, just for an instant, but it was enough.

Something was wrong; Ari could see it in the woman's forced smile. Even with the expression plastered on her face, her eyes couldn't lie. Ari fought with everything she had not to scream and demand information. She hoped she was wrong, but her instincts told her she was right.

"Well, she said she saw him this morning," Rich said, pointing accusingly at Hattie.

All eyes turned to the deformed girl, who looked shocked.

Another fucking tell, Ari thought.

"Is that true?" Davey asked, looking around Beulah to the girl.

Hattie froze, put on the spot, and nodded. "Yeth. I was in da woos and saw him walking to the houth. But maybe he wenth into da woos on da side." She pointed across the field to another patch of trees.

Davey shrugged. "I was busy all morning and didn't see him, but I guess that's possible."

Beulah shot a glance at her daughter.

Another lie had been told, but Ari wouldn't say anything without proof. The worst thing she could do was fight with the owner with her boyfriend still missing.

Looking up at the sun, Davey said, "Well, we're burning daylight, so let's not waste any more time. Hattie, lead the way."

Even from behind the mask, Ari could tell the girl was smiling. She shot a glance at Danielle when the others weren't looking. Even without words, she knew Danielle could feel her emotions.

Together, the six of them set off looking for the missing teen.

4

They returned to the farm as the last rays of sunlight

fell behind the horizon. Tired, sweaty, and losing hope, they ended where they started: in front of the farmhouse.

It was strange for Davey to feel emotions other than lust or greed, but watching Ari cry did something to him. Yes, he would've fucked the girl in a heartbeat, missing boyfriend be damned, but he genuinely felt bad for her. He remembered teen love and how strong it could be. But he also remembered the heartache of losing that love. His girlfriend didn't disappear, but broke up with him after one too many times catching him with his dick where it didn't belong. It was his fault, but still, he blamed her for the breakup.

"Come on. Let's get back to the cabin and clean up," Danielle said, throwing her arm over her sobbing friend.

Davey took a quick glance at the sweaty asses of the girls and broke his gaze just before getting caught by Rich.

"Hattie, why don't you go inside and shower up. I'll make us something for dinner when you're done."

Hattie didn't move. She stared at her mother and Davey in the growing twilight. Finally, and silently, she walked back into the house.

Beulah moved close to Davey.

He could smell the combined scents of their sweat. Even exhausted and sore, he was turned on.

"Well, it's late. I should be going. I have to clean up and get some rest for tomorrow."

Beulah took his hands in hers, which did not help his growing erection. "Why don't you stay the night? I have a spare room and some old clothes. I'll cook you a nice meal, and then…maybe…we'll see what happens."

Her smile was one Davey had seen many times before. But there was something else in her eyes: fear.

He didn't understand where that came from, but it was there. It was the same look he'd seen in his mirror time and time again as a boy when he heard the heavy footsteps of his father marching up the stairs to his room.

"I…ah…" A homecooked meal and some pussy did sound like a great way to end the night, especially after the day he had. Besides, he was dead tired from the night before.

"I'll give you half pay for the night, if that helps your decision," Beulah said.

Davey had stolen money from one-night-stands before, but he'd never been paid to fuck. It made him feel like a whore, but that didn't bother him in the least. "A home-cooked meal, you say?" He threw his arm around her shoulders and started toward the house.

He stunk, but Beulah moved closer and looked up at him. "Whatever you want," she said, and pecked him on his bearded cheek.

His hand ran down her back and grabbed her ass. "Whatever I want?"

Beulah nodded and, together, they walked into the house.

CHAPTER 19

1

They ate another meager meal that was courtesy of whatever crap they could find in town.

Ari wasn't very hungry, and she only picked at the slop on her plate.

Rich's appetite wasn't bothered by his missing friend. What the girls didn't eat, he did.

Each of them had showered and changed, making them feel slightly more human after traipsing through the woods for the last few hours.

The day's events weighed on Ari. Though she was tired and stressed, she felt like sleep was miles away. Her body was fatigued, but her mind was racing like a hamster on a wheel. She sat at the small table with her friends, moving the few grains of rice Rich hadn't eaten.

"I think it was the girl. Whatever the fuck her name is. Hattie, is it?" Ari tossed her fork down and leaned back in her chair. "Th-that little bitch. She did something. I'm almost positive."

Rich and Danielle looked at each other, gauging how to respond.

Danielle sighed as Rich stuffed his mouth with the last bit of food, signaling it was up to her to talk.

"Ari, be serious, okay. What could she have done? JD is practically a grown man. Do you think a girl who's not even out of high school could hurt him? Even with a weapon, you would've heard the struggle in the woods." She leaned forward and put her hands out, beckoning her friend.

Sighing, Ari gave her hands to Danielle, who rubbed the backs of them.

"This is fucked, I know, but to think something foul happened is only going to make things worse. Tomorrow, we'll do what we should've done in the first place: go to the police station. We have the car, so we don't need a ride. That'll ensure Hattie or her mom can't stop us. We'll take a drive into town first thing in the morning and rally the troops," Danielle said enthusiastically.

Ari nodded, but the look of despair didn't leave her eyes. "I just hate knowing he's out there alone."

"Me too."

"Holy shit!" Rich said, abruptly sliding his chair back.

Both girls jumped at the outburst and looked at Rich's smiling face. He wasn't looking at them, but at the window.

JD was looking at them from behind the glass. His eyes were wide, like he was trying to scare them, but it was him.

"Oh, you motherfucker. You had us worried sick," Rich said, moving toward the door.

Ari's heart felt like it was in her throat. The elation she felt was unreal, but something was wrong. She'd know JD's face anywhere, but he didn't look right.

Rich, with Danielle in tow, opened the door.

"Wait!" Ari yelled, but it was too late. She dashed behind them, seeing the horror that awaited them outside the cabin.

A beast, a monster made only in nightmares, was standing just outside the door. Part pig, part man stood holding JD's severed head. The dead boy's hair was twisted in a mangled-looking hoof.

Even with the macabre trophy, that wasn't the most horrifying thing the monster held. In its other hand—a human hand—was a rusted pickaxe.

Rich and Danielle's smiles fell as quickly as they'd risen at seeing the horror brought to life.

The dim light from the windows illuminated just enough of the monster, leaving the rest of it bathed in shadow.

With a flick of its mutated hoof, the monster threw JD's head, striking Rich in the face.

Stumbling back, Rich tripped on his own feet, landing hard on his ass. Coagulated blood from his friend's severed neck blotted his face like globs of jelly.

Ari watched everything happen in slow motion.

Danielle's eyes, even with the beast in front of her, followed the head's arc as it struck her boyfriend. She watched as he went down, and turned as the monster swung the pickaxe.

A scream was stuck in Ari's throat.

The axe pierced Danielle's chest, forcing the air from her lungs with a hiss and grunt. Rusted steel penetrated her back, dimpling her shirt.

The pig monster growled, drooling from a hellish mouth full of crooked, yellow teeth. It ripped the weapon from Danielle's chest with a slurp and crack of shattered ribs.

Rich crab walked backward as his girlfriend

collapsed.

Blood poured from her wounds and open mouth. With shock etched on her face, her hands came up to stem the rushing flow of oxygen and blood.

"Run!" Ari screamed, bending down to help Rich to his feet. Even though she knew the creature would kill them if they stayed, she couldn't take her eyes off Danielle.

Knowing the girl was mortally wounded, the monster looked at Rich and Ari and shrieked again. Globs of spit fell, landing on Danielle, who was doing her best to stay alive. The beast raised the axe high above its head, its beady eyes locked on Ari and Rich, and swung.

Danielle pulled her hands from her ruined chest and raised them to defend herself. It did nothing.

The pickaxe smashed through her hands, snapping weak bones as it found her jaw.

A loud crack echoed as bone shattered and Danielle's lower jaw disappeared under the heavy tool, leaving her face locked in a state of deadly horror.

The cartilage and blood vessels of her neck ruptured and poured forth their life-giving cargo.

The beast fell on her corpse and plunged into her belly with long tusks, tearing open the white flesh like tissue paper.

Rich and Ari stood frozen as the monster ripped loops of intestines from Danielle's gut.

Shredded, wet offal fell from the monster's maw as it chewed, looking up at the stunned teens. Its eyes, even though animalistic, had the intelligence of a human.

Ari grabbed Rich's shoulder and pulled him. "Fucking run!"

His eyes were still locked on his dead girlfriend, but the yank from Ari was what Rich needed to jumpstart his escape.

Sprinting into the darkness, Ari headed toward the house and the car. She fought the urge to look back, fearing she'd trip, giving the monster an easy target.

The sound of racing footsteps closed in on her, and she prayed it was Rich.

Her shoulder blades itched as if waiting for the pickaxe to enter her flesh.

Rich ran up next to her, then overtook her, pushing branches out of his way.

Ari followed in his wake, rushing toward the lights of the house.

2

The towel felt more like sandpaper than fabric, but Davey had used worse, and he felt better after the shower.

He was tired and sore from the day and desperately needed some sleep.

The old sweatpants Beulah gave him were loose, and he needed to pull the drawstring tight to keep them up.

Shirtless, with only the towel draped over his shoulders, he walked out of the bathroom.

The old farmhouse needed some repairs, but it was far nicer than his place.

Davey wandered into the room Beulah showed

him before his shower. It smelled old and musty like it hadn't been lived in in quite some time. The bed was freshly turned down with clean sheets, so again, much better than his place.

He tossed the sodden towel on the floor and looked around.

Plaques hung on the wall, some adorned with pictures. Davey could only assume they were from the former man of the house, Mr. Winslow.

In the short time he'd worked at the farm, Beulah talked little about her father. Davey didn't think much of it; he had his fair share of dealing with a shitty father, and if Beulah wanted to talk, he'd listen, especially if it would get him laid. But the way she acted earlier in the day, he didn't think she was the sensitive type.

The door creaked behind him and Davey turned, expecting to find Hattie watching him. Ever since arriving at the farm, he knew the girl was hard up on him.

It wasn't Hattie who crept into the room, but Beulah. She stood in a long shirt with faded images of a farm show from decades ago. Her hair was wet and tossed up in a messy ponytail, and her threadbare shirt was almost translucent.

Davey wondered if she was wearing panties. He doubted it.

The sweatpants perfectly framed his cock as it began to stiffen at the thought of round two.

"I hope this is okay," Beulah said. She stepped into the room and pushed the door shut.

The old door swung, but didn't catch, leaving it ajar.

Her eyes drifted toward his pants, rising over his tattooed abdomen.

He flexed, ever so slightly, making his abs more prominent. "Oh yeah, this is great." He sat; if she wanted to fuck again, she could come to him.

After the performance he put on earlier, he didn't think she'd be able to resist.

Davey pulled the pants tight, framing the shape of his manhood in the gray fabric.

Beulah looked toward the window for a second, but her eyes shot back to him. "I appreciate your help today. Hopefully the other two can get back in the morning. I just spoke with Wayne while you were in the shower. The client was being a pain in the ass, which is nothing new. They were delayed, so I told them to take the farm truck home and bring it back in the morning."

He didn't give a shit what she was saying; his mind was only focused on what was under her shirt.

With every step, her breasts wobbled and swung.

"No problem. I don't mind a hard day's work. And looking for the missing kid was the right thing to do. Besides, it got me some fresh air and a little exercise for the day."

As she stepped closer, Beulah's tongue snaked out just for a moment.

Davey's dick jumped at the thought of being inside of her mouth. He opened his legs, allowing Beulah to step between them.

"Is there anything I can do to repay you for your hard work?" Beulah asked, descending to her knees. She rubbed his inner thighs, caressing his erection.

"I'm sure you can think of something." He lifted

his ass from the bed as she grabbed the elastic of his waistband.

She pulled his pants down, yanking them over his feet, and tossed them in the corner. Beulah grabbed his cock, pointing it straight up, and licked his balls. Her warm tongue teased each testicle before she put them in her mouth. She let out a moan, vibrating his most sensitive organs.

His wet sack fell from her mouth.

Gently, she licked him again, starting at the base of his shaft. Her eyes locked on his as she worked her way up to the tip.

He wanted to grab her head and force himself down her throat, but he was enjoying the show.

Sucking his dick like a pro, Beulah swallowed him.

If he hadn't already cum earlier in the day, he probably wouldn't have lasted long.

Beulah cradled his balls as her mouth and hand went to work on his erection. She slowed before taking his cock from her plump lips.

Davey thought she was going to leave him hanging as she stood up, but he was pleasantly wrong.

Lifting the hem of her nightshirt, exposing her wet sex, Beulah said, "Let me do the work this time." She straddled him. "Just relax and let it feel good." A whimper escaped her throat as she impaled herself on him.

The bed creaked and groaned under the carnal passion of their second fuck session of the day.

Neither of them noticed the sound of breathing at the door.

3

Hattie listened to the screams through her open window.

It was happening.

Her grandfather was untethered and on the loose.

In her hand, Hattie held the knife from the slaughterhouse—the blade that had opened many throats and helped end the lives of the farmhands. There was no going back.

The house creaked and groaned, but another sound caught Hattie's attention. She knew the sound; it was one she'd heard many times.

Slowly, she left her room with the blade clutched tightly in her grasp.

A sliver of light cut through the gloom of the hallway. It was a room that hadn't been used in years, but that was not the case that night. From the sounds drifting out, it sounded as if the room was in use.

Rage boiled up inside of her. Again, she was playing second to her mother. It wasn't anything new, but it still hurt. Her heart raced, thumping against her ribs as she looked through the crack in the open door.

For the second time that day, she felt as if her heart was ripped from her body.

Her mother straddled Davey, riding him like he was a mechanical bull. Her hips bucked, each thrust eliciting a squelch.

Davey's face and hands were occupied, squeezing and sucking Beulah's breasts.

Hattie wanted to throw the door open and set

upon them with the blade. She didn't know if she could kill them, but she could probably catch Davey off guard. Before he knew what was going on, she could run the razor-sharp knife across his throat. His gore would spray, coating her mother's nude body in crimson. If she was quick enough, Hattie could probably get her mother, too.

One hand touched the knob, with the other death-gripping the handle of the knife.

She stopped.

There were worse fates than a quick death with a knife. That execution was reserved for the pigs, which gave the farm value. It was swift and relatively painless.

There was another fate for the lovers.

When Hattie heard dull screams closing in on the house, her mind snapped away from the murder of her mother and the man she'd come to love.

The teens were coming. And if they were coming, that meant her grandfather was coming too.

She stilled her emotions, knowing she had to take care of the others first. They couldn't escape; she'd never allow it.

Quietly, yet quickly, Hattie left.

4

Sprinting toward the house, out of breath and panicking, Ari and Rich raced toward their car and stopped.

"Fuck!" Rich yelled, noticing the slashed tires.

The car sat on the dusty ground, clearly out of commission.

Ari was a few steps behind him, and her stomach dropped at seeing the disabled vehicle. "No, no, no," she muttered.

She pulled at her hair and looked around in desperation. It was as if she expected the pig creature to be right behind her, but it was nowhere to be seen. She didn't know if that was better or worse. At least when the beast was in front of her, she could watch it.

With it disappearing, she had no idea where it was. There was no way it could've beaten them to the house, but then again, such a creature shouldn't exist in the first place.

Rich looked around frantically. His always-perfect hair was in disarray, but for once, he didn't care. Tears and snot ran down his face. In a matter of minutes, he'd lost his best friend and watched his girlfriend be brutally murdered. His brain was in overdrive, looking for an escape.

His eyes locked on Davey's truck. "The truck!" he yelled, sprinting toward the vehicle.

Ari wanted to run into the house screaming for help, but she didn't know where the girl was. Ari was sure she was behind this, setting them up. As much as her instincts were telling her to get help at the house, she knew that could be disastrous.

Rich reached the truck.

A shiver ran up Ari's spine.

Something moved in the shadows below the truck.

In the dim moonlight, she saw a glint of light reflect off a blade.

Rich screamed and stumbled away as Hattie

slashed the back of his ankle. He fell forward, stumbling on his one good leg as his Achilles tendon separated, cut to the bone. A throat-tearing scream erupted from his lungs as the freakish girl crawled from beneath the truck with a knife in her hand.

"Rich!" Ari yelled. She took a step toward her wounded friend as he limped away from the knife-wielding girl.

Hattie brandished the weapon in front of her, a warning to Ari.

"Heth's coming," Hattie mumbled.

Ari turned but saw nothing.

The darkness of the woods swallowed everything.

5

Beulah's grunts were animalistic. Her body was slick with sweat and Davey's saliva. She heard yelling outside, and hoped Davey didn't.

At any time, she could've reached her orgasm, but she knew once she did, Davey would get his. She had to keep him distracted and in the house. Once he blew his load, she hoped he'd want to sleep, leaving her to clean up the mess her daughter created.

Another scream ripped through the night, this one louder and sounding like pain.

Davey pulled his mouth from her chest, but Beulah didn't slow her pace.

She rode him with a new plan: forgoing her orgasm and making him cum.

"Hold on," Davey said, grabbing her hips. He was deep inside her.

"Don't stop me, baby. I'm so close," Beulah cooed. She ground her wet pussy against him, feeling the electric buzz of pleasure.

"Shh." Davey put a finger to his lips.

More yells and screams shattered the silence.

"What the fuck is going on?" He pushed at her hips, but Beulah resisted.

Davey threw a little more strength into his attempt, knocking her from him. His cock slipped out of her with a wet slurp.

"Don't leave me hanging."

Ignoring her, he threw on his sweatpants, but couldn't find his shirt. "You didn't hear that?" Davey asked, pointing to the window. "I know you did, so what the fuck is going on?"

Beulah knelt on the bed and touched her pussy, spreading her wet lips with her fingers. "Probably just the kids fucking around. Now, bring that big dick back over here and finish what you started." She put her wet fingers into her mouth in a final attempt to keep him in the house.

On cue, another scream tore through the night.

Davey looked at her nude, glistening body.

For a split second, she thought she had him. The pants hardly contained his erection, and she still craved a release, even with the chaos erupting outside.

Davey didn't answer. He slammed the door behind him as he left the room.

"Fuck," Beulah muttered.

6

Rich wasn't a big guy, but with his weight leaning against Ari, she felt every pound.

Blood poured from his wounded leg, soaking into the ground.

Hattie stood by their ruined car with the knife still in her hand, but pointed down. Raspy, labored breaths came from behind her mask.

Ari couldn't see her face, but she knew the deformed bitch was smiling. An almost imperceptible glance from Hattie made Ari alert. She knew the monster was somewhere lurking in the shadows. Her head snapped with every sound of the night. She didn't know where to go. She had to assume Beulah was involved. There was no way that vile creature could roam the grounds without her knowing.

Another sound came from the shadows, and Ari's head snapped, her breaths coming in ragged gasps.

Footsteps rushed her, and she turned just in time to see Hattie coming toward her. The girl had the knife held high, as if readying a slash.

Instinctively, Ari moved back, letting Rich fall to the ground.

"Fuck!" Rich yelled as he hit the dirt. He tried to brace himself on his good leg, but couldn't.

Ari danced away from the blade, but the attack was weak. It was almost as if it weren't meant to cut her, just move her, to herd her away like they did to pigs as they ushered them to their deaths.

Fighting her instincts, Ari spun away from the

attack and looked at the shadows she was approaching. It was the only thing that saved her life.

The head of the pickaxe swung out of the gloom.

She stumbled to the side as the rusted tool narrowly missed the top of her head. Ari stared in fear at the monster.

The creature locked its black-eyed gaze on her. It roared with an almost-humanlike sound, as if vocal cords were being tortured and amplified through the wide snout of a pig and broken tusks, yellowed and crooked, meant to tear flesh with ease.

"Ari!" Rich yelled. "Run!" He kicked with his good leg, trying to get back to his feet.

Ari moved away from the monster as it worked the buried tool from the earth.

The black, soulless eyes that locked on her turned, focusing on easier prey.

Her eyes darted around, looking for safety.

The slaughterhouse.

I need a weapon. Anything to defend myself. There has to be something in there.

It wasn't quite a plan, but it was a start. With a final glance at Rich, she ran. Her tears streamed behind her. She didn't risk a look back, fearing what she'd see.

The screams were enough.

7

The pain in Rich's leg was like nothing he'd ever felt before. He was in agony, but the fear he felt staring down the beast tempered the pain to something bearable. He kicked and worked himself to his feet as the abomination closed in.

"Get the fuck away from me!" He stumbled and lurched as the monster stalked closer. With his full attention on the beast, Rich forgot about Hattie.

Sharp pain ripped into his lower back. He turned and staggered again, seeing Hattie with the bloody knife in her hand.

She laughed as Rich reached around his body, finding a new wound leaking blood.

"Fucking bitch!" Rich swung at the girl, hoping to inflict some damage on her deformed face. He missed, throwing him off balance.

His already injured leg screamed as it tried to bear his weight.

He crumbled and fell to the dusty ground.

Roaring, the monster raised the pickaxe. Its head of horrors blotted out the moon.

The tool descended, impaling Rich's thigh.

Bone shattered, and blood flew as he howled.

Rich grabbed the steel head of the axe and pulled, but he was pinned to the ground.

Hattie shrieked with glee. "Kill 'em, Grampa."

The pig creature stood over Rich, dripping saliva onto his wounded leg.

Rich kicked at the monster with his last leg. His paltry attacks did nothing. He thrashed as the beast circled behind him, but his efforts were for naught as the tool in his leg kept him immobile.

Shattered bone ground against steel and unleashed more gore from the wound.

"Loo at hith pwethy hair. Like a girl. I wanth it."

Even with death looming, Rich feared losing his hair. It was an irrational thought, but at the end of his life, it was what popped into his mind. He turned his head just in time to see Hattie hand the curved blade to the monster—her grandfather.

The beast took the knife in one hand and grabbed Rich's hair with the other.

Reaching up, Rich scratched at the rubbery flesh of the monster. "Fuck you!" He pulled and ripped at the beast. His nails bit into the meat, and blood ran, warm and tacky, down his hands.

No matter what Rich did, the monster didn't release its hold on him.

The edge of the knife was cold against his hairline. A quick sting made him wince as the blade bit into the thin flesh. The edge glanced off his skull as the monster cut and ripped. A sound like tearing paper was loud in his ears as his scalp pulled away from the bone.

The beast grunted as it yanked, unceremoniously taking Rich's hair from his head.

A new type of coldness greeted him. A chill that he'd never experienced as the night air kissed his skinned skull.

Blood ran down his face, mixing with tears. Through his blurred vision, Rich watched Hattie step before him.

On top of her head sat his scalp. His blood ran down her faded, cracked mask.

"Am I prethy now? Don'th I looth prethy?"

Rich wept.

Then, he screamed as fat fingers plunged into his mouth from behind.

The monster snapped his head back, giving Rich a glimpse of the knife-wielding creature.

A cold blade pressed against the strained flesh of his neck.

He swallowed hard, feeling his Adam's apple scrape the edge.

Drool fell from the open maw of the beast as it cut.

Warm ichor cascaded down Rich's chest as he gasped for air, but nothing came. Blood filled his lungs as the knife sliced through his windpipe and arteries.

Hattie danced in the moonlight with Rich's scalp on her head.

It was the last thing he saw as the world faded to black.

CHAPTER 20

1

He thought he'd died from the rough sex and landed in Hell. That would've made sense, at least. What Davey was seeing, did not. Nothing in his short existence on Earth could've prepared him for what confronted him in front of the farmhouse.

A monster, a thing that had no business existing, was sawing the head from one of the teens. It hunched over the mangled corpse of the kid as it brutally decapitated the boy.

Davey stood frozen with fear as the monster lifted the head high in the air.

The beast looked big, even as it hunched, but Davey almost lost control of his bladder when it came to full height. He wasn't a short man by any stretch, but the creature looked a whole foot taller than him.

Something moved to his side.

Hattie was twirling without a care in the world. Something was on her head as she danced to a song only she could hear.

"Hattie!" he yelled, snapping her out of her trance.

The girl stopped moving, realizing he was there.

"Get away from it. Come here."

Davey's brain was malfunctioning. When she didn't move away from the creature, something clicked. It was as if his brain rebooted and started working again.

She wasn't scared of the monster. No, she looked at it lovingly. She wasn't against the beast; she was with it.

"Oh Davey, we cooda been togeda foreva. Buth oo ood never love me. Mama had oo hath you to herself. Buth I don'th need oo, Davey. I have Grampa to love me. Heths always loved me." She walked over to the monster and put her arm around its waist—a loving gesture between two creatures.

Hattie bent down and picked up the bloody knife, tucking it into her pants. "Kill him," she said as she walked toward the house.

The pig monster grunted and, somehow, smirked. It threw the dead boy's head into the darkness, where it landed with a *thump*.

Davey's eyes bounced between Hattie and the monster.

The pig beast ripped the bloody pickaxe from the thigh of the headless boy and lumbered toward Davey.

There was no way he could fight the creature with his bare hands. He'd been in a bar fight—or twenty—but hand-to-hand combat with an armed giant would not go his way.

The truck.

He needed to reach his truck. In the bed of the beat-up vehicle, he had tools. He wasn't sure what he had, odd bits and pieces he collected over the years, but something was better than nothing.

What he didn't have were his keys.

The Davey he knew and loved would run away,

leaving the rest of the kids—if there were any left—and Beulah to fend for themselves. It would've been another act of selfishness in a life full of them.

He could probably outrun the monster, but shoeless and miles from town, he didn't know how far he'd make it. And frankly, fighting the beast, exhausted and in the dark of the woods, was even more terrifying than slugging it out right then and there.

The creature closed the distance.

Davey glanced back at Hattie, who watched him as she disappeared into the dark house. He wanted to warn Beulah, but she might have been involved the entire time. That was probably why she tried to keep him in bed.

With a burst of speed Davey wasn't prepared for, the creature lunged. It easily swung the heavy tool, aimed directly at his bare midsection.

Dancing back, Davey narrowly avoided the weapon. A gust of wind from the attack brushed his torso as it swept past him.

It was the opening Davey needed.

The monster expected an easy kill, and was thrown off balance at the miss.

Davey rushed toward his truck. His feet slapped in the bloody mud around the body of the dead boy.

Quickly, he reached into the dark bed of his truck, keeping one eye on the raging monster. He felt the wooden handle of a tool and grabbed it.

The framing hammer felt good in his hand as he tested the heft of it.

The beast was more cautious as it squared up with Davey once again. Something human still lurked in the swine brain.

"Come on, you cocksucker." Davey crouched, spinning the hammer so he'd strike with the claw.

His plan was simple: allow the monster to swing again, dodge it, and bury the claw in its brain. It seemed easy enough.

The combatants moved closer, and Davey knew he was within range of the pickaxe. He needed to time his attack.

Before he had time to react, the monster struck. Instead of swinging the axe, it jabbed with it, hitting Davey square in the nose.

Flashes of light danced in his eyes as his nose bent and shattered. Blood ran down his face, and he moved back, knowing the killing blow was coming.

He was right.

Another gust of air blew by him as the weapon missed again.

He was still alive, but with his blurred vision and pain, he didn't know for how long.

Blindly, Davey swung the hammer, realizing how paltry it was compared to the creature. He slipped as he swung, falling to his knees.

His attack went low, but struck flesh. The claw of the hammer weakly bit into the unnatural meat of the creature's thigh.

A hellish squeal pierced the night sky as the monster spun.

Davey was on guard, looking for the pickaxe to strike him. He wasn't expecting the beast to throw a backhand.

The meaty, human-like hand struck him on the jaw, sending another starburst into his vision.

He slid out of the mud and found dry ground, maneuvering away before the axe could find his skull.

Once again, man and beast squared up, but the monster didn't rush in. A glimpse of human caution shone in his beady eyes.

Davey's face hurt, but his body was alive with adrenaline. He had to end this fight quickly before the chemical wore off; it was his only hope. Soon, he'd tire and not be able to avoid the monster's weapon. His luck had brought him far in life, but it felt like his odds were dwindling.

The mutant snarled. Mucus ran from its wet snout. Hot breath came from the open mouth. Tusks flashed in the moonlight. It wound up, shifting its feet as it launched another attack.

Davey had to get the weapon away from it if he had any chance of survival. But the strength of the beast was unnatural. He watched as the pig creature lifted the pickaxe over its head.

It was intelligent; Davey would give it that. He wasn't sure if the attack was a feint, so he stood as long as he dared.

Once the steel head began its descent, Davey moved. On dry ground, his footing improved, hopefully giving him enough speed and power to escape. He shuffled his feet to the left, narrowly avoiding having his skull impaled.

The heavy tool plunged into the ground.

The creature paused for a moment as it tried to work it free.

Davey struck. He spun the hammer, exposing the flat head, and brought it down onto the back of the monster's hand with everything he had.

The bones felt harder than they should, but then again, Davey never struck someone with a hammer.

Under the steel head, bones broke.

The grimy fingers released their grasp on the wooden shaft of the pickaxe.

Again, the pig beast threw a backhand strike at Davey, but he was ready for it.

Shattered bones scratched his face, gouging his cheek, but the blow didn't ring his bell like before.

Then, standing next to the creature, Davey went on the attack.

The head of the hammer struck the creature in the neck, eliciting another shriek.

Staggered by the blow, it stepped back and clawed at the wound.

Davey looked at the pickaxe. It would end the fight much quicker, but his energy was sapped. He'd only have one chance to put some power behind an attack with the heavy tool.

And if he missed, he'd be dead.

He threw the claw hammer down and yanked the pickaxe free. The weight difference was staggering. It felt deadly in his hands.

With the pig monster still stunned from the neck shot, Davey struck. He used the same tactic as his adversary and jabbed with the head of the pickaxe.

The steel caught the beast in the mouth, further cracking the already-broken tusks. Blood ran from its mouth and snout as it staggered backward.

Davey jabbed again, moving it back.

A cold dampness touched his toes, and he realized they were back by the puddle of muddy gore.

The mutant looked up with mad rage in its eyes. Any semblance of human calculation had gone by the wayside. Unarmed, bloodied, and angry, the beast was still dangerous.

Davey knew he was winning, but the fight was far from over. He planned on ending it in one strike if his luck held.

Stepping out of the gore, he backed up, gauging his strike. His feet were on solid ground when the monster lowered its head and charged.

Cold mud squished underfoot as the pig beast slipped as it moved forward.

Davey cocked the pickaxe back, summoning every ounce of strength possible. He pictured himself in a simpler time, a time when his father still loved him and Davey still made him proud.

He wasn't a thirty-something, drunken womanizer anymore. He was ten again, and standing in the batter's box of a baseball game.

The fastball hummed when the pitcher released it. Watching the seams as the ball spun, Davey knew it was right down the middle. He just needed to keep his eye on it and swing.

There was a glimmer of human fear in the eyes of the mutant when its footing went out from under it as it staggered forward.

Davey swung.

He put everything into that strike, knowing it would be his last, one way or another. It was every snide comment from his father, every bit of self-loathing he felt after waking up drunk next to a stranger, and every time he finessed his way out of trouble.

The point of the axe met flesh and bone as it carved a path of carnage through the monster's skull.

His hands stung like they did when he hit his first home run. It hurt like hell, but it was a good pain—the pain of hard work and redemption.

A loud croak escaped the mutant's throat as its life flashed out. It fell face down in the mud, dead.

The weight of the corpse yanked the tool from Davey's hand, but he didn't think he could've held it for a moment longer.

Pig blood mixed with human as it ran from the wound.

Black eyes, filled with blood, wept.

Davey staggered back and fell hard to the ground. His broken nose shot a jolt of pain into his brain, but he was alive. With the back of his hand, he wiped his face, gently around the shattered bone. He didn't know if he'd be as attractive after the ordeal, but that was a problem for another day.

He was alive, and right then, that was all that mattered.

Davey's head snapped back as shouting erupted from the house.

2

Beulah stood at the window watching the carnage below. A cigarette burned in her fingers, producing a halo of smoke.

Davey was smart and strong, but there was no way he'd defeat what her father had become. She selfishly kept him for that reason, knowing it was an impossibility.

The fight went back and forth, but she could see Davey was tiring. She knew he had no chance, even with a weapon, which looked feeble compared to the bulk of her father.

She crushed the cigarette against the windowsill and left the room. It was her job, *hers*, not his. She had to end it.

Beulah walked through the darkened hallways to her father's room. She was ready to do what she should've done years ago. And this time, she wouldn't let her curiosity get the better of her. This time, she'd end it with a blast of a shotgun, not start a new horror.

The closet door creaked open, and Beulah looked to the corner where the big gun was kept.

Fuck.

The gun was missing.

And then it clicked.

I took it downstairs. It's in the kitchen.

Beulah rushed toward the stairs, but even in her haste, she heard the door squeak as it opened.

Hattie! Hattie did this; she is to blame for the bloodshed outside, and God only knows where else.

"Hattie!" she yelled, rushing down the stairs, hoping to draw the girl's attention before she found the big gun.

Hattie sat at the kitchen table bathed in darkness.

"Ha-Hattie?"

The girl didn't move. She sat motionless, her breath raspy behind the mask.

Beulah looked to the corner, but the gun was gone. Slowly, she turned on the lights.

Her daughter was covered in dried gore. Across

her lap was the black death of the shotgun. Her hair hung over her face like a hospital shroud, covering the mask. A mangled scalp rested on her head, dripping fresh blood. A wet laugh built in the girl's throat, coming out in distorted croaks.

"What have you done?" Beulah asked.

Hattie's head rose, but she didn't move the hair from her face. Dark eyes peeked through the plastic holes.

Beulah had stared into those eyes for years, but something was wrong with them. Something was missing, replaced by a darkness she'd seen in her early life.

"Whath hath *I* done? No, whath hath *oo* done?" Hattie stood and put the butt of the shotgun into the pocket of her shoulder, still keeping the muzzle pointed toward the ground. "Dis is aw becauth of you, motha."

Beulah had to keep her talking, but she didn't know if it would do any good.

Davey couldn't save her; he was probably dead by then.

And after her father killed him, he'd come for her and finally finish the job he has wanted to do since day one.

She saw the hatred in his eyes her entire life. Beulah knew he didn't see his daughter, but his wife, a wife that left him, and for good reason. If he was as bad as he was with his daughter, she could only imagine what he'd done to his wife.

She still held hope in talking to her daughter, but why should she? Had she been a better parent to Hattie than her father had been to her?

For the early years when she was still doing sick porn and fucking for cash, the countless times she left Hattie in a cage while she went out to get fucked and high, hoping the drugs would erase the pain of her life that had been thrust upon her by her father. The same torment she'd put on the girl in front of her. Maybe Beulah deserved to die. But she sure as fuck didn't want to, just like her father didn't when she killed him with the big gun her daughter now held.

She was going to do it; Hattie was going to shoot her.

The girl's muscles tensed just before she racked the gun. A shell flew like a wounded bird, landing on the dirty linoleum.

Beulah's eyes instinctively followed it, but snapped back in time to see the black maw of the gun pointed at her face. It swallowed her; the blackness drinking deeply from her soul.

Her mouth was impossibly dry, but a withered scream rose from somewhere deep inside of her.

Hattie didn't flinch as Beulah screamed.

3

Davey opened the door. His injuries plagued him, and he only wanted respite from madness. But what he was greeted with was far from that.

Hattie had a shotgun pointed squarely at Beulah's face.

When the door opened, Beulah looked at him and screamed.

Hattie didn't flinch, but she lowered the gun.

For once in his life, Davey knew he looked like

shit. He might never look the same again, but he was alive. Years, or even months ago, he would've gladly traded his life before losing his looks. But the insanity he faced left him with a new lease on life.

"You're alive," Beulah said. She flinched like she wanted to run to him, but Hattie snapped the gun back toward her.

He didn't want to be on the receiving end of the firearm, but it only felt right to stand by Beulah.

With the monster dead, Davey thought they might have a chance to get out alive, but it would take some smooth talking—something he specialized in. At least, he hoped, especially with his ruined face.

"Hattie," he said. The broken nose distorted his voice and hurt like fuck, but he saw something change in the girl's eyes. "Please, put the gun down."

The muzzle of the shotgun was pointed at Beulah's head. It was heavy, and the girl's arms were tiring from the weight.

"Don'th tal oo me!" Hattie yelled. Her eyes glistened with tears. A wet sniffle came from behind her mask, sounding wetter thanks to her deformity. "I love you, Davey. Buth oo hate me. And-and oo illed Grampa." Her voice rose and shuddered.

The gun wasn't pointed at him yet, so Davey took a step closer. He thought if he could inch his way, he might have a chance at grabbing it. He was no action hero, though he may have looked like one. In reality, he was on the verge of pissing his pants.

Another step closer and Hattie hadn't noticed. One more, and he should be in range to snatch the big weapon.

Hattie's grip wavered, and she adjusted the butt

of the gun in the pocket of her shoulder.

It all seemed to happen in slow motion.

Davey watched as her dirty finger curled around the trigger.

He lunged, but he was too late.

The gun spat fire and lead, aimed right at Beulah's face.

A gout of flame erupted with a crack of thunder. The pellets impacted Beulah's head.

Her flesh puckered and dimpled with each strike.

The lead shot tore through her skin, mashing bone as it destroyed.

A pink mist painted the wall behind her. Blood, bone, and bits of brain shot from her corpse.

Davey expected the shot to throw her back like it did in the movies, but what happened was worse than fiction.

Beulah dropped like a puppet with the strings cut. Her brain stopped giving commands to her body, ceasing to work. She hit the ground with a wet *slap*, her left leg bent at an awkward angle. Blonde hair turned red as blood ran from the massive exit wound in the back of her skull.

Hattie racked the shotgun, expelling the empty cartridge.

A smoking husk of plastic and brass flew through the air, bouncing on the kitchen floor.

She looked at the gun for a moment before throwing the action forward, chambering another round.

Davey lost the fight with his bladder, and hot piss ran down his leg. Beaten, broken, bloody, and covered in urine, he watched as the girl turned the gun toward him.

He wanted to cry, to plead with the girl, anything to save his life, but his throat was dry. There were no words left in him, only infantile croaks. "P-please," was all he could mutter.

Hattie's chest rose and fell. Her breath sounded almost distant behind the mask. She, again, looked at the gun.

Davey wasn't overly familiar with firearms, but the way she kept staring at it led him to think she may have been out of ammo. But was he willing to risk his life on that hunch? No.

He used the only weapon he had: his charm. His voice returned as the piss began to cool on his leg. "Hattie, baby." The lies were already coming to life in his mind, rushing down to his tongue, one that had hurt as many women as it pleasured over the years. "Now we can be together." He risked a glance at Beulah's corpse.

A halo of blood was spreading on the kitchen floor around Beulah's face, locked in a death mask he'd never get out of his mind.

"She was keeping us apart, but now that she's gone, we can be together."

Hattie's eyes filled with tears.

It was working. The same lies he used to talk girls out of their panties could also tug at their heartstrings. Who would've guessed?

Slowly, the gun lowered.

Davey didn't like that it was pointed at his cock, but it continued the trajectory and eventually stopped, pointed at the ground.

"Give it to me, baby. And if you're good, I'll give it to you." He looked at her with his best *fuck-me eyes,* hoping it would work.

Davey only needed a moment to gain her trust and get the fuck away. He wasn't a killer, at least in cold blood. For as fucked up as the girl was, he didn't think he could kill her unless he absolutely had to. Escaping with his life was the only priority on his mind.

The gun fell from her hands, hitting the ground with a clatter that made him jump.

He wanted to turn and run, but held firm. He did what he'd done a million times: opened his arms for a hug. "Come here, baby. Come hug your man."

Snot and spit ran from beneath Hattie's mask as she sobbed. She pressed her masked face against his chest as Davey wrapped his arms around her.

He felt the warmth of her sobs and mucus on his chest, but didn't care. He didn't know if the nightmare was over, but one chapter was.

Hattie's sobs increased, growing louder. But something about their pitch changed, something that made Davey's blood run cold.

The girl wasn't sobbing any longer; she was laughing. As quick as any punch he'd ever taken before, Hattie struck. Her fist hit him in the gut, knocking the wind from him. She ran her hand across his belly.

The look of shock on his face must've been priceless as a spool of severed gut spilled from his opened abdomen.

Hattie stepped back, the long knife in her hand.

Davey grabbed at his innards, wetting his hands

with shit and blood.

The fucking knife. The bitch picked it up while I was fighting that fucking thing.

Backpedaling, Davey slipped in the slurry of gore from his wounds and Beulah's. His feet went out from underneath him, and he landed hard on his ass.

"I don'th need oo. I can run dis plath by myselth." Hattie wiped the blade on her shirt and tucked it behind her back, where she must've had it hidden. "Dis is my farm now."

Davey was growing cold, even though he felt warm from the tacky blood on his clothes. Each breath was agony, and with each beat of his heart, more crimson drooled from his wounds.

Darkness was closing in on him.

Hattie stepped close, bending down and putting her masked face to his.

He wanted to punch her, to damage her, even with just a strike, but the energy was gone.

She didn't say another word, only staring as the life ran out of him onto the dirty floor.

CHAPTER 21

1

The night was almost over.

Hattie looked at the corpses of her mother and the man she thought she loved, the man who tried to trick her at the last moment.

They were all the same, men. They'd do or say anything to help themselves. Well, maybe it wasn't only men. Her mother had been a pretty good liar. She could manipulate and use people as well as the worst man.

But now they were gone—dead and cooling on the floor of her new house.

She wanted to shoot Davey with the gun. She wanted to put a shotgun blast into his dick, blowing the thing she'd thought about to red paste. But after killing her mother, the big gun was empty. She was just glad Davey didn't realize it. She didn't think she would've won in a fight against him, even with the knife. But her fake tears worked perfectly as bait. She had cried enough real ones that whipping up fake ones was easy.

Hattie had her mother to thank for that. All the years of torment that woman put her through had finally paid off.

Making herself cry was the easy part. The hard part was keeping it going and not laughing until Davey took the bait.

She never thought she could kill a person. Animals, yes, that was life on a farm, especially one with a slaughterhouse. But after that night, Hattie knew nothing could stop her. She was reborn, baptized in the blood of those who wronged her. And from that day forward, she swore no one would ever wrong her or use her again.

With her tacky fingers, she reached up and took off the mask. She almost forgot she was wearing it. It was just as much a part of her as her hair or nails. It was what made her *her*. It was the shield she put up against the world. It hid her shame, but she realized she had nothing to be ashamed of.

If the world didn't like how she looked, then fuck them.

She was perfect in her eyes, and no one would ever convince her of anything different again.

But she knew she would be judged. That was, if she managed to get away with what had happened on the farm. It wasn't every day a half-dozen people could go missing and not raise suspicion. But that was a problem for another time.

One of those problems still existed.

If she had any chance of escaping prison or the death penalty, Hattie had to tie up the loose ends.

And there was still one unaccounted for.

When Hattie first saw Ari, she felt something new in her body. She didn't know what gay was, but laying eyes on the dark-haired beauty made her feel something between her legs she'd never felt before. Hattie had only ever felt that heat for men, especially Davey, but the slick lust she felt thinking about Ari was new and exciting. Caressing her in the woods made Hattie tremble. The softness of her breasts and the acrid smell of her freshly fucked pussy had her soaked.

She didn't think it was love, but there was a lust for the female form that was undeniable. Hattie wanted to find her and offer her a truce. If the girl could keep her mouth shut, Hattie would let her live her life on the farm. She and Hattie could start new together, running the farm as partners. And maybe, just maybe, Ari would grow to love her. Or, at least, lust for her.

Together, they'd share passion, pleasuring each other after a long day's work, bathing together, caressing each other's soapy bodies.

No, not again; she wouldn't let herself drop into the pitfall like she did with Davey.

She was incapable of being loved. It was the hard truth, and the sooner she realized it, the better.

There was no way she could let Ari leave the farm alive. But if there was a way she could keep her...

Hattie looked at the discarded mask one last time. Her fingers itched to grab it and pull it over her deformed face, but that chapter was over.

And another was beginning.

2

The slaughterhouse stunk like death, and for good reason.

Ari used the ambient light from the moon to make her way around, hoping to find something to defend herself with, or even just a place to hide.

The yelling outside had stopped. The only

remaining noises were the grunts of the animals and the chatter of night bugs.

She didn't know if the lack of sound comforted her or added to the terror.

A dark alcove called to her.

She played to the child inside of her, looking for a spot to hide during hide-and-seek. But the childlike fear of the dark toyed with her psyche. What lurked in the deep dark? What monsters awaited her in the crevice beneath the counter?

Steeling her nerves, she prepared herself to plunge into the gloom. But something caught her attention: a smell.

It wasn't the overpowering smell of unwashed swine or the always-lingering stench of death; it was the scent of a thunderstorm, the electric smell of ozone and rain, but the night was quiet and clear.

Something shuffled behind her, and Ari turned just in time to see Hattie. She screamed at seeing the deformed girl's unmasked face.

Her cleft was turned into a wet sneer, and she held what looked like a pair of giant tongs in her hands. They were connected by a thick wire.

It was the last thing Ari saw as the tongs clamped around her head.

A quick jolt shot through her body, and her world went dark.

3

The first thing Ari realized was that she was naked. It wasn't the first time she'd woken nude in her life, but it was the first time she awakened strapped to a table.

Usually, if she was waking up naked, it was next to JD, not tied down.

Her head was throbbing, and she smelled burnt hair. The odor of death lingered, but was fresher than before. She didn't know if the shock she received was playing with her sense of smell, but an unpleasant aroma wafted through the air.

Ari looked around. Her vision blurred at the slight movement, and she found the source of the stench and nearly vomited.

Hattie was crouched over a few fresh pig carcasses. The girl's clothes were wet with blood as she carved through the flesh of the dead beasts. Delicately, she decapitated one of the pigs with a long knife. Her deformed face was contorted in concentration as the blade made short work of the flesh.

Ari let out an involuntary groan. She pulled against her restraints, but the old chains were tight.

Cocking her head to the side, Hattie paused her cutting, but didn't turn. She listened to Ari's grunts and groans.

The chains rattled against the metal table, but held firm.

Hattie resumed her dissection, finally removing the pig's head. She set the knife down and stood, holding the ghastly trophy. Gently, she set it on the table next to Ari.

Ari looked at the gory face next to her.

Dead, black eyes gazed back. A wet tongue lolled from the pig's mouth, hanging over yellowed teeth.

The big tongs hung from the ceiling. Even though they were far away, Ari could smell the electricity running through them.

Wiping her bloody hands on her shirt, Hattie looked Ari up and down.

She felt violated by Hattie's gaze, but when the girl's bloody hands touched her, she screamed. "Get your fucking hands off me!"

Hattie stared at her thighs, squeezing her muscles. Like a lover, the girl continued north, spreading Ari's vagina with a bloody finger. She gently pressed her clit as she continued up her stomach. With both hands, she caressed Ari's breasts, pushing them together.

If the freak put her finger anywhere near her mouth, Ari was determined to bite it off.

Hattie was smarter than that, stopping her probe at the hollow of Ari's throat. "Mama made Grampa down here. I'm noth sure how she did ith, buth I hath penthy of pigths to geth ith righth." She crouched down and picked up the knife.

Ari screamed and thrashed. Her wrists bled as the chains bit into her delicate flesh.

Mucus ran from the twisted openings of Hattie's mouth and nose as she laughed and laughed. It was as if she heard the best joke in the world. Her laughter doubled, turning to snorts, like that of a pig.

As the cold steel of the blade touched her throat, Ari screamed. And as her flesh surrendered to the edge, her screams turned into wet moans.

Hattie squealed with glee as she sliced. Her grunts and snorts washing away the gurgle of the dying girl.

She might not have been as pretty or as smart as her mother, but she had a stack of bodies and all the time in the world.

ACKNOWLEDGEMENTS

This book started as a short story many years ago. I was in my infancy as a writer, but I had this vile idea about a man who loved his pigs more than his family. He'd do anything to keep the pigs happy, no matter what. I wrote that story, which turned out to be around 15k words. It was fun and gory, but didn't feel long enough.

I shelved the idea for years and let it sit. The story began to manifest, and as it did, I knew it was going to be a novel. It wasn't until I started outlining that I realized how long it would be. This book is my longest to date, and might remain that way for quite some time.

I started and stopped this book more times than I'd like to admit. I flew through the opening and stalled out with other projects looming.

It wasn't until I went to a writing retreat in the Pocono Mountains that this story came back to life. Thank you to Wrath James White, Aron Beauregard, Kristopher Triana, Shane McKenzie, Lucas Mangum, and Judith Sonnet. These fine folks helped me a lot during the retreat and got me moving again.

Thank you to my editor, Mary Danner, for once again cleaning up my mess and making this book something special.

Nick Justus and Len Danovich killed it with this stellar cover and are two artists I highly recommend working with.

And finally, to one of my literary icons, Edward Lee. *The Pig* was my first extreme horror book, and it stuck with me. So much so, I asked Ed to use his most popular opening line in this book as an homage to his filth. He agreed and I was honored to carry on his legacy of women taking shots of pig jizz. If you haven't read his work, get on it ASAP.

Thank you to all of my readers. Without you, none of this would be possible.

ABOUT THE AUTHOR

Daniel J. Volpe is the Splatterpunk Award-winning author of PLASTIC MONSTERS, TALIA, LEFT TO YOU, and many others. His love for horror started at a young age when his grandfather unwittingly rented him *A Nightmare on Elm Street*. He can be found on Facebook @ Daniel Volpe, Instagram @ dj_volpe_horror , X @DJVolpeHorror , TikTok @danieljvolpehorror1

www.ingramcontent.com/pod-product-compliance
Lightning Source LLC
Chambersburg PA
CBHW051525250626
47156CB00001B/227